Eddie felt a desperate anger boiling in his chest, ready to burst because it had nowhere to go. He wanted to get even, to strike back at all those silent organizations that sent him bills through the mail and didn't care what happened to him, whether or not he could live with what they were doing to him, whether or not he got anything in return for the money they squeezed out of him in greater and greater amounts. The gas company. The government. The goddamned car dealer and the banks.

Then it hit him. He knew an awful lot about computers. Enough to turn those wicked machines into his own faithful servants . . .

# THE
# Programmer

■ ■ ■ ■ ■ ■ ■ ■ ■ ■ ■

## Bruce Jackson

BALLANTINE BOOKS • NEW YORK

**For Diane**

Copyright © 1979 by Bruce Jackson

All rights reserved. Published in the United States by Ballantine Books, a division of Random House, Inc., New York, and simultaneously in Canada by Random House of Canada, Limited, Toronto, Canada.

Library of Congress Catalog Card Number: 78-20078

ISBN 0-345-29079-8

This edition published by arrangement with Doubleday & Co., Inc.

Printed in Canada

First Ballantine Books Edition: December 1981

# Part One

■ ■ ■ ■ ■ ■ ■ ■ ■ ■ ■ ■ ■ ■ ■ ■ ■ ■ ■

## ONE

When Eddie got home, Betty was in the living room watching television. She yelled a hello to him and he answered her. The kitchen was exactly as he had left it. The dishes were neatly stacked alongside the sink and the papers and envelopes were neatly stacked on the kitchen table. He poured a cup of coffee and sat down to attack the envelopes. He didn't feel very well.

He looked at the neat pile of envelopes directly in front of him on the bare Formica table. He looked at them for a long time. They didn't move and neither did he. He knew they wouldn't go away. He had to make them go away. There was no way he could make them all go away.

To the left of the pile was his checkbook. The plastic cover was supposed to look like leather; it was bright red and had his name in small gold-leaf letters in the lower right-hand corner of the front. To the right of the pile of envelopes were his pen and the green coffee mug. He drank some of the coffee, got up and poured some more, then opened the first envelope.

Sounds of commercials burst from the other room. He hated the way television stations doubled the volume for commercials. They didn't want you to get away for free. Betty came into the kitchen, took a beer from the refrigerator, and went out again without saying anything to him. Different theme music came and went. More commercials.

After a while he leaned back in the chair, his body stiff. He hadn't moved for some time. The coffee in the green

mug was cold. He thought about dumping it back into the
Norelco coffee maker, which was now one-third full, and
pouring hot coffee back into the cup. But he had already
had four cups and he knew another would keep him from
falling asleep. As it was, he was feeling that odd twitchy
sensation in his arms he got when he'd had too much
coffee. It was starting to affect him more and more lately.

"Shit."

"What?" Betty said from the other room.

"I was talking to myself."

"You're doing that more and more lately."

He looked through the doorway. She hadn't turned
around. The back of her head was absolutely motionless.
She was watching "The Price is Right." Sometimes when
she watched it she wrote her guesses on a small pad; when
the announcer told the real price of the items, she wrote
those in a parallel column. After the program, during the
commercials, she would show Eddie how well she had
done.

All the envelopes except one contained current bills.
The one not a bill was a letter from the office of the deputy mayor telling Eddie his complaint would be investigated immediately. The letter was three weeks old and
nothing had been investigated.

The incident had happened two months earlier. Eddie
had just finished shaving. He was standing in the dark bedroom, near the window; he was still in his bathrobe. His
trousers and shirt were hanging neatly in the closet. He
looked out the window and saw, in front of the house, garbage collectors lifting his green plastic containers to be
dumped into the large city garbage truck. They looked
eerie under the streetlamp. Something seemed wrong, out
of place. It took a moment to realize what it was: all the
wheels on the left side of the garbage truck were on
Eddie's lawn. The driver had parked on the grass so the
crew wouldn't have to walk so far.

Eddie ran downstairs to yell at them, but by the time he
got to the front door, the truck had moved two houses
down the block. He would have chased them, but he felt
foolish standing there barefoot in his orange robe. It was a
cold morning.

There was a large muddy track across the lawn, exactly

the width of the garbage truck's double tires. There had been a melting of a heavy snowfall not long before, and the relatively warm two weeks since then had seen the first of the heavy spring rains. There might be more snow and freezes later, but for now the ground was soggy and soft. The wheels had cut an ugly trench several inches deep.

He went into the house and furiously wrote a letter of complaint to the mayor. He didn't even make his morning coffee or read the *Courier* or have his muffin; the letter was more important. He waited a week, but there was no reply. He sent another letter, which was also ignored. Then he saw in the morning paper an article announcing that the mayor was not going to run for reelection; he said he had been in government a long time, had done a lot of public service, and was this year eligible to collect a pension. He said a pension was no good if you didn't use it, and he intended to use his immediately at the end of his term. The political reporter for the *Courier* asked about a rumor going around which said the mayor had arranged with the governor to be appointed to a state regulatory commission on his retirement. The mayor had no comment. The reporter pointed out that it was possible to receive a full salary as a regulatory commission member from the state while continuing to receive a full pension from the city. The mayor had no comment on that either. The county chairman, who was present at the press conference, said the Democratic Party candidate would be the present deputy mayor, a young man named Lester Fogg.

Eddie wrote Lester Fogg that night. Three days later he got a call from a man named Wister, who said he was Fogg's executive assistant. Wister said he was at the office of the Sanitation Department. "I'm going to put someone on the phone," Wister said. "You explain it all to her. She's in charge of this sort of thing."

Eddie wondered how often the garbage trucks drove on people's lawns if they had to have a woman in charge of it.

"Now, sir," a nasal voice said, "what seems to be your problem?"

"Did you read my letter?" Eddie said.

"Of course. I have them right here. All three of them."

"It's all in there."

"Your letter doesn't specify the extent of the damage to your lawn."

"Sure it does. I said the rut goes clear across my lawn and it's the width of a city garbage truck's rear tires. That's the extent of the damage."

"But how *long* is it, sir? I have to know that."

"You want me to go outside with a ruler? It's raining."

"I have to know how long it is."

"Twenty-seven feet." He made up the number, the first time he had ever done such a thing. He felt very good about it.

"Thank you. That's all we had to know. If you had told us that before, we would have fixed it immediately."

"What the hell does that have to do with anything?"

"We have to plan things. Everything will be taken care of."

"When?"

"That's not up to me. We don't handle these repairs. The Parks Department does that. It depends on their schedule. Very soon." She hung up.

A month passed. The spring rains intensified. There were days when one could go outside without a coat. The neighborhood foliage greened and thickened. The grass on his lawn did not grow in to cover the dark tire tracks, which curved across it like a saber scar. No one from the city ever came. Eddie wrote Fogg, the deputy mayor, again and got in return the letter thanking him for his inquiry, the three-week-old letter promising an immediate investigation.

The only change was that the garbage men seemed to leer into his windows as they dumped the contents of the green plastic containers into their enormous silver truck, and the containers were now usually left on their sides out in the street rather than standing up in the driveway.

The tracks of the garbage truck were a thorn, but the bills were like spears. Sometimes at night Eddie dreamed about the bills, dreamed he was suffocating in an enormous storm of envelopes with shiny glassine address slots.

They lived frugally, but it didn't seem to matter. He had gotten, in the past three years, a 6 percent cost of living increase, the maximum allowed city workers who were not political appointees. That was less than one quarter of the real increase in the cost of living. His raise didn't equal the increase in real estate taxes. And the 6 percent increase had lifted him a tax bracket, so even though his money now bought less than his smaller previous salary, the federal and state governments taxed him more heavily than before.

Utilities had skyrocketed. He had lowered the thermostat, as the President suggested, even though Betty complained about the discomfort of wearing a sweater in the house. But it still cost twice as much to heat the house as last year and four times what it cost three years ago. In addition, the utility bills included an 8 percent sales tax, so he was being taxed on the inflation. The school taxes and sewer taxes had gone up, as had the city water bill and the Social Security deduction.

And silver garbage trucks drove across the goddamned lawn.

He wrote checks and slid them into the envelopes with their little windows. By the time he was halfway through the pile, the balance column in the checkbook said he had $7.27 left, which was not enough to neutralize any more of the bills. It was probably just enough to pay the monthly service charge on the checking account. The bank ran advertisements that said it gave free checking service, but a small line at the bottom of the ad revealed that the service was free to people who maintained a minimum balance of three hundred dollars through the entire month. It had been years since Eddie had been able to maintain a minimum balance of three hundred dollars. If his account got any smaller, they would bounce one of the checks rather than wait for his next deposit to collect their service fee.

He closed the checkbook and put it in a drawer, along with the bills still to be dealt with. He put stamps on the envelopes he had sealed and put them in the mail slot, where the mailman would pick them up the next morning. It was the last week of the month; Eddie was sure that the bills he would find in their place would leave him even deeper in the hole.

He put the green mug into the machine with the other dishes, dumped some Calgon into the slot on the door, and pushed the button to start the washing cycle. The kitchen was neat and clean now, except for the letter from the deputy mayor, which was still on the Formica table. Eddie read the letter again, then threw it into the garbage pail.

Betty was watching another television program, a rerun of "Bonanza," which he knew she had seen at least a half dozen times. A can of beer sat on a cork coaster near her left hand. It was partway off the coaster, and condensation from the cold can had dripped onto the tabletop, making an oblong puddle. The water went toward the table's edge, curved a little, then disappeared under the framed high school graduation photograph of Eddie junior, now a sophomore at Cornell.

Eddie junior came home twice a year, never for more than three days. He wrote letters twice each semester. He was going to be a hotel manager in some interesting place, he told them the last time he visited. Eddie senior had said he hoped it paid well because Cornell was a very expensive school. Eddie junior's face was blank: it was no problem of his. Eddie senior asked if Eddie junior would be having a job this summer. Eddie junior said he would think about that and he was going out now; could he have the car? Their longest conversation in five years.

Eddie knew it was his fault as much as the boy's, but it was too late now to change things, and he knew neither of them really wanted to: they didn't like one another very much.

Betty was still watching television when Eddie went to bed.

On the bus to work the next morning, Eddie had a terrible headache. His eyes hurt. He knew he would have to change his life soon or he would go crazy. Or die. Every time he looked at the growing stack of envelopes he felt a cloying constriction in his chest, as if cold fingers were, one by one, closing off the spaces for air, the passages for blood. And every time he looked at Betty sitting there on the sofa, her feet up on the gray ottoman and the can of beer always within reach, he got an acid feeling deep in his stomach.

The bus stopped to admit some passengers waiting in front of a branch of the Marine Midland bank. Even though spring was several weeks old, the morning wind was sharp and damp and they clustered close to the door, jamming against one another in their rush to get inside. Two men stood by the coin box, arguing over which was first.

"It don't matter," the driver said in a flat voice. "The bus ain't going nowhere until you've all put your money in. Why argue?"

"I was first," the taller man said.

"I was," the other one said.

"Why don't you both get off and start over again?" a black man in the second row said.

"You can go fuck yourself, that's what," the taller man said.

Eddie looked at the bank. It was dark inside, except for a small fluorescent light in the back.

Perhaps he could rob the bank. A daring daylight robbery. The newscasters on television always said that, especially on Channel 7: "A daring daylight robbery occurred today at the Main Street branch of . . ." When else *could* you rob a bank? he thought. They're locked at night. He pictured himself in the wide space between the tellers' cages and the front door, wearing one of those ski masks with slits for the eyes and mouth and little round holes for the nostrils. He lightly held a black sawed-off shotgun, the muzzle of which he moved constantly around the room at the people he had ordered to lie down on the floor, their hands clasped behind their heads. He wondered if their noses would hurt. He thought it must be hot inside those masks. And most bank robbers seemed to get caught. It would be his luck to be one of the bank robbers who got caught. Or whose getaway car wouldn't start.

Eddie's boss looked at the clock on the wall as Eddie came into the office. It was eight thirty-two. The boss didn't say anything. Two minutes wasn't enough of a lateness to say anything. But he made sure Eddie knew he had noticed the time. The boss was a short thick man who always wore three-piece suits that never quite closed properly. He liked to wear brown bow ties.

"You're working on the motor vehicle violation program today," he told Eddie. "They want printouts on all cars with more than two outstanding parking violations. They

want it by owners, correlated to show multiple owner-
ships. They're having a campaign against scofflaws."

"They usually do that in November," Eddie said, "after
the elections. How come they want that stuff now?"

"I think it's only certain scofflaws they'll be going after.
Well-known Republicans. You know how that works. Two
or three leaked articles to the *Courier*. 'Councilman Bar-
ber, who is up for reelection, has twenty-two unpaid tickets, a reliable source close to the investigation revealed
today.' The *Courier* loves tips like that. Anyhow, that's
none of your business, or mine either. You just work up
the program they want and put it on the machine."

"What about the water bill survey? You told me yesterday you wanted that finished immediately."

"Finish it tomorrow."

Eddie spent part of the morning at the motor vehicle office getting the information category codes. He talked
awhile with a woman who worked there, Edna Kringle,
who was first cousin to some political person in town. She
always seemed to spend a lot of time talking on the phone,
and no one ever yelled at her about it. Unlike other people
in City Hall, she didn't seem to be afraid of being caught
doing something wrong, nor did she spend her time hus-
tling or even trying to catch someone else doing something
wrong. She had always been friendly to Eddie.

During his lunch hour he sat on a concrete bench outside and watched a crew begin tearing down the wall of
red bricks the mayor had recently put up around the monument in the plaza. Bricklayers had spent most of the previous month putting up the wall. Then some people
noticed that it made the plaza almost inaccessible. The
mayor said the wall created little private spaces in the ur-
ban environment, small concealed areas where people
might find some isolation during the day. The construc-
tion, when looked at from the top of City Hall or the hotel across the street, was like an ancient maze. There were
four entrances, one at each major compass point; no path
went directly through to another side. The several interior
walls created small cul-de-sacs, each of which had a stone
bench against the wall at its dead end. The *Courier* article
on public opposition to the project quoted a criminologist
who said the brickwork was a paradise for muggers and

rapists, both of whom could now work in full confidence all day long. He said the plaza was now dangerous in the daylight and absolutely unusable at night.

The mayor responded to a reporter's questions. "No one comes downtown at night anyway, and where were those people when the arrangement was going up? You can't just come in with objections when something's finished. That's not how public works *works*." The reporter offered no response, but everyone knew the answer: City Hall was on the lake front and no one, without a compelling reason, went there between November and April. The icy winds blowing down from Canada could freeze tears to your eyes in seconds.

The pressure became so great the mayor got a second federal grant, this one to pay for tearing the wall down. Because of increases in labor costs the wall cost more to tear down than it had to put up.

Eddie went inside the building at twelve fifty-seven and got to his office exactly at one. He spent most of the afternoon preparing the program. When he had finished, he took it to the computer center and told the clerk that it was to be run immediately and the printout was to be hand-delivered to the police commissioner's office.

"We don't have any errand boys here," the clerk said.

"I'm telling you what I was told to tell you. You do what you want."

"Goddamned place. We're not goddamned errand boys, you know."

"I know that," Eddie said.

"Those fuckers upstairs don't know that."

Eddie shrugged and went back to his office.

The bus home that night was crowded and he felt a slight rawness in his throat, perhaps the beginning of a cold. He sneezed once near his stop and several people scowled at him. He pretended he didn't notice.

Betty was watching "Star-Trek," the episode about small furry animals called Tribbles. Tribbles multiplied at an exponential rate and filled portions of the ship by the third commercial. It was one of her favorite "Star-Trek" episodes. She yelled out to him that his dinner was on the table.

He hated eating so early and she knew it, but if they ate later it meant she missed "All in the Family" and the first of the evening movies. When he argued it once, she said, "You've got your work down there at City Hall making those computer programs and whatever else you do. What do I have? Nothing, that's what I have. Don't take what little I have away from me."

"I thought you said you had nothing. You can't take anything away from nothing."

"You know what I meant, Eddie. Don't try to get me upset. I hate getting upset."

He sat alone in the kitchen and ate the overcooked roast. He wished he had had the sense and nerve to get out years ago, when he still might have done something with someone interesting. Now it seemed pointless: where would he go and what would he do? He wondered how many other men he knew lived lives so secretly desperate. You only found out when one of them did something crazy, like blowing his brains out or blowing his wife's brains out, and then everyone said, "Who'd have thought it of him? He was the quietest fellow in the world. Never fought with anyone." People like that, Eddie thought, don't fight because they can't find the proper thing to vent the anger and hurt upon. Maybe they're too worn out to waste it in an exercise that will do them no good.

He and Betty had started going out during their last year of high school. She wouldn't put out until they were formally engaged. The night after he gave her the ring and there was an announcement in the paper, she permitted him to do it to her—that was her term: "All right, you can do it to me if that's what you want"—in the car. They had parked on a side road near Delaware Park and she accepted his clumsy penetration as if it were some kindness women bestowed on men, as if the act were something in which women had only a passive role, as if the entire idea were some annoyance invented by men. It was years before he understood what a hustle that was, and years more before he appreciated how perfectly he had helped himself get perfectly trapped by it.

He somehow became responsible for her. She never quite said it, but if he married her as he promised she would still be a good person, and if he abandoned her he would have taken something under false pretenses. It wasn't just the virginity—evidence of which he hadn't observed—but the years she said she had already devoted to their relationship. And it seemed a good enough idea at the time. They were married during his second year of college. She worked as a secretary then, first for a lawyer and then in an industrial office of a firm that manufactured elastic yarn sold all over the world. Just before the wedding Eddie panicked and thought about simply fleeing the city for a while. It would ruin the semester at school, but he could perhaps make up the work the following summer. His two best friends—one of whom was then in dental school and the other about to become an insurance salesman—both assured him that all men felt that panic just before the wedding, they had felt the same way themselves. They walked him down the aisle and led the toasts at the dinner. Eddie later learned that both of them had girls with whom they secretly went out regularly. When he asked the dentist how he could live that way, the dentist offered to fix Eddie up with his receptionist, a woman who had, the dentist said, "monumental jugs and a pussy that won't quit." The accountant said that Eddie was a married man now, but he obviously had a lot of growing up to do.

Betty got pregnant almost immediately and quit her job in her third month. She got headaches during the day and grew dizzy every afternoon. She never went back to work, and now had no skills left with which to get a job if she wanted one, which he knew she didn't. Her shorthand hadn't been that good to begin with and she hadn't touched a typewriter in twenty years. Eddie had, a few years ago, tried to get her to go back to school. The state college on Elmwood Avenue had a lot of programs especially for women who had been out of school for a long time. She said she would think about it. She never wrote for the booklets or the applications.


She came into the kitchen while he was drinking his cup of coffee. He had decided to have only one tonight because his stomach was not handling a lot of coffee very well. "The program is completed," she said.

"What? What are you talking about?"

"The TV program." She offered a rare smile. "You

thought I meant the other kind, your kind, didn't you?" He nodded. "I didn't. I meant my kind."

"Oh."

"I went to the store today. Shopping."

"Good."

"That's not why I'm telling you. I got a ticket. A parking ticket. What do you think I should do with it?"

He didn't tell her what he was thinking. "Give it to me," he said.

"I'll see if I can find it." She went into the other room. Five minutes later she hadn't come back, so he went looking for her. She was sitting on the sofa, her feet up on the ottoman. She looked at him. "At the next commercial, okay?"

"There it is," he said. The orange parking ticket was sitting under her beer can. It was wet and soggy. "Goddamn," he said. "Parked by a fire hydrant. That's twenty-five bucks. What's the matter with you? You know better than to park by hydrants."

"I couldn't find a parking space near the store. There were a lot of people out shopping today, I guess. I didn't think I'd be inside so long. And by the time I got out, there it was."

"Twenty-five bucks," he said again. Large letters on the bottom of the ticket said if the fine weren't paid within ten days it would double.

"Don't get so angry. It wasn't deliberate. Can't you fix it? You work for City Hall. You're down there every day. What's the point of working down there if you can't get a simple traffic ticket fixed? Everybody gets them fixed. I think—" She was starting to say something else, but the commercial ended and Archie Bunker appeared, saying something to his son-in-law, a moustachioed fart Eddie found more offensive than Archie. The sentence died in her throat and her face relaxed as she listened to the conversation on the screen. There was a brief lull while Archie went upstairs. "He's married to Laverne," Betty said.

"Laverne?"

"Of 'Laverne and Shirley.' Archie's son-in-law. They're married. In real life, I mean."

"That's wonderful," he said sarcastically.

"Yes," she mumbled, listening to Archie and his son-in-law argue again.

Eddie went into the kitchen and poured more coffee. It smelled very strong and would not only upset his stomach but keep him awake. He dumped it into the sink and poured himself about two inches of scotch into the same cup. He added a little water. He rarely drank liquor because it tended to make his thinking blurry very quickly. Right now he felt like being a little blurry.

Another twenty-five bucks to the goddamned government. City, county, state, federal: they all took. Every time he looked, they were taking again. The fourteen thousand they paid him every year and the twenty-one days' vacation and six holidays came to piss: they took it back every time he turned around, or they authorized others—like the gas company—to take more and more of what little was left.

He wished there were things he could do to make the government spend less of his money, but nothing came to mind. The papers were recently full of terrorist acts, but he thought that was silly. Sometimes innocent people got hurt, and he didn't think that was justified. And blowing up installations accomplished nothing because they just built new ones which cost more to build than the old ones that had been destroyed. Stopping operations wasn't good enough: the workers came in anyway, got paid anyway, and then had to work overtime later, after things got fixed up, to make up the lost production hours. And Eddie Argo wasn't the kind of man who went around making bombs. Eddie Argo was the kind of man who got depressed and paid his goddamned bills and wondered just how much longer he could manage not drowning.

The next morning, during the bus ride downtown, Eddie thought about what Betty had said. Maybe she was right.

He told his boss he was going to lunch a half hour early.

"Make sure you're back at twelve-thirty then."

"Of course," Eddie said.

He walked down the high-ceilinged hallway and took the long corridor left to the motor vehicle office. He peeked in, saw Edna was alone in the room, her hands folded neatly in her lap. She was looking at her telephone.

"Edna," he said, "can I talk to you a minute?"

"Sure, Eddie. I'm always here for somebody to talk to." She smiled and pointed to the chair next to her desk.

"I got a little problem," he said, looking down at the floor.

"Tell Edna." She lighted a cigarette and smiled at him. Her teeth weren't very even, but Eddie decided she was better-looking than he had thought. He realized he hadn't ever thought about her at all, nor had he looked at her for years. She leaned back in her leather chair and he knew she was doing it for him. He also knew that it wasn't a movement that meant anything, it was a movement she would have done for any man who sat down to talk, showing she still had it. He wished her sweater weren't pink; he hated pink sweaters.

Eddie reached into his jacket pocket and took out the parking ticket. "Betty—my wife—got this yesterday. Fire hydrant. I just wondered if . . ."

Edna laughed. "You wondered if I could get it fixed for you?" She laughed again, forgetting she had just inhaled the cigarette, and immediately had a violent coughing spasm. Her breasts heaved up and down inside the pink sweater. He looked away, slightly embarrassed.

"You guys," she said when she got her breath again. "Who knows what you're going to come up with? I thought you'd popped out of your cocoon."

"My what?"

"Never mind. Let me see it." He took it from his jacket and handed it to her. "What were you doing, trying to wash it clean? The writing's all blurred."

"Betty put a beer can on it."

"That won't make it go away. And neither will I. I can't do that anymore, not since they computerized the tickets. I used to could, but not now. You're the only guy who can disappear them now."

"What do you mean? Me?"

"It used to be that we could just make a ticket disappear by pulling it. Now they all exist in triplicate. One goes to the citizen, one to the city court, and one to the state records office. They all have to be disposed of properly, and the state audits the ticket records to make sure none of the municipalities misses that fine source of revenue. If you have a friend in court, a judge can dismiss the charges, but that's a big deal, for people with connections, and that's not you. Even people with connections don't do that much anymore because then they owe the judges favors. It's just not worth the small change. The other way to make the ticket disappear is to tell the computer it's gone. It's the computer that keeps all the records. Nobody looks at the tickets themselves after they get encoded the day they're written. The computer gets the dispositions. Tickets that are paid or dismissed are of no interest to it; tickets that are outstanding too long get kicked out in occasional surveys. You're the programmer for the city, right?"

"My boss is the programmer. I'm his deputy."

"That waddly turd couldn't program his way out of a phone booth and you know it. He got that job because he was Costanza's cousin, or I should say, because he was the only one of Costanza's cousins who could count to ten without getting confused. All the others work for the Fire Department or the Police Department. You do the actual programming. Just type out a disposition and the ticket is abolished."

"Abolished?"

"Yeah. It doesn't officially exist anymore. Here, look it up." She pushed across the desk a small red booklet.

"That's the city program manual," he said. "I've got a copy. I wrote most of it."

"That's what I've been telling you. Just go up to your console and take care of your problem. Clickety-click."

"But that's . . ." He paused, looking for a nice word.

"Illegal?"

"Yes. That's what I was going to say."

"Then pay the ticket." She picked up the phone and dialed a number. "I've got to call my sister now," she said.

Eddie went to the ground floor cafeteria and got a sandwich and container of coffee, then went back to his office to work on the water bill survey. No one else was there; the others were still out on their regular lunch hour.

Why not? He asked himself. It took only ten minutes from start to finish: eight to find the code, one to decide how to do it, and one more to type the orders into the computer console. When he finished, the screen told him that the violation number had been removed.

A few minutes later his office door opened. It was his boss. He was back ten minutes early from his lunch hour.

"You're here," the boss said.

"That's right," Eddie said.

"Good," the boss said, leaving without bothering to close the door.

# TWO

Eddie waited at the corner of Delaware for the bus. It came late, and when the doors opened he saw there was no room to get on. They had been cutting service lately and the bus was probably doing the work of two.

"You gettin' on or not, mac?" the driver yelled.

Eddie stepped back to the curb and the doors hissed shut. The bus growled into the rush hour traffic, leaving in its wake a thick layer of black smoke. He waited for the light to change, then crossed over Delaware. A car, making a right turn against the light, honked at him. He gave the driver the finger in return and felt good about that.

Instead of walking along Delaware to West Ferry, he walked along Niagara, which for part of the way went near the river. It was a lot further going that way, almost twice as long, but he was in no hurry. It was a pleasant, cool evening. It wouldn't be dark for two hours yet and there was a nice breeze blowing down from Canada. He doubted Betty would notice his absence.

He was thinking about his adventure earlier in the day—how he had erased the records of the parking ticket. For an hour or so he had felt guilty about the act and had half expected his office to be suddenly flooded with large city policemen, ready to drag him away for meddling with official records. No one came. He looked over the program again later and was sure Edna was right: if you got into the right dialogue with the computer, no one could ever know later what had been said or done. If you told a computer to forget something, it immediately reached into its memory for the appropriate length of tape, and within seconds its powerful magnetic heads so realigned the iron molecules on the tape that no machine in existence could reconstruct what was now gone.

Once when he was a kid, someone had facetiously asked the teacher where the letters went when she erased the blackboard. She began a lecture on the bits of chalk that collected on the eraser and on the chalk ledge, then noticed that the boys were all giggling. She made the boy who had asked the question stay after class and wash perfectly clean all the blackboards in the room. Unlike the blackboard's letters, erasures on the memory tapes left no bits of dust with which one might know that writing and erasing had gone on. As he thought about it, he decided there were few things in life that could be perfectly ended and erased the way information on the tapes could. Real-life things hung around for a long time, and even when they were supposedly over there was the memory or the bills that kept coming. On the machines an absence was perfect: once the programmer told the machine something didn't exist, it disappeared for good.

The stores along this part of Niagara Street reflected what the neighborhood had become: there were Italian and Puerto Rican and Indian enclaves all along the way. Once it had been Irish, but they had moved to another section of the city when the Italians came. The blacks mostly lived on the east side of Main Street, far across town. But the high schools and the downtown area were all mixed up. Eddie knew that was what those people really moved to the suburbs for, why they paid the extra money for houses that would probably fall down in their lifetimes: to get away from the spics and niggers. They wouldn't say that. They would only say, "There's a better class of people out there and the schools are better."

The city council had tried passing a law forcing all city employees to live within the city boundaries, but one of the unions fought that law and it was soon declared unconstitutional. Eddie was the only person in his department who still lived in the city.

One man he knew, a lawyer, had been up reading late one night and all his front windows suddenly came crashing into the living room. The lawyer thought someone was shooting at his house. He crawled across the floor and dialed the police emergency number, 911. The operator asked him several questions until he yelled, "They're shooting out my goddamned windows! Get somebody over here!" A patrol car came to his house twenty minutes later.

"I would have been terrified," Eddie said to the man.

"I was. And so was my wife. We kept looking at the

clock above the fireplace and wondering if those people would come right into the house next. I was afraid to peek out because I thought, if they saw a head at the window they'd start shooting again. When the cops came, they looked around and told me it was nothing, just rocks. They went around the room picking up the rocks. I hadn't seen them before. The cop said it was probably some kids, maybe they got drunk in the park. 'You didn't know that,' I told him.

" 'How could I know it before I got here to investigate?' the cop told me.

" 'Then why did it take you guys twenty minutes to come? The police station is only four blocks away. You couldn't know beforehand that it wasn't a real shooting.' You know what he told me?"

"No," Eddie said.

"He told me, 'We're very busy. You people don't understand that we've very busy these days.' "

The lawyer told Eddie that he and his wife put their house on the market as soon as the windows were repaired and the moldings repainted. They bought a place out in Amherst. "The Amherst police probably don't come any faster," Eddie said. "That place is more spread out than the city."

"Sure," the lawyer said, "but you don't have those crazy animals roaming the streets with the rocks at night out there. All you have out there are burglars, and burglars you got everywhere."

No one had ever bothered Eddie and no vandalism had ever occurred on his street that he knew about. The kids did things on Mischief Night and Halloween, but that wasn't the sort of thing you called the police about. He had never had occasion to telephone the police for help. His only problem was with the garbage department truck that drove across his lawn.

And the Volvo agency on Delaware Avenue. They were after him.

He had brought the car in because he was having trouble with the brakes and the muffler was getting noisy. They told him they had to replace the entire exhaust system and the brakes all needed relining. He had them go ahead and do the work. He went to pick up the car three days later, paid the bill—which was $86 more than the estimate—and drove out onto Delaware Avenue. The car still sounded terribly noisy. He drove it back into the shop and asked the mechanic to put it up on the rack.

"I got another car going up there now," the mechanic said. "We're real jammed up here."

"You have to put it up. There's something wrong."

The man finally agreed. When the car was in the air, Eddie walked underneath. He didn't know much about cars, but he could see that they hadn't changed any of the pipes between the two mufflers, though he had been billed for them, and the rear muffler wasn't the right size. When he looked at it closely, he saw a Volkswagen symbol on the end.

"Who's responsible for this job?" he asked the mechanic.

"Not me. I don't do mufflers."

"Who, then?"

"Damned if I know."

"How come there's a Volkswagen muffler on here? I bet that doesn't cost a third of what a Volvo muffler costs."

"Damned if I know," the mechanic said.

The assistant service manager said the service manager was the fellow who had handled the job, but he wasn't around. Eddie said he had been around when he paid his bill fifteen minutes earlier. "He ain't around now," the assistant service manager replied, but then said he would replace the cheap muffler with the one Eddie had paid for and would install the missing pipes. He said he couldn't understand how it happened. Eddie said it was clear enough to him what happened.

Two days later, Eddie was picking up some packages at the food market on Elmwood Avenue. He stopped for a light and almost crashed into the car directly in front of him. The brakes barely held and the pedal traveled to the floor. He very carefully drove to a Mobil station nearby. The mechanic put the car up on the rack and fiddled with the front wheels for a while, then said, "Caliper on the left front wheel is gone. Tell me, did it. . . ." He described the symptoms that the car had shown before Eddie had brought it into the Volvo agency.

"They told me it was linings, bad linings."

"Maybe. But not likely on a car like this. Betcha they just pumped it full of fluid and sealed the left wheel. It doesn't hold, doing that. A couple of days later and it's just as bad as it was to start out with."

Eddie thought about writing the Better Business Bureau and the District Attorney, but what could he prove? He didn't have the defective linings, the linings they had told him were defective, and they had made the changes on the exhaust system. He had to let it go.

But the Volvo agency didn't let it go. They had started sending him bills for $75, which they said was due for additional work done to his car. The bills didn't say what the additional fee was for. Lately, they were threatening to take him to court if he didn't pay what he owed. The company had just moved to Hamburg, about ten miles away, and changed its name. He supposed it was to escape their conniving reputation. They continued sending him bills.

Eddie wrote the national office of Volvo in Rockleigh, New Jersey. A vice-president answered by return mail. He thanked Eddie for bringing the problem of deceptive service and improper billing to his attention and suggested that in the future Eddie deal only with authorized Volvo dealers. He gave Eddie the name and address of the authorized Volvo dealer in his area, the dealer in Hamburg who had lied about the brakes and substituted the Volkswagen muffler and was presently dunning him.

Eddie had gotten the Volvo because of their ads, which promised a car that would last for years. Buffalo was rough country on cars, not so much because of the hard winters but rather because of the tons of salt that were deposited on the roadways every winter. The salt ate away the car bodies quickly. One saw few cars more than three years old without ugly brown rusted-out holes on the fenders, doors and rocker panels. Volvo was supposed to be a good winter car, even in an area that used a lot of salt, and the ads said it had a fine service system. The car had been more than he could afford, but he reasoned that amortization over seven or eight years would in the long run make it cheaper than an American car.

He had been an idiot. The Volvo company didn't care. They knew he wouldn't be buying any more Volvos.

It hadn't been that easy getting the damned car in the first place. It had cost nearly seven thousand dollars, which meant Eddie had to take out a large automobile loan to pay for it.

CitiBank had been advertising heavily on television and in the papers about its four-year loan plan. The ads said the extra year increased the interest only slightly and gave a person a whole extra year to pay for a car. "Which means you can have more car for yourself," the commercial said. The monthly payments would be much lower than they would have been on a thirty-six-month plan, the maximum offered by all the other banks in town.

Eddie went to the branch on West Utica, not very far from where he lived. It was next to a supermarket in a small shopping center that had been created when a half block of two-family houses had been ripped down the previous year.

As Eddie waited his turn to talk to the loan officer, he felt an uncomfortable sensation radiating into his abdomen from his stomach. Things felt more tumultuous and liquid than they should have been. He looked around for the toilet. He knew there was no reason for such nervousness, that it was just the way he always felt when he had to tell a stranger that he was a worthwhile and responsible person. He wished there were some way to handle the transaction by mail.

The person sitting next to the loan officer's desk got up and left. The loan officer yelled, "Next!"

Eddie walked across the highly polished floor to the desk. The loan officer—a small engraved plaque said his name was Mr. L. Beaver—pointed to the empty chair. Eddie sat down.

"Well?" the loan officer said. "What can we do for you?"

"I want to buy a car. A Volvo. It's seven thousand dollars. I need a loan for it. The four-year loan you advertise."

"We're the only bank in town that gives a forty-eight-month payback period," Beaver said.

"I know," Eddie said. "That's why I came to Citibank."

"That's brought us a lot of business. Must be hard times, these days."

Jesus, Eddie thought, you're a banker, don't you *know?* "Everything's going up," Eddie said, "except for salaries. They don't seem to go up very fast."

"And what's yours?" Beaver said.

"What? Beg your pardon?"

"Your salary. What's your salary?"

Eddie told him. He also told him, in response to a series of questions Beaver asked in a flat voice without once looking up from his form, about his previous loans (one with the Marine for the car they currently owned, an old Buick; the mortgage, held by the Big E; and a loan he had taken from the Big E five years ago when the furnace went in December and had to be replaced immediately), about their charge accounts, and about other income ("None," he said). When he was done reading his questions, Beaver asked, "How come you didn't go to Marine or Big E for this loan?"

"Because of the forty-eight-month option you've got. That's what I said before."

"That's what I thought," Beaver said. "They don't offer that option."

"I know," Eddie said.

Beaver looked up again and stared straight into Eddie's eyes. "Now, Mr. Argo, think carefully. Is there anything else you want to tell me?"

"About what?"

"About your financial affairs."

"What else do you want to know about?"

"Nothing, but it's hard asking about what you don't know about, if you know what I mean."

"I know what you mean," Eddie said. "There's nothing else in my financial picture. I have no debts except for the charge accounts and the mortgage. I've never defaulted on a debt or been more than a few days late with a payment. Is that what you mean?"

"That's the sort of thing I mean. Anything else?"

"What do you have in mind?"

"I don't know."

"Well," Eddie said, "neither do I. I can't think of anything else."

"All right then, Mr. Argo. We'll let you know." Beaver turned to his papers and began writing on some forms. Eddie sat there a moment, then understood that Beaver had quite finished with him.

"When will I hear?" Eddie asked.

"You can call me at three tomorrow afternoon. I'll have the credit report on you by then."

"Fine. Thank you."

"You're welcome."

Eddie stood up and didn't move for a moment. He wondered if he and the banker should shake hands. But Beaver didn't look up again, so Eddie turned and walked to the door. At the moment his hand reached out for the door, he heard Beaver's voice bark out, "Next!"

When he got home, she was watching "Bewitched." He put up some coffee and watched it start dripping through. Before the pot was full, she came into the kitchen.

"What happened?" she asked. "Did they give you the money?"

"Banks don't *give* you money," he said. "They rent it to you. Nobody gives anybody anything."

"You don't have to be nitpicking. You know what I mean. Did we get the loan? Can we go pick up the car?"

"Not yet. I have to call tomorrow. They have to run a credit check."

"But why do they have to check up on you? You're perfectly reliable, anyone can tell them that."

"They have to check it anyway. That's how they do things."

"I know some people I'd like to have checked. Like the Sullivans down the street. I've heard some strange things about them. Do you know what goes on in that house?"

"It's not that kind of check. They just ask a computer if you've been a bad credit risk, if you've defaulted on a loan or something. There's no problem. I have to call him tomorrow and then they'll let us have the money."

But that wasn't what happened. When Eddie called the next day at three, a woman who answered the telephone took his name, went away for a moment, then said that Mr. Beaver couldn't come to the phone just now, that he would call back in a few minutes. Eddie waited until almost five o'clock, which was when that bank closed. He called the bank again.

"Oh, yes, Mr. Argo," Beaver said. "You're calling about your loan application." Eddie said that was correct. "I'm afraid we won't be able to give you the loan," Beaver said.

"Why? I don't understand this. You said my income was adequate."

"Because of your unpaid accounts at Penney's and Harper's. Which you neglected to mention, though it wouldn't have mattered in the end."

"There's some error, Mr. Beaver. I don't have any accounts at either of those stores and I never did. I told you where all my accounts were."

"Mr. Argo, I'd like to help you. I really would. But we can't give you a loan with those defaulted accounts. You understand that."

"I just told you. I don't have any defaulted accounts. There's a mistake."

"Mr. Argo, we have to go with the credit bureau. And if they say you've got bad accounts, then you've got bad accounts. You can't expect me to take your word over theirs, can you?"

"I'd prefer that you would."

"All you people would. But that's not how banking works."

"What is this credit bureau? Give me their number. I'll call them and get this straightened out."

"It's confidential information, Mr. Argo."

"You can't deny me a loan on the basis of incorrect information and then tell me I can't know where you got the incorrect information. You have to give me a chance to clear myself. I'll write to 'Newspower.' "

"Newspower" was a column in the *Courier*. Consumers who thought they had been treated dishonestly or unfairly by local businesses could write in and a reporter would be sent to check out the accusation. If the consumer was right and the business didn't immediately make amends, they printed the name of the offending merchant in the paper so other people would know about him and his business style.

"Just a minute," Beaver said. "I'm going to put you on hold."

"All right," Eddie said.

There was a long pause, during which time Eddie listened to sugary music. He supposed the music was to let the person waiting know that the circuit hadn't been broken. But it was awful music.

The msuic stopped and Beaver said, "It's TRL."

"Pardon?"

"TRL. They're in downtown Buffalo."

"Do you have their telephone number?"

"All I know is, it's TRL. In downtown Buffalo."

"I'm going to put you on hold a moment," Eddie said. "All right?"

"I'm very—"

"Good. Be right back." Eddie pushed the button and got out his city telephone book. There was no entry for TRL. He activated the phone line again and told Beaver that.

"Maybe their number isn't listed," Beaver said. "Or maybe they're in the book under another name. Maybe they just moved down there. I don't know what to say."

"I think you'd maybe better get me their number."

"I don't have it," Beaver said. "I don't deal with them."

"You must call them to have them run the credit checks. Unless it's all made up."

"Mr. Argo! We don't make things up here, as you put it. My assistant handles that. Calling for the credit check, I mean. I'm really very busy here right now."

"Ask her, then."

"I'm going to put you on hold," Beaver said. The music came on again. It was as if the melody and strings picked up in the same place they had been cut off the last time. It was the kind of music you could enter and exit with no sense of interruption or incompletion.

Beaver came back on the line. He recited the number. "Is that all?"

"That's all. Thank you, Mr. Beaver."

Beaver hung up without responding.

Eddie called TRL immediately. The receptionist told him they did not discuss cases over the telephone. If he wanted information about his dossier, he would have to come to their offices. He asked what their hours were. They coincided exactly with his. He said he would come the next day.

"You need an appointment," the woman said.

"At twelve noon. No: make it twelve-five, so I have time to walk over there. I'm only a few blocks away."

"All right, Mr. Argo. Twelve-five."

The next day, Eddie managed to get out of the office a few minutes early. He walked across the square and along one of the streets behind the Statler. The building in which the TRL offices were located was old and dilapidated. It was directly opposite the YMCA. It would soon be destroyed to make way for a new convention center the city was planning, and that probably explained the state of disrepair. The elevator was out of order and a sign said all TRL offices were on the fourth floor.

If he hadn't known it was a credit agency, Eddie would have thought the place was one of those CIA fronts he had read about in mystery novels. Nothing in the lower part of the building gave any hint of what TRL actually did, not unless the initials meant something to bankers he knew nothing about. No one seemed to be moving in the halls of the first three floors.

When he reached the fourth floor, he saw no signs at all. Along the hallway were a dozen office doors, all of them closed. He walked to the end. On his left was a large room in which about twenty people typed rapidly on computer consoles. None of them looked up. At the far end of the room a person without a console watched the others. It was like a movie he had seen with Anthony Perkins, called *The Trial*. The man at the far end of the room looked at Eddie, but he made no gesture of acknowledgment.

Eddie stepped into the room. There was no sound except the chatter of the IBM typewriters. The supervisor glowered at him and raised his arm. He pointed down the hall behind Eddie and said, "That way. Inquiries are that way. No admittance here."

Eddie backed out of the room into the corridor. A branch angled off to the right. At its end was a door with a sign: TRL: INQUIRIES. BY APPOINTMENT ONLY.

A large woman sat at a desk just beyond the door. The desk was positioned so you couldn't move into the office complex beyond without walking around it. The woman was very fat and had bright yellow hair. A gold chain disappeared between her breasts.

"Yes?" she asked without smiling.

"My name is Argo. I want to examine my credit file. There are errors."

"You have an appointment?"

"Yes."

"For what time?"

"Twelve-five," Eddie said.

"It's twelve-five now."

"That's right," he said.

"Fill this out"—she handed him a sheet of paper— "then go sit over there." She turned away, letting him know the conversation was over. As she moved, the object on the bottom of the chain was briefly visible. It was a gold name tag with large letters in script—*SARAH*—and it had been completely hidden sideways in the flesh. When she leaned forward, the name tag again disappeared completely. She sighed loudly and scratched her arm, then didn't move at all.

"What do I do with the paper when I've filled it out?" Eddie asked.

"You'll be told," she said without looking at him.

Along the far wall of what appeared to be a waiting room was a long high bench bolted to the wall. Two men were leaning against it, filling out the same form the woman had given him. Short stubby pencils, the kind no one would steal, were attached to the bench by pieces of white string.

The form asked for his name, address, Social Security number, employer, previous employer, address, previous addresses, charge accounts active and charge accounts inactive.

It was obvious to Eddie that one function of the form was for TRL to get more information than they perhaps had. He filled out only the top half.

At twelve forty-five a man came out of a small cubicle. He was shaking his head and mumbling to himself. He called to a small boy who had been sitting on the bench in front of Eddie.

"Who's next?" the woman inside the booth called out.

"I have an appointment for twelve-five," Eddie said.

"I asked who's next?"

"Me," said one of the men who had been filling out the form when Eddie got there.

The fat woman at the front desk permitted Eddie to use her phone. She asked if it was a local call, he said it was, then she watched carefully while he dialed, making sure he didn't stick an extra three digits in there. He told Gladys, his boss's secretary, that he would be back late. Gladys said the boss wouldn't be pleased. Eddie said he was aware of that, but it was unavoidable.

At one-fifteen the woman in the booth told Eddie it was his turn. She took the form he had filled out and looked it over quickly. "You didn't fill out the bottom half," she said, scowling at him over glasses that covered the lower halves of her eyes.

"Do I have to fill it all out?"

"We prefer it," she said, holding the form over the desk.

"Do I have to?"

"We need it for identification," she said.

"Here," he said. He showed her his driver's license, his city employee identification card, and his Mastercharge card.

"All right," she said, annoyed. She put the form squarely in the middle of the desk in between them. "What is it you want to know?"

"I was turned down for a loan. They said I had some accounts that I hadn't paid. I've never *not* paid my accounts. They weren't mine, the ones they had records of. I want to know how they got into my file and I want them taken out."

"Just a moment." She picked up the telephone. "Citibank rejection. Argo. SS number . . ." A few minutes later a young girl came in with a brown manila folder.

The woman began looking through it. "It says here that . . ."

"May I please look at that?"

"No. Of course not. This is confidential information."

"But it's about me. I should be able to look at it."

"It's in code. You wouldn't understand it. I'll read the significant portions to you. That's all you're entitled to."

"That's not right," Eddie said.

"That's the law. Now do you want me to read it to you or do you want to terminate this inquiry?"

"Read it."

She read off the parts of his indebtedness. The mortgage on the house. Charge account at Sears. Mobil card. Mastercharge card. She read with her eyes down at the page, below the upper rim of the glasses, hardly pausing after each entry. When she said "Penney's and Harper's," he interrupted her.

"No," he said.

"I beg your pardon?"

"I said no. I don't have accounts at Penney's or at Harper's. I never have."

"Of course you do. It says so right here. In our records." She looked at him over the tops of the rims and moved the glasses slightly down her nose so her line of sight wasn't cut in half by the steel frames.

"Well, your records are wrong," he said. "I don't have an account at either store. I've never had an account at either store. I demand you take those entries out of my file."

"It's possible that there was some error," she said, pushing the glasses back up. "If you're sure—"

"Oh, I'm sure," he said. "I'm damned sure."

"Perhaps they confused you with someone else with the same name. Sometimes that happens."

"Then you'll remove those entries from my file? They've ruined my credit rating, and it's not fair. They're not my accounts."

"Oh," she said, turning the pages in the file, "I can't do that."

"Then I'll sue you."

She smiled and leaned back in her chair. "A lot of people say that. It doesn't do them one bit of good. See, we're just a data collection and transmission agency. We don't guarantee anything. All we do is print out for the banks the information we have in our computers. All of our reports carry a disclaimer saying that the information is as reported to us by merchants and fiduciary institutions and we are not responsible for the contents. We're fully protected. If you get Harper's and Penney's to write us requesting that we withdraw the entry, then we'll do it. Otherwise, no way. You can sue all you like, but you know what'll happen? Nothing, that's what'll happen. We always win those suits. We're protected."

"But that's wrong," Eddie said. "It's wrong to ruin a man's credit without even being sure your information is correct, especially when a guy comes down and shows you where the errors are."

"That's not my concern. Is there anything else I can help you with? If not, we're very busy." She closed the file, took off her glasses, and smiled at him from across the desk.

The waiting room was nearly full when he went out. None of the people there talked to one another. They all looked slightly embarrassed about being there, as if they had been trapped and exposed doing something secret and immoral. At the far end of the hall the silent workers still sat before their ranks of computer consoles, getting and storing bits and pieces of information. Eddie's shoes tapped loudly on the steel stairs as he walked down. In the dark corner of the turning flights on the second floor, he met one man coming up. Even though the stairway was narrow, neither man looked directly at the other.

"Where the hell have you been?" his boss yelled when he got back to the office. The boss clutched a fistful of papers. He always seemed to be clutching a fistful of papers.

"I got tied up. I called Gladys."

"You called Gladys forty-five minutes ago. What do you think this is? We're swamped with work and you take two-hour lunch hours. Let me smell your breath."

"You know I don't drink."

"I don't know a damned thing about you, Argo. I never did."

Later that afternoon, when his boss was out, Eddie called Harper's credit department. He explained the situation. The clerk asked him to wait a moment. Eddie said he couldn't wait very long.

"You're the one who called," the clerk said.

"All right," Eddie said.

There was some of the same kind of music he heard when he called Citibank. Then the clerk came back on the line. "You're right, Mr. Argo, we did have you mixed up with someone else. I don't mean *we* did. I mean one of the machines must have mistyped a name. It seems to have been an Edward Arko. He lives on West Utica."

"But I live on West Ferry. They knew that at the bank and at the credit agency."

"They probably assumed the address was an error. It's an easy error to make."

"Will you call TRL and have them fix it?"

"I'll have to talk to my supervisor first. I've never done that, just cleared a delinquent account on my own."

"It's all right. You know what the error was. Just call them right away. Please."

"After I talk to my supervisor, Mr. Arko."

"Argo." Eddie spelled it out.

When he hung up, he saw his boss was standing in the doorway, frowning and doleful. "That wasn't city business," his boss said.

"No, it wasn't. Something I had to take care of."

"City time, city business. I don't want to have to tell you again."

"Yes, sir," Eddie said, hating him. He realized he'd always hated him. He also realized the feeling was reciprocated. He knew why he hated his boss, but he wondered what reasons his boss could have. As Edna had said, if it weren't for Eddie, the department wouldn't be able to function because the boss didn't know enough about information systems to do any of the work himself. That, Eddie decided, was probably the main reason behind the boss's feeling. Eddie wouldn't like to have a job where his subordinates knew more about the work than he did. But, then, Eddie would never have the kind of political influence necessary to get jobs like that in the city government.

That night, after dinner, he called Penney's. He was told their credit department was open from nine to five. He asked if there was anyone in the office who could take down the information. "No," the operator said, "there's no one here." She broke off the connection.

He called them again the next day during his lunch hour. He explained the situation carefully, and said that he had never had an account with Penney's and their erroneous report of it was ruining his credit. The clerk said she would check. She asked for his present address.

"Can't I hang on while you check?" Eddie asked.

"It takes a long time. The information isn't here, it's at the national accounting office in Pittsburgh. It doesn't respond very quickly to inquiries from the branches. Penney's is a very busy firm, sir."

Three days later Eddie got a letter from J. C. Penney thanking him for letting them know about his new address. There was also a letter from the Volvo dealer wanting to know when he was going to come in and pick up the car. Four days after that he got a bill from Penney's for the amount the woman at TRL had said he owed. He called again and pointed out that his name was Argo and the name on the bill was Arko. The woman again said she would look into it. Then he got another bill in the mail; this one had his name spelled correctly and the right address.

He wrote the national office of Penney's. He got no answer. He wrote another letter, slightly more militant. They didn't answer that one either.

The Volvo dealer was threatening to keep the deposit and sell the car to someone else. Finally Eddie went to another bank. The loan officer was very sympathetic. Eddie explained the entire situation. The loan officer said he understood how those things happened, but given that Eddie had explained it all beforehand, he didn't think there would be any problem. He said he would call Eddie in a day or two. That was on a Tuesday. Eddie called him Friday afternoon.

"Ah, Mr. Argo. I've been intending to call you."

"Do I have the loan?"

"Well, there are certain problems."

"What problems?"

"The report shows that you've cleared up your difficulties with Harper's. They list you as a slow payer, but they say you did make good on the account. And—"

"Wait a minute," Eddie said. "I don't *have* an account at Harper's."

"Not now you don't," the loan officer said. "They canceled it after the outstanding balance was taken care of. And—"

"But—"

"Mr. Argo, may I finish?"

"All right," Eddie said in a low voice.

"And Penney's still lists you as delinquent."

"That's not me. I told you. It's a man named Arko. He lives on West Utica."

"They have the name and address correct, Mr. Argo. I'm looking at the report right now."

"But I explained all that to you," Eddie said, his voice rising again.

"So you did, so you did. But I have this report here and there is a committee at the bank."

"Can I come in and talk to the committee? Maybe if I explained it all to them? I can bring all the letters I've written to Penney's."

"The committee, Mr. Argo, never meets with anyone."

It took two more weeks. The fourth bank he applied to agreed to let him have the loan. They made him put down a thousand dollars more on the car than he had planned and they charged him a higher rate of interest than was usual. They said it was because he was in a high risk loan category, and when he complained, they pointed out that they didn't usually make any loans at all to people who had defaulted on major store accounts like Penney's.

Penney's never answered any of his letters.

And as it turned out, he rarely used the car. It was easier taking the bus to and from work. On rare occasions, like today, he walked home.

After walking a little over two miles from City Hall he reached West Ferry, his street. His house was a mile to the right. Just before he made the turn he noticed at the bottom of the hill to the left, just in front of the iron drawbridge, a cluster of flashing red and blue dome lights. They were bunched together where West Ferry ended at the canal. It was five-twenty. He had time. All the time in the world.

A small crowd had gathered around the cars. There was an ambulance, a sheriff's car, and two city police cars. Down by the concrete wharf to the right of the iron bridge deputies in wet suits and snorkels were pulling something out of the canal. Eddie leaned against the bridge's black railing and watched the ropes come dripping over the gray concrete edge.

Then the crowd made an ooohing noise. Someone

pressed against Eddie's back. He felt for his wallet. He had read about people getting their pockets picked at scenes like this.

"Well, pardon *me*," a woman's voice said loudly in his ear. It was she who had been pressing against him, forced by someone standing behind her who was also trying to glimpse what was going on. She had thought Eddie was feeling her thigh. He felt himself blushing, but he said nothing. There was too much noise to explain. And what could he say: "Sorry, lady; I thought you were picking my pocket"?

Dozens of people had arrived in the few minutes since he had gotten there. He was amazed how rapidly the crowd had collected.

"How long's he been in?" a woman asked.

"Hard to tell," a policeman standing nearby said. "Looks like a while."

A teen-age boy who was down on the concrete wharf shouted up to a friend on the bridge. "He doesn't have any eyes. His eyes are gone clean out."

"The fish eat them," someone said. "They're shiny in the water, like lures."

"They float up here all the time," the man standing next to Eddie said. "It has something to do with the currents between the river and the lake. Sometimes they float out to the lake and then they float back into the canal and they stop around here. It can take months. Sometimes they get drunk and fall in right here. They put fences up and down the other side, but not along the jetty. And people prefer fishing along the jetty, I don't know why. A lot of 'em fish here weekends, go to sleep, and fall in. They don't know how cold and fast the water is. They find out. Weird thing is, some of those people disappear for a month or two, then come back up right here. Just about the same place they went in."

"How do they know who the people are?" Eddie asked, still looking over the rail. If he had known the man they had just pulled out—he assumed it was a man because of the clothes and short hair—he wouldn't have been able to recognize him.

"Sometimes they don't, I guess," the man who had just spoken said.

"We hardly ever don't find out who it is," the policeman said, making his voice sound professional. "We go through the list of who is missing. Somebody always reports somebody missing after a while. Then, if we've gotten one out of here that disappeared about the same time, we try and put them together. A wallet, teeth, fingerprints. Fingerprints aren't any good after they've been in a week or more, though, especially since the fish have started coming back into the lake. Sometimes somebody's standing right here when they go in and we know who it is even before we find them. It used to be you couldn't read the stuff in the wallets because the ink would all fade away, but now people have plastic credit cards and things and they last forever."

"Do they all come back up?" Eddie asked.

"Who knows?" the policeman said. "We only know about the ones we know about."

Eddie stared at the body without any eyes. What if some part of that person had been aware of the fish coming and poking and nibbling away, had wanted to scream out against the violation through a throat clogged with black cold water?

Sometimes Eddie wanted to scream out, but there wasn't anyone to listen. Sometimes he felt like he was drowning and that screaming was pointless.

As he walked along West Ferry toward his house, Eddie looked at some of the old people sitting in their windows, looking down at the cars. He wondered if the body in the river was some old person who decided it wasn't worth bothering anymore. They must get all those bills too, the city and the state and the federal government must take it away from them too, their utility bills must be dearer and dearer. There had been an article in the *Evening News* a few months before about an old couple who had frozen to death in their small house because the gas company cut off their service after they were two months behind in their payments. The couple had been found after the mailman noticed their Social Security checks were still in their mailbox three days after he delivered them. He called the police and they broke the door open. The two bodies were huddled together, locked tightly under blankets in the living room. The old bodies hadn't generated enough heat for the blankets to do them any good.

Eddie felt a desperate anger boiling in his chest, ready to burst it because it had nowhere to go. He wanted to get even, to strike back at all those silent organizations who sent you bills through the mail and didn't care what happened to you, whether or not you could live with what they were doing to you, whether or not you got anything in return for the money they squeezed out in greater and greater amounts. The gas company. The government. The goddamned Volvo agency and the banks. The clerks who cared only for the smooth operations of their electronic machines.

He had nothing to withhold, which was what made them all so powerful. None of the poor and none of the lower middle class any longer had anything to withhold. Who cared if someone like Eddie disappeared from the face of the earth? Someone else just like him would take his place, move into his job and into his house. If Betty were still living there, she probably wouldn't even notice that a change had occurred, not so long as the TV set continued functioning properly.

Nothing he could think of would do any good. Should he throw a pie at the governor, the way he saw a kid do on the news a few months earlier? They'd probably shoot him and he'd probably miss anyway. Vote NO for something? It made no difference who got in: prices went up, taxes went up, Betty still had nothing to say and watched with passion reruns of "All in the Family," and the bony old people froze to death in dark silence.

There were soon to be state senate hearings in the county hall chambers. He could strap sticks of dynamite around his waist and set himself off during those hearings. But he would only get himself killed and open jobs for a new bunch of idiots to do the same things done by the present bunch of idiots.

No: if he were to do anything, it would have to be done so he could be around afterwards. He wasn't courageous enough to opt for the martyr's faith—that it was worth it before you know the results. He wanted to know that what he did really happened. The only problem was, he had no idea what he could do or how he could do it. If he were the president of a large corporation, a man with a lot of money and a lot of power, then he would know. But he was just Eddie Argo, a clerk for the city, a designer of conversations for computers that talked to one another over telephone lines. Nobody.

A long black car was parked in front of a liquor store. It was also directly in front of a bright red fire hydrant. Signs all along the street said, "No Parking 4–6 P.M." Cars behind and in front of the long black car had tickets on them. A police car was parked at the corner. Through the window of the liquor store he saw two policemen talking with a man leaning against a wall. The two of them came out, each carrying a package. Neither paid any attention to the long black car.

What if he went downtown tomorrow and erased the tickets on all the small cars and entered them all in the record of the long black car? It would be easy enough to do. By the time the next scofflaw readouts went through in the fall, the actual tickets would have been destroyed and there would be no way for the owner of the long black car to prove he hadn't gotten the citations. You can't prove something *didn't* happen, you can only infer that from things that did happen.

As he crossed the street, he was almost hit by a red Chevrolet van. The driver cursed at him. "You blind or something?" the driver yelled. Eddie was thinking about the man with the fish-eaten eyes.

Three pieces of mail were in a neat pile on the kitchen table: a flier from Harper's announcing a spring sale especially for charge account customers, a pitch for contributions from a home for Catholic delinquents, and a notice from the telephone company that the local rates would soon rise by 22 percent to meet rising costs.

The lead article in the *Evening News* was about further layoffs in the steel plants surrounding the city. The steel company said its two reasons for closing down operations were the increase in Japanese imports and the stifling accumulation of state, county, and city taxes, which cut heavily into the profit margin. The equipment in the Lackawanna plant was due for replacement anyhow, and they were thinking about replacing it in Alabama, where they could negotiate a better tax deal.

At the bottom of the page was an article about the telephone company's bid for more money. The writer said the city's basic telephone rate was now three times the basic rate in San Francisco. He had asked a telephone company executive to explain the difference, since the process and equipment were probably exactly the same. "People in the Buffalo area," the executive said, "have access to more telephones without tolls than people in San Francisco. From Buffalo you can call Cheektowaga and Lackawanna and Depew without a toll. People in San Francisco can't do that. They can just call people in San Francisco."

Eddie felt the anger starting again. He never called anyone in Cheektowaga or Lackawanna or Depew, and the fact that he had access to those grim towns was no compensation for the 22 percent rise in rates that were triple what people paid in other cities. The utilities commission would hold a hearing, then it would approve the increase, just as it always approved increases requested by utilities companies.

There was nothing to be done. He had once heard a comedian say, "If you don't like the telephone company, you know what you can do? Two tin cans and a piece of string, that's what you can do. That's the only alternative you've got." The people in the audience had laughed. Eddie thought about it now and decided it wasn't funny at all.

As always, she was in the other room watching television. If he put a shotgun to his mouth and blew the top of his head away, she probably wouldn't discover the mess until the commercial gave her time to get a beer or head for the toilet.

That was one way to solve everything. But he didn't have a shotgun.

He could get one. Anybody could get one. And there were other ways if someone didn't want to waste the money on something that was just going to be used once. You could sit in the garage with the motor running, the way Fred Astaire had done at the end of *On the Beach*. There was a lot of music during that scene, rising over the mellow roar of the motor. In real life there was never music at the critical moments, though if you were sitting in the car with the motor running in the garage you could put the car radio on loud. They'd probably cut in with a commercial for cat food as you passed into unconsciousness. How would that be—for the last thought on your mind as you passed into oblivion to be about what to feed a finicky cat?

How, he wondered, could anyone who was as terrified of dying as he was calmly think about how he might commit suicide?

The answer was, he could contemplate it calmly because he knew he wasn't going to do it. But he could see how it became attractive to some people. It resolved all the ambiguities, terminated all the fears people who were afraid of dying—and who wasn't?—worried about.

When will it happen? *Seven minutes.*

Will it hurt? *Not if you don't yank the barrel out of your mouth. You'll be dead before the noise reaches your ears. You won't hear a thing.*

What about all those bills? *Who cares?*

What about afterwards? *Um . . .*

Ah, that one.

Eddie thought again of the eyeless men. The last of the ice had melted in the lake now. He wondered if some of the eyeless men were frozen in it for the winter, preserved beyond their time because they had the misfortune to drown just as winter was closing in. He envisioned the little fish nibbling at the parts not in the ice, the feet and hands that were dangling lower when the locking began. In the spring the police might discover a body with a perfect head and nothing but bones below the neck, like an animal assaulted by those tiny South American fish with the vicious teeth. Piranha.

He had seen a tank of piranha at the pet store in the mall on Niagara Falls Boulevard once. The owner said you could feed them almost anything: hamburger, steak, veal, hot dogs. But they preferred little animals. There were a lot of people in the store at the time, and he put on a show. He took a white mouse from a glass bowl and held it along the face of the tank so the fish could see it. Some of them banged their heads against the glass so hard you could hear it. Then he dropped the mouse into the water.

There was a terrific thrashing about. The water churned wildly. "People think they bite off pieces of flesh," the owner said, "but that's not so. They're like sharks. They clamp on with their teeth and then they rip. The pulling by the fish on the other side gives them the traction they need. Or whatever you call it."

By the time he finished talking, it was all over. The tank's water had turned a pale red. The bones of the mouse dropped to the sandy bottom. The fish were absolutely motionless. Only the small fins on the sides of their bellies moved.

"How awful," a woman said.

"It's no problem," the owner said. "The filter clears it up. In ten minutes that water will be clear as a bell."

"That's not what I meant," the woman said.

The man shrugged. Some people talked about how interesting it had been. A man asked how much a pair cost and if they produced offspring in captivity. Eddie wanted to say that the kind of clear a bell was was not the kind of clear water was, but he didn't. He remembered the way he felt every month when the bills came and grew more and more oppressive, the accompanying letters more and more hostile, and he identified with the mouse.

Eddie sat at the kitchen table. He turned and saw the back of Betty's head, and beyond her movement on the poster-colored television screen. He realized he had begun to smile. There was a possibility that his evenings in the kitchen were finite now, this would not go on forever. The black car by the fire hydrant and his idea of shifting to it a thousand parking tickets and the vision of the eyeless men had given him the key to freedom.

# THREE

The problem now was how to do it, where to start. He was thinking of escape, of leaving it all for good like someone in a romantic novel. But there was no wild country west of the Mississippi in which he could disappear, as men could a hundred years earlier; nowadays everyone had an identity printed out on laminated or embossed plastic cards, and the numbers were so much a part of one's life they may as well have been tattooed on your wrists.

Escape was his need now, it filled his mind but for one small corner. That corner was concerned with another subject entirely: revenge. How do you revenge yourself on faceless corporations that deal only through voiceless machines? You attack them through their machines. Impossible, unless you're a faceless corporation yourself, which Eddie wasn't.

So escape, escape first.

And that produced three problems, three needs: adequate information, sufficient money, and good equipment.

On the bus going to work the next day, he felt a heady excitement, almost like being a little drunk, except for the splendid fact that his mind was perfectly clear. It was like a dream he once had in which he walked down a street and took his glasses off, to find that he saw everything much more clearly without them, and knew that for years they had been part of the cloud over his eyes. Everything glistened. Then he woke up, and needed his glasses to read the newspaper.

During his lunch hour he stayed in the office and Xeroxed all the city and county computer programs. The material was in a file cabinet next to Agnes' desk. Everyone else had left exactly at noon; he worked without being disturbed. The telephone rang once, but he didn't bother to answer it. He obtained access codes to the state computer data banks and the federal data banks with which they were currently in direct communication as a result of various federal programs currently in effect. When he was done, his briefcase was full. He pushed the briefcase under his desk and was busily at work on a revision of the city's office equipment and supply accounting program when his boss came back.

He told his boss he wanted to attend a refresher program at IBM. He showed him the descriptive brochure he had gotten that week. The boss was surprised; he thought Eddie knew all he needed to know for his work.

"You never know all you need to know," Eddie said.

"Can't argue with that, I guess. But I can't spare you to go to school now. You know how busy we are."

"The classes are at night. Tuesdays and Thursdays."

"On your own time?" Eddie nodded. "Then it's fine with me." He initialed Eddie's application, which meant the city would pay for the training program.

Most of the men in the class—there were no women at all for some reason—were younger than Eddie. He knew only one of them, a fellow who had once worked for the city but who now worked for the university out in Amherst. His name was Brown and he said he liked working for the university much better than he had working for the city because now it didn't seem to matter very much if things got screwed up; you just did it over again. The computer center out there was divided into two sections. One section handled research programs, the other handled university operations such as purchasing and student registration. He was in the second section, which meant he didn't have to deal with any of the accounts on federal contract, which had a lot of paperwork, especially when you made big mistakes. He told Eddie that last spring the computer had misregistered four thousand students and they were calling for days trying to get straightened out. "It was kind of crazy out there," he said. "See, we didn't have any manual way to handle the student records anymore and we didn't know what had gone wrong with the program, so there was no one who could help these people, and it went on for weeks and weeks."

"What did you do about it?"

"Stopped answering the telephone. Set it up differently the next semester."

"What about the people who got closed out of their classes?"

"I don't know," Brown said, "that's not my department."

He told Eddie another incident that produced a lot of telephone calls. The computer program—its acronym was SARA, which made Eddie think of the fat lady at TRL—had to have a room for every class, and it would not permit more students to register than it had been told would fit in the chairs assigned to the room. The English Department had over a hundred students who registered for thesis work, which didn't require any classroom. It was all done at the library and at their homes. But because of the computer's program they had to pick one empty room as the theoretical place of activity. The computer permitted thirty of the students to register, then kicked all the others out. "That was a real mess," Brown said. "Since they couldn't register, some of them lost their fellowship checks for three or four months. They'd call and we'd say, 'It's not our fault. It's the computer's fault. We can't do anything about it.' They're a foulmouthed bunch, you know that?"

The classes were held in a room of the local IBM office building, which was the reason Eddie had registered. During the third session he performed the second felony of his life: he burglarized an office in which access codes were developed and scored. He did it by leaving class a half hour before it usually finished. He left his coat on his chair and his notebook on his desk. If anyone were paying attention, it would seem he had gone to the toilet.

Eddie went to the stairway and walked down one flight to a large room that had been included on the tour the class had taken during the first session. It was the room where IBM's own local programmers worked. All the offices on the floor were open. There were no doors, just partitions setting off areas. There was no problem with security, the instructor had said, because when everyone left for the night the entire building was locked and there were supersonically activated burglar alarms on all the floors and all the stairways. No one, Eddie decided, had planned for a burglary while people were still in the building; the kinds of burglars they expected didn't do that sort of thing.

The address codes were in small brown books bound along the left margin with a black plastic assembly that passed through a number of rectangular holes. That was so the books could lie flat when they were being used. A large carton of the books sat on an oak table in the manager's office. The table was anomalous: almost everything else was black Formica and steel. The box was half empty, which meant it was highly unlikely anyone would notice that one had disappeared. It wasn't the sort of thing anyone would steal.

Eddie opened the book at the middle so it would be as thin as possible, and tucked it under his shirt. He fluffed the shirt out a bit so it wouldn't show the book's outlines, then returned to the classroom. He took his seat and wrote down in his notebook what the instructor had put on the blackboard in his absence.

If he wished, he could now talk with every computer in the district handling major commercial work. He had captured the unlisted telephone numbers of the computers used by the banks, the mills, and even the airlines reservations offices. Many of the firms did not use IBM equipment, but that didn't matter: they all handled information the same way and they all used telephone lines to do it, and they were all compatible with one another because of the necessity of information sharing and distribution.

The wonderful thing about stealing information, he decided, is it is there afterwards to be used by the rightful owner, or even stolen again by someone else. It doesn't deplete. Marlene Dietrich had said something like that in a movie once: information, she said, was like sex, you could sell it over and over and over again.

Eddie's previous felony was minor; it had happened while he was in college. Only two other people knew about it: his physics instructor, a fine old man named Putter who had died some years ago of a coronary, and a classmate named Michael Lee.

They had read articles in the papers about people using things they called "black boxes" to make long distance calls without having to pay for them. The boxes apparently imitated the audible frequencies that controlled access to long distance lines, and they could bypass the local automatic accounting devices. One blind kid in Florida did it without a black box: he was able to whistle the proper tones into the mouthpiece and get the long distance access. At times he amused himself by calling from long distance system to long distance system, sending his calls all around the world several times before getting the party he was trying to reach, which was sometimes himself. He would get to the end of his game and hear a busy signal from his own phone, or the telephone in the next booth would ring, and if he had a friend with him, they could talk to one another separated by two feet of physical space and fifty thousand miles of telephone lines.

Michael Lee asked Professor Putter how such an operation was possible. The old man thought about it a moment and said, "It's really quite simple." He drew some diagrams on the blackboard. "You have to have some electronics to understand this," he said, "and I'm not going to teach you that too."

They saw it was really simple. That night, Eddie and Michael Lee went to the physics lab and assembled a simple black box. Its input was a telephone jack; its output, a line leading to a jack plug. The entire job took about three hours and cost less than ten dollars.

"Who are we going to call?" Eddie asked.

"I don't know. You got anybody in mind?"

"No. I don't know anybody long distance to call."

"Whose phone we going to use? What if it's traced?" Eddie said.

"Maybe we should use a pay phone."

"They're not on jacks."

"Then we have to give this thing an audible output so it can work with jack phones or pay phones. That's easy enough. I'll pick up the things we need on my way to school tomorrow."

They met by the library after classes. "All done," Michael said. "Look." He opened his briefcase. Their simple black box was now slightly larger. It had a telephone touch-tone board attached and there was a space for a small battery. "It uses so little current there's no need for an AC connection. It's got both electronic and audio output. I put a little speaker jack here." He pointed to the side. "That way we can put the speaker directly against the telephone mouthpiece."

"It seems awfully complicated," Eddie said.

"No, it's quite simple. You mean it's cumbersome, and that's true. But it's a prototype. Let's go find a pay phone."

"Maybe we should wait until later," Eddie said. "Until after dark."

"No. Things are more suspicious after dark. Anyway, telephone booths have lights in them and people can see in. It's better now. You can stand on the side where I have the box and no one will be able to see a thing."

They called Grauman's Chinese Theater in Los Angeles and made a reservation for dinner for six in the name of T. A. Edison; they called Michael's uncle in Ardmore, Pennsylvania; they called the White House, but got frightened when the operator asked them to identify themselves and say where they were calling from.

Michael Lee later made more and more sophisticated black boxes. The last model Eddie saw was about the size of a pocket calculator. Eddie never used any of them, mostly because he didn't have anyone to call and found the silly calls boring. After graduation Michael Lee got a graduate degree somewhere and took a job with NASA. Eddie wondered if he were now making toll-free calls from outer space.

Eddie later read in the newspaper that the blind kid had finally gotten caught. The telephone company then hired him to help capture other black box users. Some of them were caught, though it was never clear whether or not the blind kid really had turned into a telephone company rat. He said in an interview that he only gave them technical advice. One article said that the users who were caught were careless: they used the same 800 exchange to channel all their calls through, and after the 800 exchange accountant found a lot of obviously spurious calls (one of the lines was for information about local dealers of car undercoating; none of its inquiry calls was over two minutes, but a scan showed occasional two-hour conversations on the line), they started monitoring the number, and it was easy to trace it back to the point of origin.

The few arrests made terrified most black box owners, and so far as Eddie knew, hardly anyone used them anymore. The telephone company said it would spend any amount of funds necessary to capture cheaters and protect their stockholders' interests, and they talked about supersophisticated tracing equipment they had developed at their Murray Hill laboratory.

Eddie doubted they had developed equipment to trace black box users; it wasn't necessary: the regular tracing equipment was all they needed, and he had read in *Scientific American* about some of the devices they had developed for government agencies.

He still owned the last black box Michael Lee had made, a small one that worked on jacks or audio, ran for a year on a hearing-aid battery, and fitted into a shirt pocket. It was somewhere in the basement, along with his other things from college, things he no longer needed or even had the curiosity to examine. It was in a dry carton high on a shelf and probably worked as well as the day it had been made.

Eddie went after the money first. He decided he should have about $25,000. There was no reason for picking that amount, except it was more than twice his annual take-home pay and about $22,000 more than he had ever held in cash in his entire life. And it seemed like an amount he could steal without anyone noticing.

The design was quite simple, almost elegant. His real estate tax was due. When he made out the check—as always, larger than the previous one and still infuriating, even though he knew he was going to steal the money right back—he overpaid by twenty-six dollars. That was on a Tuesday. The following Tuesday he called his bank and asked if the check had cleared yet. The clerk said it hadn't, but he shouldn't be concerned, the city was often quite slow about its deposits. Eddie called again on Friday and was told that the check had just come through. It had been processed and his account had a current balance of six dollars and twenty-seven cents.

That evening, Eddie mailed to the city a form requesting a refund of the twenty-six-dollar accidental overpayment. Such errors happened all the time and there was a program to handle such applications. It was set to take care of small homeowners who juxtaposed digits on a check or misread their tax bills, and large corporations that misplaced a few decimal points in their payments. Eddie knew about the program because he had prepared it, and he also knew when the refund operation would come through the computer's printing operation.

On the appropriate Tuesday, Eddie introduced to the tape a set of instructions to print, in the name of William Artis, a check for $25, 624.34. The name of William Artis immediately followed Eddie's on the alphabetical tax roll (which was how the checks were printed). He made the amount uneven because a neat number like $25,000 would be noticeable, should someone later do a visual scan.

The checks were printed between 4 and 5 P.M. That evening, Eddie stayed late at the office, working at his desk. When everyone had gone, he had his console open a line to the tax-refund tape. He erased the order to print the $25,624.34 check. There was now no existing record that would show how or why that check had come into existence.

Like the traffic tickets, the physical checks weren't looked at once they came back from the banks. The machines typed them, they went out to people, with addresses typed by machines. A real name and a real listed address had to be used because the computer automatically addressed the envelopes and it was cross-programmed to reject the insert-into-envelope order when there was an unverified address. When the checks came back, a computer read their punchmarks automatically and informed its central accounting memory that the funds had been deducted from the city account. The checks themselves were subsequently destroyed.

At nine-fifteen Wednesday morning Eddie told his secretary he had to go downstairs for a few minutes. He picked up a file so it would look as if he were doing something he was supposed to be doing. He went directly to the tax office and stepped behind the counter. The clerk on duty, Milton Rook, paid him no attention: Eddie's work frequently required him to poke around the files.

The checks were in their envelopes in two long boxes on a radiator.

"One of these is mine, Milton," Eddie said. "I'm going to pull it and save the city a stamp."

"And save yourself a couple of days waiting for it," Rook said. "Sure, go ahead." He didn't even turn around.

Eddie thumbed through the checks and found the one with his name on it. Immediately behind it was an envelope addressed to William Artis. He made sure there wasn't another addressed to Artis—there was the distant possibility that he might be getting a check of his own and Eddie didn't want to pull the wrong one. Artis wasn't getting a refund this year, it turned out. Eddie slipped the two envelopes into his inside jacket pocket.

By the time the county realized it was short $25,624.34, Eddie would be no more, and it was entirely possible the source of the error would never be found anyway. Hundreds of thousands of checks were processed every year and the place anyone seeking an error would look would be the computer tapes, not the canceled checks. The checks were held for a short time, the tapes for years. But the tapes would reveal nothing. The $25,624.34 had gone the same place as Betty's traffic ticket and Nixon's eighteen-minute conversation about his part in the Watergate cover-up: out of this world forever. The important difference was, these tapes wouldn't show an obvious gap.

Eddie wondered if some smart operators in the tax office hadn't, from time to time, helped themselves to great amounts of county and city money using this process. It was easy enough.

If the check for Artis had for some reason been out of order in the box, then Eddie would have had a slight problem. It would have gone out in the mail and Artis would have perhaps called the city to find out why they were sending him so much money. But perhaps he would have decided not to question a stroke of luck and would have cashed the check, and then it would have disappeared just as if Eddie had used it as he planned. They still couldn't trace the encoding operation.

Computers, Eddie knew, have no idea where their sources of information are in the world. They look upon the world as one great big fat wire bulging with information and instructions, a wire with no beginning, middle, or end. The world for a computer is merely an electrical input saying, "Here's what you should know," or, "Here's what I want to know," or, "Here's what you are to do now," and an electrical output for them to talk back: "Here's what I must know to answer your question," and, "Here are your answers." To the computers, all interrogators and commanders speak with the same voice and the same authority; all listeners have the same ear.

Like guns. It doesn't matter to a gun who pulls its trigger. Guns have awesome power, but they are entirely dependent on the hands that use them. Morally guns and computers are out of it all, though they are regularly the instruments for people who make things happen.

Twice now—first with Betty's parking ticket and now with his $25,624.34—Eddie had been someone who made things happen. It was a very exciting sensation, one he hadn't previously experienced.

He had seen, not long before on the "Today" show, an airline pilot who talked about his affection for the 747. He loved it more, he said, than any other aircraft he had ever flown, and he had been a pilot for twenty-five years. The interviewer asked him to explain his enthusiasm.

"I sit there in that little room in the front," the pilot said, "a room just four stories off the ground when we're parked, but at the top of the world when we're in flight— and I move little knobs and dials. None of them takes more than a few ounces of pressure. In an instant a machine weighing a hundred tons responds more smoothly than if I were moving it myself. It's like the aircraft becomes an extension of myself because so little effort is needed to make it do what I want, and it does whatever I want it to do. It's very exciting."

"You make it sound almost sexual," the interviewer said.

The pilot frowned. "I don't know about that. I never thought about that." His face brightened. "It's not sex. It's better. It's *real* power."

Eddie sensed that his entire relationship with the computer had started a radical change. Before, he had been the machine's servant, bringing it little orders and loads of information to feed upon. The questions weren't his and the answers never mattered to him. He was merely an intermediary in the affairs of others. Now he was having his own affair.

And his own affair required further action before the check in his pocket became anything but a useless piece of paper.

On his way back to the office Eddie stopped in the motor vehicle section. Edna was there alone, as usual, talking on the telephone, also as usual. She was wearing a different pink sweater. She held up her hand, the fingers all extended. At first Eddie thought she was showing off her rings—there were four of them, all different—but then he understood that she was telling him she would be on the phone five minutes longer. He waved his hand to indicate he was in no hurry. She leaned back in the chair, her pink breasts pointing toward the corner light fixture.

Eddie wandered around the office, acting as if he were bored. He looked at some papers. She was paying no attention to him. He stopped at the drawer where blank drivers' licenses were kept. He looked over his shoulder. She was still talking, her back to him. Her left hand held the telephone and her right hand slowly rubbed the back of her neck.

He quickly took from the drawer ten forms, then leaned on the counter and quietly stamped each of them with the tricolored state seal required for validation. He put the forms into his jacket pocket along with the two checks. Now he had only to type out whatever names he wanted to use and he would have official New York certification.

He was perspiring heavily under his jacket. He hadn't realized what tension he'd been feeling during the few seconds of his theft. Now that it was done, he felt very good. He wiped his face with his handkerchief, then walked to the front of Edna's desk. She was frowning at the telephone.

"No," she said into the mouthpiece. "That's not what I did at all. First of all, he—"

"I've got to get back upstairs," Eddie said.

She covered the mouthpiece. "I'll be done in a minute. Don't rush away." She smiled at him and moved her shoulders so the pink breasts slowly rose and fell. She smiled a different smile.

"Later," he said. "I'll come back later. It's nothing important."

"I'll be here," Edna said. Her face reassumed the frown as she started talking to the telephone again.

The rest was easy. During his lunch hour, when the office was empty, Eddie typed William Artis' name and address on one of the license forms. He copied the address from the check. Then he called the Marine Midland bank, said he was a clerk at a store in Cheektowaga, and asked if a William Artis had an account there that could cover a seventy-eight-dollar check.

"Do you have the account number, sir?"

"Gee," Eddie said, "I don't."

"Then it's very hard to say," the woman at the bank said.

"Could you please look it up? His wife wants to cash a check. She called to say she was coming in to pick up this package and we wanted to be sure. We've had some bad checks on the Marine lately."

"Just a minute, please." The woman put him on hold. Music came over the phone, not at all like the music he had heard when he dealt with Citibank. "I've inquired of the computer," she said after a few minutes, "and there is no account in that name in any of our branches."

"Oh, dear," Eddie said. "Perhaps it was the Big E. Oh, I think it was. I made a mistake. I'm sorry to have bothered you. Thanks a lot."

"You're welcome," she said.

After he replaced the phone in its cradle, he sat there and watched his fingers shake. He had just made a mistake. It wouldn't cause a problem, but it shouldn't have happened. There was no need, he knew now, for him to have talked with anyone. He should have addressed the bank's computers through his own terminal—it was simply a matter of dialing the proper number and using the tape access code, which was among those he had stolen from IBM. He had needlessly had a personal contact with someone.

Whenever he could manage it, future contacts would have to be made only with machines. Personal contacts should be made only when absolutely necessary, when purchasing objects that could be gotten only in stores, for example. But there was no reason at all for Eddie to request information from any person. There was no information people had that wasn't already stored in some machine. He might have to work a little harder to find the correct machine and the proper memory bank, but that was better than exposing himself and risking identification.

His entire plan rested on two factors: first, that most of what he was going to do would escape detection entirely, and second, that what was detected could in no way be connected with Eddie Argo.

Thursday afternoon he went to the main office of the Marine on lower Main Street. He had considered using one of the branches, then decided that a transaction so large would cause a lot of attention in one of the smaller banks, while the downtown office, which handled many of the city's business accounts, wouldn't pay any attention at all.

The bank was crowded. It was payday in a lot of offices and people were in getting cash for the weekend. He looked around carefully. High overhead, on a balcony, two guards looked down at the crowded lobby. The bank was deceptively open, one of those modern structures that give a feeling of having full freedom. The entrance was a wide area directly off a large shopping mall, and it seemed one could go in and out with no hindrance at all. Until you noticed that there were no other visible exits, that the wide doorway was the only way in or out, and that the guards on the balcony and two more on the main level kept it constantly under surveillance. A robber wouldn't get very far.

A robber using a gun, that is. One using a piece of paper had a far better chance. Robbers with guns, Eddie decided, were anachronisms, relics of a dead past when people could count on a faster horse to get them away. Cameras that operated off foot buttons and radio communications changed all that. By the time a man with a gun reached an exit from this building—one hundred yards and down a flight of stairs from the bank's doorway—city police could have the building surrounded.

To his right were a dozen desks for bank officers. Eddie walked to the wooden rail separating them from the open section of the bank. A woman sat on a chair behind one of the desks. He caught her eye and she immediately put on a professional smile and motioned for him to come right on in.

"May I help you, sir?" she asked.

Eddie noticed that bankers who didn't work in the loan department were a lot more friendly than those who did. Here you weren't one of the beggars of the world, and if they weren't nice to you, it was their loss when you walked out and took your business elsewhere.

"I want to open a time-deposit account," Eddie said. "And I want three cashier's checks."

"Yes, sir," the woman said. "Will you please fill these out?" She gave him four forms. One was for the deposit account, the other three were for the checks. He asked for two checks for $10,000 each and one for $4,000. He said he wanted the other $1624.34 to go into the savings account. She smiled and pointed at the forms. "Just write it out the way you want it done, sir."

She began writing on another form. She explained that if he withdrew any of the money before a certain period of time, the interest would drop to the interest paid regular accounts. Eddie said he had no intention of withdrawing any of the money before the minimum period was up. She smiled again and went to type his checks.

In fact, he had no intention of *ever* withdrawing the $1624.34. Nor would he ever again return to this bank. He created the account only so the clerk wouldn't get suspicious. Perhaps it wasn't necessary. But he was sure the bank official would assume that anyone putting that much money into an account was legitimate. Eddie wrote the $1624.34 off as his first business loss. He had never before had occasion to suffer a business loss on anything. He loved the sensation of throwing away over sixteen hundred dollars.

She returned a few moments later, still holding the forms he had filled out. No checks. Eddie had been perfectly calm, but as soon as he saw her moving back from behind the teller's stations he was weakened by a sudden terror. He looked toward the large doorway. The guards were all still in the same positions. There was no way out. It seemed that the bank had just gotten very quiet.

"Mr. Artis," she said.

"Yes?" Eddie said, working hard to keep the voice steady and almost succeeding.

"I forgot," she said. "We'll need some identification. It's a bank rule with transactions of this size."

"Will a driver's license do?"

"Best identification in the world," she said. "Or at least the state. Certified by the State of New York."

He took out his wallet and began to take from the plastic holder the license he had typed with William Artis' name on it.

"Oh," she said, "that's all right. I can look at it in there. Don't bother to take it out." She reached for the wallet.

Eddie hesitated a moment, then pushed it across the desk. She looked at the license for what seemed a long time. It was in the first plastic pocket. Just next to it, in a leather half-pocket of the wallet itself, the edges of his Mobil and Mastercharge cards protruded; the names on them were hidden by the leather. If she moved either of them out, she would see the name Eddie Argo. If she turned the plastic pocket, she would see a Social Security card with the name of Eddie Argo. He felt awful.

"Fine, Mr. Artis," she said. "That's all I needed. I'll be right back."

Five minutes later he left the bank with a new bankbook showing a current balance of $1624.34, and with three checks in his wallet worth $24,000. As he passed the two guards at the door, he smiled, and one of the guards tipped his fingers to the patent leather bill of his gray cap.

He walked through the wide avenue of the shopping mall, feeling taller than he had ever felt before. In his pocket was more money than he had ever had in his entire life. He could use it anywhere in the world. He could walk into any of the fancy stores he was passing and walk out with the most expensive things he could carry. That had never been the option for Eddie Argo before.

The next morning, he left the house as usual, but he didn't take the bus to work. Instead he walked six blocks to a small restaurant. He ordered breakfast, ate it slowly, and thought about what he would do. When it was time for him to be at work, he went to a pay telephone and called in to say he was sick.

His boss complained and said there was a lot of work to do. Eddie reminded him that he hadn't taken a sick day in seven years. "I just wish you'd picked some other day," the boss whined. "We're really busy this week."

"We're always busy," Eddie said. "If I feel better, maybe I'll come in tomorrow morning."

"No," his boss said. "The contract says you have to get overtime for Saturdays. You know that. I'll see you Monday."

Eddie took the Greyhound bus to Rochester, two counties away. The bus was nearly empty. It sat in the station awhile, then rolled out into the city streets. As it headed toward the Kensington Expressway, which would connect with the Thruway, it stopped a long time for a traffic light on Main Street.

What if someone looked into the window and recognized him? Say they called Betty or his boss? How would he explain? He didn't have a story ready; there was no story that would quite work.

Then he laughed at himself as he realized he wouldn't need one. He was the kind of man people didn't notice. For years Eddie had envied people who were distinctive, people who were remembered even after a brief meeting. He had always been the kind of man who met someone a week or two later and had to be introduced all over again. Clerks in stores often ignored him, almost as if he were transparent. Now, for the first time, that old pain was a fabulous asset. He could move in and out and around his city and he was nearly invisible. It was a special kind of freedom he had never before appreciated.

The bus moved along the Thruway from Erie to Orleans County. The land dropped and flattened even more. He slept, and didn't wake until the hissing of the air brakes and an end of the rocking let him know they had arrived at the Rochester terminal.

He walked through it quickly. It was the kind of place that made him nervous, though he knew that was irrational. Some old black women with large shopping bags sat on one of the benches. Most of the people on the other benches seemed to be drunks, sleeping. They were all sleeping upright. Eddie assumed there were guards who would come and prod them if they tilted over and tried to stretch out on the smooth wood seats. Along one wall three young men talked intensely about something. One of them kept looking at the clock on the wall and then back to his wristwatch.

The neighborhood was run-down. Nearby were some boarded-up stores and a few dingy apartment houses. There were two cabs out front, but he had decided he wouldn't take one unless he had to. The street seemed safe enough.

Eddie walked the twelve blocks quickly, occasionally looking over his shoulder to see if anyone was behind him. No one ever was.

The dealer had a lot of used cars and vans on his lot. The ad had said he specialized in vans. Eddie walked around the lot for almost fifteen minutes before one of the salesmen spotted him. The salesman came out of the office, not walking very fast. He was dressed in shades of brown: brown shoes, brown polyester suit, brown knit tie, brown plaid shirt. He wore an enormous gold watch on a brown leather strap. His tie was held in place by a garish diamond stickpin, and he wore a diamond pinkie ring. Eddie wondered if maybe they were artificial. He didn't know any men who wore diamonds, though someone had once told him that vice squad detectives wore a lot of them.

"I want a van," Eddie said.

"Something for yourself or for your kid?" the salesman asked.

"What?"

"Sorry. Vans are very popular these days. Some of them are very fancy. Whorehouses on wheels, if you'll pardon the expression. The kids like them with fancy seats and upholstery and hi-fi. Someone your age, well, you know, someone who wants one for business—"

"Yes," Eddie said. "It's for me."

"My name is Flekon," the salesman said, "Charlie Flekon. But my friends call me Fritz." He smiled and put out his hand.

For some reason he didn't quite understand, Eddie didn't want to shake hands with the man, but he didn't feel strongly enough about it to be insulting. "Why do they call you Fritz?"

"I don't know. That's what they call me." Fritz laughed. Eddie didn't.

Eddie pointed to a van he had been looking at the last several minutes before Flekon came out of the office. It was light gray, with no external markings at all. No pinstriping, no designs, no painted figures, no decals. There were no side windows in the body. The windows on the front doors and the back were much more darkly tinted than the windshield. There was a small rectangular cover on the roof, the sort that usually covered an exhaust fan.

"How is that one over there?" Eddie asked.

"The seventy-five? That's a great van. Yes, sir. Perfect for you." Flekon smiled again. Eddie was sure Flekon would have found any vehicle he selected *perfect* for him. He wondered if the man's mouth ached at the end of a day from all the deliberate smiling. They walked toward it, stopped near the rear doors, then walked in silence all the way around to the other side. "This is a clean vehicle, sir," Flekon said, "as I'm sure you can see. Really clean. It's got everything. Everything you could want."

"I doubt that," Eddie said, "but it may do."

Flekon opened the side door. The area behind the two front seats was empty. There was a gray carpet on the floor, faded much lighter on the side closest to the door.

"The previous owner had a sofa there," Flekon said, "so it didn't get much wear. Not that this van has had much wear anyway. It's in A-number-one shape. That's all we sell here. A-number-one vehicles."

Eddie walked around and opened the driver's door. He closed the door and listened to the sound, then opened it again.

"Go ahead," Flekon said. "Sit in it. See how it feels to you. Those captain's seats are top-of-the-line."

The van had an automatic transmission, air-conditioner, and a very fancy radio. Flekon explained that the radio was also a tape player and a CB. "It's the top-of-the-line, just like the captain's seats. You can be listening to the radio—AM or FM—or to the tape, and if you have the CB turned on too and a transmission comes over, the tape or radio drops in volume so you can hear what's coming over. That way you can listen to both and not be bored. You know, you can be driving along when you're using the CB in most cars and the damned static drives you crazy. Not with this baby. The only time it talks, it's working. That's a no-nonsense unit, take my word."

"How's the motor?" Eddie asked.

"Perfect, I told you. You want to try it out?"

"Yes."

"You're really interested in this van?"

"What do you think I'm doing here, making surveys?"

"Okay, sorry. It's the kids. They drive me crazy. They come in, they talk like they want to buy, we go for a ride and they scare me half to death, and then I never see them again."

"I'm not one of the kids."

"Right, sir. I'll get the keys from the office."

While Flekon was gone, Eddie tried the other doors. They all moved easily and closed securely. He looked along the sides, sighting as if he were checking a board for straightness. There were no irregularities in the surface. He heard Flekon's footsteps on the gravel behind him, but he paid no attention. He yanked on the tops of all four wheels. They barely gave at all. He had read an article in *Consumer Reports* about how to buy a used car.

Obviously he could have bought a new one, but he had decided that a vehicle a few years old in good condition would be just as useful and a great deal more innocuous. He wanted a van rather than a car because he was going to be carrying a lot of things very soon. From the van he would be in touch with the world.

They drove across the city and then onto an expressway. Again Eddie did all the things *Consumer Reports* suggested. The van behaved very well.

"All right," he said when they got back to the lot. "How much?"

"Only fifty-eight hundred . . . and that's a steal, a real steal. But we've got a bunch of vehicles to move this month. Got a bunch coming in. You came in the perfect time. It's a great bargain."

It seemed reasonable enough to Eddie, but he knew that only a fool would take a car dealer's first offer on anything.

"No."

"You don't want the van?" Flekon looked stunned.

"Not for fifty-eight hundred. That's too much. Way too much."

"But it's got air-conditioning and that super radio-tape-CB. With AM and FM. You don't find that very often."

"But I know where to get it," Eddie said. "The air-conditioner costs an additional two-ninety when the vehicle is new. The radio unit costs under two hundred. And they're not new now. I'll tell you what: take them out and I'll give you four thousand."

"I can't take them out. They come with the van. Maybe you want to look at another one?"

"Four thousand. Take them out." Eddie looked at the cars moving along the street. Neither of them said anything for a while.

"Fifty-four hundred and I'll leave them in," Flekon said. He smiled. "You want a cigarette?" he asked. Eddie shook his head. "You're bleeding me to death. I'm losing my commission as it is, but I've got to move some vehicles. I'll tell you what: fifty-one hundred and it's yours. A clean deal."

"Forty-two hundred, and that's all I'll do," Eddie said, watching the cars again. His hands were folded neatly in his lap.

"Impossible. That's five hundred under my cost. I can't take a loss on it. You can't expect me to sell it to you at a loss."

They settled on forty-five hundred. Flekon looked pleased. They went into the office to do the paperwork. When it was done, Eddie handed Flekon one of the ten-thousand-dollar cashier's checks. Flekon's face went white.

"I can't take this, Mr. Artis. I'd have to give you over five grand in change. I don't have that kind of money." His face brightened as he got an idea. "Look: I've got a brand-new van out there. It's got a dynamite motor. Hand-painted designs on the sides and back. Television and a couch that opens into a bed. You can have it for eight even. It's got a dynamite motor, like I said." His voice was desperate, and Eddie knew that he was thinking Eddie had come in planning to spend the entire check.

Flekon began to perspire along his forehead: a big one was slipping away and he didn't know what to do.

"No," Eddie said. "What I've agreed to is the most I can afford. I need the rest of the money for something else."

"Maybe you'll take my check?"

"No," Eddie said. "You have to get plates for the van for me anyway. I don't have a car now. Let's stop at a bank and cash this on the way to the registration office."

To save time Flekon had Eddie fill in blank registration forms he kept in his desk. He dropped Eddie at a branch of the Marine while he went a few blocks away and picked up the plates. Eddie was waiting outside when Flekon came back.

"I had a moment of fright," Flekon said.

"Why?"

"That this was maybe some kind of scam. People run ā lot of scams these days. I wondered if you'd be gone when I got back here and then I'd have a van registered in the name of somebody who didn't exist and then I'd have to go through all kinds of crap getting it changed back."

"Oh," Eddie said, smiling, "I exist all right."

"I can see that," Flekon said. He was looking at the sheaf of bills in Eddie's left hand.

"When we get back to the lot," Eddie said. All the way, Flekon chattered, but Eddie didn't listen to him. He was listening to the sounds from the engine and the transmission. The van sounded fine.

When they reached the lot, Eddie counted out the money.

"It's not often people pay in cash anymore," Flekon said. "It's all checks and bank loans."

"Would you prefer my check?" Eddie asked.

"No, sir," Flekon said, laughing and counting the money again. "Your money is just fine."

Eddie drove back to the Thruway, listening carefully to be sure there was nothing in the van that needed repair. It continued to sound fine.

He now had slightly less than twenty thousand dollars—still more money than he had ever had at one time in his entire life, but he knew it wouldn't last long if he started buying things with it. He had paid cash for the van, which was necessary, but from now on he would deal mostly on credit. Credit was the way everyone dealt with everyone nowadays.

Eddie had decided he would use American Express cards as his basic source of income.

American Express, Eddie felt, was like the government. It got money from everyone and it didn't give much back in return. He felt using them to pay his bills was hardly stealing since he assumed they did it all the time. He had read some time ago that the company had out, at all times, over four billion dollars in travelers' checks. Uncashed travelers' checks. There were commercials on television in which a man with an enormous nose urged people to keep their money in travelers' checks. The man said they were safer than cash, negotiable anywhere and anytime. He didn't say that the checks, for which the travelers paid a lot of money, meant that AmEx had at its disposal a continual fund of four billion dollars which it could invest as it wished—interest free. Most people came back from their trips with some uncashed travelers' checks, which the company encouraged them to keep for an emergency. Safer than cash. Good anywhere. And AmEx's investment kept making money on money. As Eddie perceived it, they were getting people to lend them money, paying them no interest, and charging them for the privilege. Hardly anyone realized that. It was like the government holding onto your deductions until you filed your return and proved they had taken too much. They sent a refund a few months later. They kept your money all year plus about five months, then paid no interest at all. The real tax rates, Eddie knew, were a lot higher than the government said because they kept your money and got the compounded interest on it for themselves, even when they were obligated to give some of the money back.

American Express also makes an enormous amount of money on its cards. Even though people paid a lot of money to have one of those charge cards, the company charged all the stores in which they were used as much as 5 percent on all transactions. He had read that in the same article. The article also said that American Express didn't pay stores on bills for many months, usually after its cardholders had made their payments, which meant even more money they were using interest free. And their secret surcharge on purchases meant that some store prices were unfairly high for people who bought things without the cards, since some stores simply added the percentage onto all their prices.

As a result, such storeowners stole from the people who didn't use American Express—meaning that almost everybody got a piece except the poor sonofabitch without much money trying to buy some things now and then.

Eddie created for himself five identities within American Express.

He had to get the information through and the cards sent back to him without anything going through the human scanners who evaluated all new account information. To open an account you had to be rated by an account clerk. The way Eddie got around that was so clever he wanted to tell someone. He told no one, of course.

He used his IBM access code list. It had the computer address of the American Express memory banks. They were, like all the very modern large facilities, completely automated: no people were required to get tapes on and off the machines. One simply addressed a specific tape and program, and they were automatically positioned to reading and operating positions.

First, he inquired of the memory units numbers of empty accounts; that is, valid unused account numbers bracketed by accounts currently in use. Then he told the AmEx computer that five of those account numbers represented lost cards which had to be replaced. Since the information was stored by account number rather than name, he also told the computer what names to emboss on each of the replacement cards. He gave the computer five account numbers and five names. He could get more later if he needed them. All of them were sent, on different days, to a post office box he had rented in the Amherst post office on Main Street.

The five names matched the names on five of the drivers' licenses he had typed out for himself. None of them was Artis, which he would not be using for anything much longer. He held the other four licenses in reserve. He thought about getting Social Security cards in five names, but decided that was just looking for trouble. It was also unnecessary. A validated driver's license and a current American Express card were all anyone needed for anything.

Well, not anything. Some little stores didn't take American Express. But almost all of them took BankAmericard and Mastercharge. As soon as he had some time, he would get a few of those. They wouldn't be as useful around town because they maintained local on-line accounting, so the cards could become useless very quickly. He would use them later, perhaps.

The Thursday following the Friday he missed work, Eddie asked his boss if he knew what were the symptoms of a heart attack.

"Jesus, Eddie. What's the matter? You want me to call an ambulance?"

"No. I'm okay. I think. I just got kind of a weird feeling. Here." Eddie put his hand directly over his solar plexus. He felt fine.

His boss immediately looked relieved. "That's too low for a heart attack. I think it is, anyway. What makes you think it's a heart attack?"

"I don't. I was just asking you. I got this burning sensation. It's like last week, only it's worse. I don't know what it could be. I never get sick. Except for last Friday, I haven't been sick in years. Hate to miss work."

"Does it come on you after you eat? Maybe it's connected with food."

"I woke up with it last Friday. And Tuesday—"

"You had it on Tuesday too?"

"Not so bad on Tuesday."

"Eddie, you ever had ulcers?"

"Ulcers? Me? Why would I have ulcers? No."

"Did you go to a doctor last week?"

"No." Eddie made himself look embarrassed. "I just stayed around the house. It was boring, though. It got better in the afternoon. I almost came in, but by then it was three o'clock and there didn't seem much sense to it."

"Eddie, I hate having you out. We're very dependent on you here. I think maybe you should go to a doctor and get yourself checked out good. Maybe it's an ulcer, something they can give you medication for."

"I think I'll let it go for a while and see what happens."

"No. You take off tomorrow and go to the doctor. Can your doctor see you tomorrow?"

"Probably."

"Tell him it's an emergency. And take it easy over the weekend, okay?"

"Sure." It was the first time his boss had ever shown any concern about him at all.

"Do you have any idea how long it would take to train a replacement for you? Months. Maybe more than months. Jesus. It makes me sick to think about it. Finish that program you're working on and take the rest of the afternoon off."

"Gee," Eddie said. "Thanks."

"It's nothing."

Eddie looked at the clock. It was five minutes past four.

He went to bed early that night. He told Betty he didn't feel well.

"You want me to get you anything?" she shouted from the living room.

*The Omen* was on Home Box Office. She had seen it twice before. It would be over at twelve. A Clint Eastwood movie was on one of the Toronto stations at twelve-thirty. She would sleep late in the morning.

"No," he said. "I'm just tired. There's one other thing."

"What's that?"

"I'm going to be home late from work tomorrow night. Don't worry about it. A meeting."

"That's okay. I'll have dinner by myself. I have plenty to do to keep me busy."

"Fine." He fell asleep immediately.

# FOUR

He woke, as he had planned, at 4 A.M. He had always been able to wake when he wanted without an alarm clock. Even when he was in college and had been up late at night studying, he had no difficulty waking up for his early classes. Betty had always said she found it an amazing quality. "I could never do that," she said. She could hear an alarm clock go off, push the switch to silence it, and pull the covers back over her head without ever opening her eyes or remembering what had happened.

She was snoring lightly on the other side of the bed. He figured she had gone to sleep after two, which meant she wouldn't get up until at least ten. She liked to sleep longer than eight hours, but she didn't like to miss the "Phil Donahue Show." She would assume Eddie had left for work at the usual time.

The van was parked on a residential street four blocks away. It started right up and the engine made hardly any noise at all. He took Richmond to Forest, just across from the massive state mental hospital with its great pointed towers, turned right to Elmwood, and then turned left to get on the expressway. There was no traffic all the way out to the Thruway entrance, five miles away.

Shortly after he passed through the tollgate, an enormous black truck roared by him. On either side of the cab were high CB antennas. A voice crackled over the music on his radio: "Hey, little buddy in the silver van, you got ears?"

Eddie knew the trucker was talking to him. He had read articles about CB in the paper. He looked at the microphone in its neat dashboard mount. His hands moved toward it, then pulled back. He was embarrassed about sounding like an amateur.

"Hey, you in the silver van eastbound on this green stamp, you got a copy?"

The driver didn't try again after that. Occasionally Eddie heard him calling ahead to other drivers, asking if there were any bears in the area. As far as Eddie could tell, the CB wasn't much good at night because drivers coming from the other direction, the ones who would give you information about police cars hidden along your route, couldn't see what kinds of vehicles were moving all the way across the broad center island. The radio really functioned as a way to say hello in the dark, and the contents of the messages didn't matter that much, so long as another voice was found. Eddie listened to other people's voices.

He followed the truck all the way to Syracuse. It continued east toward Albany, and Eddie turned off at 690, the feeder road over to Interstate 81. It was just starting to get light then. The chatter on the radio picked up. There was more traffic, and the drivers had more to talk about. Twice he was warned about radar traps.

He drove as fast as he could without passing any of the big trucks. He decided they wouldn't stumble into radar traps. He wanted to make time, but he didn't want to get a speeding ticket. He could probably erase one if he had to, just as he had erased Betty's, but he wanted to do as little meddling as possible and to save his machine conversations for times when it really mattered. Except for the approaches to the two radar traps, the trucks kept him going a steady sixty-five.

He knew exactly where he was going because he had spent a lot of time the previous week reading the Yellow Pages for Manhattan and the ads in the Sunday New York *Times*.

With an AmEx card bearing the name Martin Conrad he purchased a good mobile scanner. He got crystals for the frequencies used by all the police and emergency agencies in the Buffalo area, as well as those used by the FBI and state police throughout all of New York. It had been easy enough to discover those frequency assignments: they were all a matter of public record, and he had gotten the information in the public library.

The next stop was the most important. His entire plan rested on it. He left the van at a parking lot on Fifty-sixth Street and walked to the enormous office building. As he went in, he was impressed by the luxury. IBM did very well for itself, he decided. An armed guard told him how to find the office he wanted.

"I'm Dr. Conrad," he told the receptionist. "I called two days ago about the console for my laboratory."

She looked up and smiled. She wore silver nail polish, almost the same color as his van. She was wearing a gray ultrasuede dress. He knew what it was because Betty had talked about ultrasuede after seeing some models on the "Dinah" show one day. She said it was the best thing ever; if he made more money she would get one or two. Betty would not look in ultrasuede the way this woman did, however.

"Do you know whom you talked with, Dr. Conrad?"

"No. I'm sorry. I don't think I do. Fellow said they'd get back to me on it right away, so I didn't bother writing anything down. Fellow didn't get back, and we really need the unit, so—"

"Please, Dr. Conrad. Don't worry about a thing. It's all right. Any one of our representatives can help you, I'm sure. Hold on just a moment." She pushed a button on her telephone. "Mr. Michaels, can you come out here, please? This is Marcy. A Dr. Conrad is here about a console."

Almost immediately a young man in a blue chalk-striped suit appeared in the doorway behind Marcy. Eddie thought he looked like an FBI agent. Michaels introduced himself to Eddie, then led him to a small office a few doors away. Eddie explained that he had called, talked with a representative a few days earlier, and detailed exactly what he needed. He looked very annoyed.

"Dr. Conrad," Michaels said soothingly, "there's no problem. Any one of us can help you. Now just tell me what you need."

Eddie said he wanted a computer terminal with a video output and a printer readout off a Selectric. Michaels asked which model he wanted and Eddie told him the model number.

"There's a newer model, Dr. Conrad. Perhaps you haven't seen the literature on it."

"I've found this one satisfactory in the past," Eddie said.

"I'm sure you have, sir. It's a fine piece of equipment. But look here." He spread out on the desk a four-color sheet that described the advantages of the replacement machine. "This does everything the other does, but it weighs less than one hundred pounds, including the monitor, and it takes up considerably less space."

"Space is not really a problem," Eddie said, "but let me see that."

Michaels went over the other features. None of them seemed to Eddie really significant, but the space and weight factors were of interest to him. And, he thought, why not have the newest and the best machine available?

"The rental is only slightly higher," Michaels said. "It's a beautiful unit. And it's nearly maintenance-free. NASA uses them."

Eddie agreed that it was a fine unit. He filled out the forms. He used the driver's license with Dr. Conrad's address—a good street on the Upper West Side—for identification. He also took out the AmEx card in case Michaels wanted verification, but Michaels said that wouldn't be necessary.

"The billing will come quarterly," Michaels said. "Unless your laboratory prefers a different arrangement?"

"Quarterly will be fine," Eddie said.

"I'll give you a permanent account number to use in all transactions with IBM in connection with this rental. If there are any problems about billing or service, make sure you include that number in any correspondence or calls. That's the way IBM knows who you are."

"I'll surely do that," Eddie said, smiling broadly. Michaels smiled back at him broadly. Eddie said he wanted a large quantity of printout rolls and ribbon cassettes delivered with the machine.

"Fine, Doctor. We'll have this at your laboratory next Thursday."

"Thursday?" Eddie made a sour face. "Oh, that's impossible. We need it immediately. That's why I came down. To make sure what happened with the other fellow didn't happen again. We've got a large grant and we're behind already. You know how it is when you're working for the government."

"I wish I could do something. All of our trucks are committed for the entire week. Perhaps someone on your staff could—I don't want to be impolite and I know it's unusual, but maybe—"

"Of course," Eddie said. "That's a fine idea. I'll have someone pick it up early this afternoon; how's that?"

"I wish we didn't have to inconvenience you, sir. It's just that we're so—"

"No inconvenience at all."

Michaels gave Eddie the address where the equipment and supplies would be waiting. He wrote something on a blue slip. "Just have your man give that to the clerk at the dock and they'll load it right on your truck." He thanked Eddie again, and again apologized for the inconvenience.

"Please," Eddie said. "It means we can have the unit in service over the weekend and that will more than make up for the inconvenience. It's a pleasure dealing with you." He smiled.

Michaels smiled back. "We do our best, sir." He walked with Eddie to the elevator and told him to be sure to call if there were any difficulties with the unit. Eddie said he certainly would do that. As the elevator doors closed, Eddie waved at Marcy, the woman in the ultrasuede suit. She waved back.

After he left the building, Eddie had a fine lunch at a very expensive restaurant. He had snails for the first time in his life and loved them. He even ordered a half bottle of chablis, but he was careful to drink only one glass. He used Dr. Conrad's American Express card and tipped the waiter very well. Then he walked along Third Avenue.

A man in front of a massage parlor promised him he would be greatly refreshed if he came inside for a while. The man handed him a slick slip of paper. The front side had photographs of five pretty girls. Two of the girls were with a rather fat, middle-aged man. The girls looked like the ones in *Playboy*, but none of the men pictured on the slip looked like men he had seen in any magazines except when they had pictures of older businessmen. The men looked like most of the middle-aged men he knew. He thought the management of the massage parlor was very smart: they knew that handsome, muscular young studs had no need of a joint like that, and that plump middle-aged executives needed to know that someone as flabby as they would be welcome. All five girls looked very happy,

even the one in the bathtub with the man who had to turn
at an odd angle so you could see his belly and smile as
well as her big breasts and smile. Everyone seemed to be
having a wet and wonderful time. At the bottom of the
back side the slip said that the establishment accepted all
major credit cards, and even cash.

Even cash. In a way New York was the *perfect* city for
someone like Eddie. Or rather it was the perfect city for
someone like the imaginary Dr. Conrad and the other
people whose made-up names he had put on the licenses
and credit cards in his pocket. Except for taxis and buses,
you don't ever need green money in New York, and he
had read in *Time* a while back that some taxi drivers now
carried a charge card machine with them because they
found they got bigger tips when businessmen had the re-
ceipted slip to turn in for their expense accounts.

Eddie had never been in a massage parlor. He knew of
two in Buffalo. One of them was always being raided and
the girls were taken away in a black police van—all of
which they showed on the eleven o'clock news on Channel
7. The other never got into the papers at all. He didn't
know if that meant that the second place paid off well or
that nothing happened there except massages. He didn't
know anyone who might know, and he certainly wouldn't
have gone in to find out for himself. Not in Buffalo.

And not in New York either, not this time. He had
taken too long enjoying his lunch. He was tempted and
slightly nervous, but he had more stops. At the first, still
using Dr. Conrad's American Express card, he bought a
twelve-inch Sony color television set, a small stereo with
both AM and FM reception, and a good cassette tape re-
corder. He wasn't sure what he would use the tape re-
corder for, but felt that as long as he was in the store he
might as well pick one up. The bill came to over fourteen
hundred dollars. Eddie felt the perspiration trickling down
the inside of his shirt as the clerk called the American
Express verification number. The clerk read off the store's
code number, the card number, and the amount of the
purchase. Eddie memorized the store's code number in
case he needed it in the future: he could find out if any of
his American Express cards was safe simply by calling up
on a regular telephone and pretending to be the store. The

American Express verification phone number was printed on a piece of cardboard over the telephone. Eddie memorized that too.

The clerk was silent for a long moment. He looked across the counter at Eddie. He made a notation with his pen.

"Sir," he said.

"Yes?" Eddie said, his voice slightly higher than usual. "What is it?"

"Is there anything else you'll be needing as long as you're in here? We have one of the best kitchen appliance departments in the city, and our prices are as low as you'll find."

Eddie felt his entire body relaxing. He hadn't realized how tight he had become during the brief space of silence while the clerk waited for the authorization.

"No, thank you," he said, letting himself return the clerk's smile for the first time. "This will be—" He paused. "Well, there are a few things I could use."

The clerk beamed across the counter. Eddie decided the store paid the clerks on a commission basis. While the clerk finished writing out the purchase order, Eddie wrote in his notebook the two numbers he had memorized. Then the clerk walked with Eddie to the appliance department and got down the group of small items Eddie asked him for. This time, when he ran the charge card through his little machine, he didn't bother calling up for verification. He knew he had a good customer.

After he signed the slip, Eddie said, "I'll be back with my car in an hour. Can you have all this stuff ready for me here? I'll just pull up out front."

"You bet, Dr. Conrad," the clerk said. "You just pull up and honk your horn and we'll bring it right on out."

Eddie thanked him. He had one more stop. He drove across town to Bloomingdale's.

He told the clerk he was going on a camping trip and he needed everything. The clerk immediately realized Eddie knew nothing about camping. The process took a little over an hour. By the end of it Eddie owned a fine pair of calf-length boots as well as a pair of British hiking boots, a lightweight down jacket guaranteed to protect him from freezing at any temperature above 20 below zero (the clerk didn't say what Eddie was supposed to do if he did happen to freeze to death at 12 or 15 below), a nice corduroy outdoor jacket for what the clerk described as "milder situations," a beautiful sheepskin coat, two pairs of gloves, two pairs of twill trousers, four stay-press khaki expedition shirts, a general purpose fishing outfit, a water-repellent camouflage suit for duck hunting, and an elegant Browning pump shot gun with a knurled grip. As the clerk was filling out the charge slips, Eddie said he decided he might as well take the Swedish hunting knife too.

"A good choice, sir," the clerk said, smiling without looking up.

"And shells for the gun," Eddie said. "I'll need some shells."

"Of course, sir," the clerk said. "I've already put that down. Four boxes should be adequate, don't you think?" He looked up, his pen poised.

"Yes," Eddie said. "That should be quite adequate." He had no idea how many shotgun shells came in a box, but he wasn't going to tell the clerk that.

Eddie handed him the card and the clerk handed him the charge slip for his signature. "I'll have to call this in for verification, sir. It's just a formality, but it's a store requirement on anything over fifty dollars. And this *is* over fifty dollars." He went to the end of the counter and picked up the handset of a wall telephone. He was too far away for Eddie to hear the store's identification number.

The clerk returned a moment later, smiling again. He handed Eddie his portion of the slip. Eddie said he was going to get his car. The clerk said the equipment would be waiting for him at the Fifty-ninth Street entrance, if that was agreeable; he could also have it on the Lexington Avenue side of the store. Eddie said Fifty-ninth Street was fine.

He picked up the van and paid the parking lot attendant. It came to six dollars, which he thought outrageous. The attendant said the lot didn't accept credit cards except from by-the-month customers. Eddie paid him.

Eddie went to the appliance store first. He honked, the clerk who had waited on him looked through the glass doorway, waved, and came out with the first of the packages. Another man brought the rest on a small hand truck behind him. "This isn't the sort of thing I expected, Dr. Conrad," he said.

"Why not?" Eddie said.

"It's not what doctors drive around here."

"Oh," Eddie said. "It's not what I usually drive either. But I've got a lot of things to do in town today and a lot of equipment to pick up somewhere else. This belongs to my son."

"Kids like these things," the clerk said. Behind him the other man neatly loaded the packages through the wide side door. "What kind a mileage they get?"

"Damned if I know," Eddie said. "I never paid any attention. I don't usually drive it, you see."

"Well, it can't be much worse than one of those Lincolns or Caddys."

"Probably not," Eddie said. "Thank you."

"You're welcome, Doc. Come back again, you need anything else."

Eddie said he would, and drove out into traffic. The salesman and the helper watched him go. He wondered if he should have tipped them. In New York it seemed nearly everyone expected to be tipped for something. The Bloomingdale's clerk frowned for a moment when he saw the van; it was clear he had expected something better. Eddie thought about telling him the "it's my son's" story, but then decided there was no reason to lie. He could drive whatever he damned well pleased.

Then he drove downtown to the IBM warehouse. He gave the dock clerk the slip he'd gotten from Michaels. "I'm suppose' to pick up some stuff here," he said. He ran his words together and dropped the terminal consonant on "supposed." The clerk assumed he was another clerk.

"Okay, mac. Where you gonna put it? You got a truck?"

"Company van's outside."

"Hang on a minute." He looked through some papers. "Okay, just back it into the bay there." He pushed a button and the wide iron door rose with a heavy clanking noise. Eddie went outside and backed the van in. The dock clerk yelled, "Okay, buddy. Hold it right there." He disappeared into the building, then came out a moment later followed by a tall black man who was pushing a hand truck loaded with four cartons. "Put 'em in the van, Eddie," the clerk said.

Eddie was about to answer him, then realized the clerk was speaking to the black man. His name wasn't Eddie today.

He made one final stop, one he hadn't planned. On his way back uptown he passed a discount record store that promised great bargains inside. Eddie parked the van around the corner, went into the store, and bought thirty-eight LP albums and fourteen cassette recordings. He wasn't sure what he wanted and he didn't want to take too much time, so he walked quickly through the store, pulling from the shelves things he had heard about and things that looked as if they might be interesting.

"Like Christmas," the clerk at the cash desk said.

"You might say that," Eddie said, handing him his credit card.

He took the West Side Highway up to the George Washington Bridge, crossed the Hudson, and then took the Palisades Interstate Parkway to the connection that would put him back on 17 northwest, which he would take to its intersection with 81 at Binghamton. Then north to the Thruway and home to Buffalo. By the time he reached Liberty, he was comfortable enough with the CB jargon to start using the radio. He liked the idea of being able to talk to people with a name everyone knew was made up. All the people talking had funny names they had designed for themselves, names they found preferable to the ones they had been awarded without their consent. Eddie understood that well enough: he had, in a period of two weeks, been William Artis and Dr. Martin Conrad. He hadn't felt like either of those people; those were just names he used when it was convenient.

When he made his first transmission on the CB, he felt perfectly at ease. "Hey, you eastbounders on this seventeen, you got the Rollin' Chargecard here. What's it look like over your donkey?"

He was answered immediately by someone who identified himself as "Snake River Jack." The man told him he was clean and green all the way into "Bingotown." A woman asked for a time check and the air was clogged with men responding. Some asked, "Hey, beaver, what's your twenty?" The woman talked back and forth with some of them for a while, then got beyond range. Eddie was astounded that she wasn't offended at being called "beaver." No one bothered to ask her for her handle.

He reached Buffalo before ten. Betty was in the living room, watching "Kojak." She didn't hear him come in. There was food on the table. The meat had dried out, but he ate it anyway. He hadn't eaten anything since the snails at lunch. "Kojak" ended and she came into the kitchen for another beer.

"Eddie!" she shrieked.

"What's the matter?"

"I didn't hear you come in."

"I've been here for a while. I didn't want to disturb you."

"Oh, dear. I didn't hear you come in. It could have been a burglar and I wouldn't have heard him either."

"I used my key. A burglar wouldn't have had a key. He would have made more noise. Anyway, we don't have anything to steal."

"What about the color TV?"

"You were watching it. How could a burglar steal it when you were watching it?"

"It's an old TV set anyway."

"So you don't have anything to worry about. Anybody call?"

"No. Who would call?"

"Nobody I could think of."

"Your dinner okay?"

"It's fine, Betty. Just fine."

"I'm going back inside, all right?"

"Sure. I'll be there in a few minutes."

He had parked the van in a nice residential block. The packages were on the floor in back, covered by an old blanket. It would be all right for a day or two.

He slept late the next morning. When he got up, she was reading the paper in the kitchen. He told her he had to go into the office for a while to finish some work.

"You never go in on Saturdays."

"It's something important."

"They pay you extra for it?"

"Probably."

"I don't think you should have to go in on Saturdays unless they pay you extra. They don't pay you what you're worth as it is."

"What am I worth, Betty?"

"What?" She was pouring coffee. "What was that?"

"Nothing. It won't take long. You want me to pick anything up?"

"No. You going to take the car?"

"Unless you need it. I can take the bus. They don't run very often on Saturdays, though."

"No. That's okay. I'm not going out today."

"See you later, then."

He drove past where he had parked the van. It looked fine. Perhaps this evening he would tell her he was going out for a walk and he would move it around the corner. It wouldn't do for people in the neighborhood to start wondering or for teen-agers to notice the van hadn't been moved in a while.

There was almost no traffic on Delaware Avenue. It was like a Sunday. Hardly anyone drove downtown to shop anymore. Anyone with a car went to the shopping centers in the suburbs. The prices weren't any better and they were further away, but the shoppers maybe felt more comfortable spending their money in the nice modern malls. And there was free parking out there.

At the corner of West Utica he saw some kids playing in the large empty lot where until a few years before had stood a magnificent copy of a Gothic cathedral. The bishop had announced that the cathedral would be ripped down because it would take a million dollars to repair the building's structural faults. Although Eddie disliked what went on in churches, he sometimes liked the buildings themselves, and this had been one of his favorites. He had sometimes stopped there and walked through when no services were going on, just listening to the echoing sound of his footsteps and watching the sunlight burst through the stained-glass windows.

He knew this cathedral was nothing compared to the great cathedrals of Europe. But he had never been to Europe and never had any hope of getting there. That was an ancient world beyond his means.

One paper said that the bishop expected the Catholic

population in the city would immediately come forward
with money for the reconstruction. But no one seemed to
pay any mind to his threat. The other paper said he had
no intention of repairing the building, that he intended to
use the property to construct a large church-owned senior
citizens apartment house, one that would be a fine source
of income for the diocese because it wouldn't have to pay
any taxes. The bishop answered neither paper, and in time
the cathedral was destroyed. It took a long time because
the lower walls were fourteen feet thick and the wrecker's
steel ball bounded off the massive gray stones like rubber.

So far nothing had been done with the property. It was
an eyesore now, overgrown with weeds and littered with
empty beer cans, broken glass, and pieces of rubble. Eddie
thought it terrible for the bishop to have destroyed that
fine old building and put in its place a vacant lot where
kids could hurt themselves on pieces of shattered glass and
rats could build nests to wait for nightfall. There would
never again be the kind of money or care needed to make
a building like that.

His floor at City Hall was empty. No one else was
there. He worked for an hour, just so he would have
something to show his boss if anyone should comment on
his having been there. He walked to the coffee machines
near the elevators and made sure no one had come in
while he was working.

When he was quite sure he was alone, he entered the
American Express access code into his console. He got immediate conversation; the line was empty on a Saturday
morning. In thirty seconds he abolished Dr. Martin Conrad's account number. As far as the AmEx records would
show, that account number was and had been empty. The
company would have to honor the purchases at the stores
since it had verified the account. In all likelihood it would
assume that by some error another account number had its
purchases charged to the empty number, perhaps one with
an eight that had worn down to read as a three. There
were too many digits involved for them to check out all
the possible accounts, too many to do anything but write
off the six thousand dollars. The slips wouldn't be connected with the deficit because they were connected with no
active account. There would be no more irregular pur-

chases under that particular number, and the company wouldn't bother checking further. It was too big for that kind of trivia. After he had finished abolishing the charges, he checked it through: he asked the AmEx computer how much that account number owed, and the computer told him that there was no such account number active.

He drank the coffee he had gotten from the machine. It was cold and awful, but he drank it anyway. He needed a pause. It seemed incredible that it was all working exactly as he had planned. There were two more things to do.

The first was the abolition of Dr. Conrad's account at IBM. That was easier than the AmEx expungement. He had picked up the direct code for account verification at the IBM school, and he had stolen the accounting paradigms. He punched in Dr. Conrad's account number, the one given him by the salesman Michaels in New York. He got an immediate readback indicating that Dr. Conrad had on rental agreement a terminal, keyboard and video, and there was an outstanding software bill of $342. He told the computer that it was wrong, the account was empty. The computer was silent for a moment, then typed back that there was no such account number.

Eddie didn't even know the real location of the computer with which he had been exchanging messages.

The other exercise was simpler. He walked into his boss's office and looked into the shredder bag. It hadn't been emptied yet. He had never been sure why his boss had any use for a shredder, but why wasn't one of the questions Eddie's position in city government permitted him to ask.

The machine took five seconds to get up to speed. Eddie opened its disposal bag and set a few pieces of legal-size paper atop the shredded bits in there already; then he closed the door. He inserted into the shredder the driver's license belonging to Dr. Martin Conrad and the American Express card. It took about three seconds. He opened the door and looked at the bits of fur atop the legal-size sheets. The shredder worked very well.

Dr. Conrad's license and credit card were gone. None of them, in fact, ever existed. No computer in the world would recognize the name, and it was only in the computers of the world that such questions could be asked. *And* Eddie had his Chevrolet van with all its fine equipment, an operational computer terminal, and a splendid bunch of other goodies. He was almost a new man.

# FIVE

Keeping the van on the street was not a good idea. He couldn't bring it home and put it in their garage. For a while he moved it every few nights to another well-lighted residential area. He had read that hoodlums were less likely to vandalize a vehicle if it was parked in a well-lighted residential area. But he was running out of them.

The danger was too great. The console would be awkward to replace if it were stolen. If some kids broke in, played with the machines for a while, and then decided the console was useless because the television set obviously got no programs (it didn't even have a channel selector), then left it all for the police to find, IBM would find out that the machines had been moved from New York to Buffalo. The police would know that a van purchased in Rochester had moved to Buffalo. That was too much for too many people to know.

Eddie was aware that it was carelessness with little pieces of information that led to the downfall of the smartest crooks. Look at Nixon and his badly erased tape. That silence, as much as anything else, brought him down. Eddie had been careful to insulate himself as much as possible from the activities of William Artis and Dr. Martin Conrad. Conrad was gone for good, and it was time to get rid of William Artis.

He didn't need the name anymore, and since it was connected to a real person, it was a potential nuisance. He didn't want people asking Artis questions and perhaps making connections to that real estate tax refund operation.

During his lunch hour he told the state motor vehicle registration computer that the Chevrolet van owned by William Artis had been totally destroyed in a wreck; the registration for it was to be canceled. Then he created three new registrations for the van, each in the name of one of his American Express and driver's license sets. He had the plates mailed to general delivery at three different post offices in small towns not too far away.

If he ever got a ticket from a policeman for speeding or any other reason, the license plate check would show a currently valid registration. If he paid or abolished the ticket, there would be no problem. And if he got into some kind of trouble, there were two sets of clean plates he could immediately use for the van. There were too many gray Chevrolet vans around for that to create a problem. He would always have valid identification for himself and his vehicle, and he could change that valid identification in as much time as it took to put on a new set of license plates.

He put an advertisement in the *Courier-Express:* "Out-of-town businessman needs private garage to park company van while in Buffalo. West Side preferred." He gave as a return address the post office box he had rented. Within two days there were eight responses. Two of them were for garages on the far West Side, the others ranged as far away as Clarence, twelve miles east of town on Main Street.

One of the two West Side garages was on a small street running into Niagara, not far from where it met West Ferry. There was a row of houses and, further down the block, a row of small cinder block garages. The garages had no windows. The streetlamp nearby was one of those high-mercury vapor types. They gave a feeling of awful cold in the winter because of their pale blue light, but that light covered a large area. It wasn't likely that someone would be busting open the garage doors with that kind of illumination on the street.

Eddie wrote the owner. He enclosed a money order for six months' rent and asked the owner to mail the keys to his box in Buffalo because he was about to go on a sales trip for several days. He said one of his assistants would be parking the van in the garage during the week.

Most nights now Eddie worked on carpentry in his basement. He started refinishing a chair he had bought at Goodwill, a pretty old oak rocker that had been badly treated. Betty was pleased because she thought it meant he was going to be watching television again. He worked on the rocker just long enough to give it a half-done look, then he moved it to the far side of the workbench.

Eddie was furnishing his van. He made a small four-drawer cabinet for clothes and other personal things. He made a lockable cabinet that would house the console and monitor. The cabinet was in four pieces, and he had only to bolt them together when he got them to the garage. He took the pieces out, one at a time, through the back cellar door. She never noticed.

Soon the van was ready. All the clothes he would need were in the four drawers, the equipment was hidden in its container, and two overhead cabinets running almost the full length of the van held the stacks of printout paper, the ribbons, the shotgun, and his other supplies. He made a narrow bed so he could sleep in the van if necessary; it also functioned as a bench for him to sit on while using the console. In a junkyard he found a small wrecked camper from which he took a butane stove and a small sink. The sink installation turned out to be more complicated than he had expected: he would have to weld a large water tank and another holding tank under the van, and he would have to install and wire an electric pump. Eddie decided to let the water go. He put the sink in and coupled it for an outside hose so if he were parked anywhere near water he could hook up directly.

While he worked in the cellar, he listened to the scanner. It was set for the Buffalo police and Erie County sheriff's frequencies.

Betty came down one night and asked what he was doing. It was the only time she came down. When he heard her steps, he moved in front of the rocker.

"I'm refinishing a chair, I told you that."

"It's taking a long time."

"It's slow work. I like to do a good job."

She pointed at the scanner. "That's a strange radio."

"It's a scanner. You've seen them on television."

She nodded and listened for a while. "But how can you listen to that program? It sounds boring."

"I'm listening to the Buffalo Police Department as they go about the city. It's interesting."

"It sounds dumb."

"You mean stupid. Dumb means no talking."

"You know what I mean. It's a lot of squawking."

"I find it interesting."

"I don't."

"That's why I play it down here. I can't stand 'All in the Family.' "

"That's not on now. 'Charlie's Angels' is on now."

"I can't stand that one either. That woman, the one with the bionic teeth—"

"That's another program."

"No, it's not. She's got the hair. You know who I mean. She smiles all the time."

"Oh, her. She's not on it anymore. They got someone else now."

"Wonderful."

"Eddie, I worry about you. Listening to this stuff. Working on old chairs down in this damp cellar. It's morbid."

"It's the life of the city. It's what you'll hear about on the eleven o'clock news. As it's happening."

"Why don't you come up and watch 'Charlie's Angels'?"

"I'm working on this rocking chair. It's a nice rocking chair."

"Maybe you should get a little TV set and put it down here if you're going to spend so much time here."

"Maybe."

"I'll tell you the next time there's a sale at Sattler's."

"Sattler's sale prices are higher than brand names' regular prices."

"But they're really nice to you at Sattler's. They have salesmen to answer all your questions."

"And that's what you pay for."

"Well, you can get it wherever you like, how about that?"

"I'll think about it. Next time we have some money to spare."

After the van was finished, there was no reason to stall on the chair any longer. He completed the work on it in one evening and brought it upstairs. She looked at it a moment, then said, "I don't think it goes with our living room furniture."

Eddie shrugged. "You're right. We can give it to Goodwill, then."

"Sometimes I think you're going crazy," she said.

"No," Eddie said. "I used to be going crazy. Now I'm not going crazy anymore."

He put the scanner in the Volvo. He was looking for a dead man, and hadn't been able to find one yet. He listened to the radio for reports of bodies in the canal. He wanted one to float up, one he could reach quickly—before the police got it out—someone who was about his size.

Eddie had thought this was going to be the easiest part of his plan, but it turned out to be a complete waste of time. Bodies came, but the confusion was never as great as he remembered from that afternoon. There was no way he could simply swap identities. The police didn't stop watching the dead people until the wagon came to haul them away. And whatever time of night it was, a crowd always gathered.

He had a van ready to go, twenty thousand dollars in small bills, sets of drivers' licenses, registrations, plates, and credit cards. He could be whoever and whatever he wished, but there was no way to become someone else if he couldn't get rid of Eddie Argo. It was like a comedy routine he had seen in a movie, where someone was trying to dump a bagful of garbage and people kept bringing it back to him, all of them friendly and helpful, so that the man was perfectly incapable of freeing himself from the absolutely useless stuff. That was how Eddie felt about Eddie Argo: absolutely useless stuff to which he was inextricably glued.

If he had told anyone what he was thinking, they would have gotten him committed immediately. Without difficulty.

For a couple of weeks Betty said nothing about his going out. Then she began asking him questions. They were almost comical. He realized during one of the sessions that she wondered if he was having an affair, and at the same time she was telling herself that no woman would be wanting to have an affair with someone like Eddie. If she were having an affair, it certainly wouldn't be with someone like Eddie. He answered her vaguely, and she soon got bored asking where he had been.

Which meant she didn't really care, which he had

known beforehand but hadn't known she knew. Maybe she didn't realize it yet. In any event, she stopped bothering him about his walks and his rides in the car. She seemed to have accepted the idea that he had gone a little crazy, and she acted as if it didn't matter in her life at all. He knew that, in fact, it didn't.

He walked a lot down by the river, sometimes very late at night. He drove the Volvo to the foot of West Ferry, parking in the lot behind the abandoned shoeshine stand, and then walked along the canal. There was a grove of trees and a parking area. Sometimes couples were there, and he knew they were making love inside their cars. He stayed far away from them; he didn't want someone mistaking him for a peeping Tom and starting a fight. Eddie had never been in a fight. The evenings were getting cooler, and he saw fewer and fewer people.

Eddie had almost given up. He had even found himself thinking about *really* doing it—jumping into the moving black water and letting the silence end his thinking about the bills and the crazy plans and the dancing account numbers. And then, one night, something happened.

There was a man who came often to the area. Perhaps he lived somewhere nearby. Eddie had seen him several times when he was out walking and when he was sitting in his car in the shadows, listening to the scanner. The man liked to walk through the parking lot and grove of trees across the iron bridge and to sit on the narrow jetty of rocks separating the canal from the river. A couple of times the man passed out and didn't get up for a long time. Eddie would stand on the iron bridge and watch him disappear into the trees, then reappear on the rocks beyond, lighted by the overhead lamps of the Peace Bridge, further down the canal. The man would be motionless for a while, and then he would make a loud sound of dissatisfaction. Immediately after that Eddie would hear a light splash, the empty bottle going into the water. Once Eddie went to work early and took the car; he wanted to look around the area in daylight. He saw the man asleep on the walk.

It was a Sunday night. Betty was home watching a Paul Newman movie on Channel 2. She was in the kitchen when he went out. They had said nothing to one another.

Eddie had parked the car by the abandoned shoeshine hut and walked down the cobblestone street to the bridge. Overhead, the massive counterweight blocked out a large rectangle of sky. He had never seen the drawbridge go up, but he knew that during the day a man worked in the small house on the left side, waiting for some boat with a high mast to come through. At night the drawbridge house was always empty.

Eddie leaned on the rail, looking toward the Peace Bridge. The lights danced on the water. From his left came the occasional hum of traffic from the Thruway extension. It was impossible to see any of the cars from down here, and no houses were nearby. Eddie wondered if muggers worked the area; if he were a mugger, it would be a perfect place.

Well, no, it wasn't: who came here but the old drunk and an occasional nut like himself? The lovers kept their car doors locked and their motors running, ready to go at a moment's notice. Muggers wanted people with money, gold watches, things like that. There wasn't enough business here to keep a mugger employed.

Eddie heard a noise in the trees, then saw at the end of the grove the drunk walking alone. He was talking to himself. He sounded angry. Eddie leaned against the cold metal, feeling the sharp edge press into his arm, and he looked at the silhouetted figure.

And then he didn't see it anymore. It had slid away somehow, perhaps during the blink of an eye. For a moment he thought his eyes had been betraying him.

But he knew what had happened. He felt a momentary spasm of guilt as he realized it was what he had been waiting and hoping for all along.

He ran to the end of the bridge and turned right, walked down to the concrete dock. The drunk would have to float by this spot. The water was very black. It was probably very cold.

Eddie was terrified. He would have to save the old man, he knew that. It was his escape hatch, but he knew he couldn't take it. He was out to get the city and the county and all those other anonymous and powerful agencies and organizations that operated without guilt or responsibility. He was not out to get some old drunk who had fallen into dark water. He couldn't be responsible for letting someone die.

He waited a long time. The water moved quietly a few feet below the dock. He leaned on a round steel mooring peg, looking into the deep water. A heavy truck rumbled high above on the Thruway. The water slapped gently underneath the dock.

The drunk didn't float by. Eddie felt panic, as if he himself were in danger. He ran to the far end of the parking area, off to the left of the bridge, to the point on the jetty where the drunk had fallen in. He walked back along the rocks, peering into the water. When he reached the place the fence began, he followed that, leaning over as far as he could.

He saw nothing, nothing at all, just the dark water occasionally shifting and flickering with the reflection of a faraway light.

# SIX

"You feeling all right?" It was his boss, standing in the doorway of the office, looking at him curiously.

"I'm fine," Eddie said. "Why do you ask?"

"You just look terrible, that's why. Like somebody died in your family."

"Nobody died," Eddie said. "I'm okay."

"Glad to hear it," the boss said. "You sure don't look it."

"I'm okay."

He walked home again. He took the long way, along Niagara. Things weren't working out well. He felt trapped and wasted. The bills kept coming, kept getting larger and larger. He had his secret money and his van and his fine equipment, but there was no way to escape. It was like he had dressed for a party and then found himself the only person there.

Wrong place, wrong time. Wrong man.

He turned left at the cobblestone extension of West Ferry and walked down the hill and out to the middle of the bridge. The water was much dirtier than he had thought. Pieces of rubbish floated along, gathering in dense bunches at some places, breaking loose and disappearing further on.

Someone stood next to him, a man about his size, wearing a uniform and a cap.

"You come down here a lot," the man said. "I've seen you two or three times."

"Who are you?" Eddie asked.

"Bobby Jim. I'm the bridgemaster. I raise and lower the bridge when the boats come through."

It seemed silly to call someone in charge of a thirty-foot bridge the master. "I've never seen the bridge up," Eddie said.

"Don't get many boats coming through anymore. Used to be a lot of boats. Now it's just people in motorboats on weekends. Don't have to raise the bridge for them. Once

in a while there's something bigger. Not often." He
pointed down into the water. "It's getting clearer."

"It looks awful."

"You should have seen it four or five years ago. First
there were dead fish all the time, and then there weren't
any fish at all. On days when there was no wind, the stink
was awful. I'd get home sometimes and my wife would
make me leave my clothes on the back porch." He took a
deep breath. His face was neutral for a moment, like a
man tasting the first sip out of a bottle of just opened
wine. "Now there's hardly any stink and people are
catching fish again. It's not too good to look at, but it's not
poisoned anymore. That's something. Not much water
around here isn't poisoned. I wouldn't want to drink any
of it, though. I think if you fell in you probably wouldn't
have to drown; you could just drink some of it and shit
yourself to death." Bobby Jim laughed, then said he had to
get back to work. He waved and went into his little house
diagonally across the bridge.

Eddie wondered what kind of work he had to do in
there. Perhaps he was going back to sleep.

Junk floated in the canal. A green Molson's bottle
bobbed up and down, then drifted over to the concrete
wharf. It bobbed again, then floated underneath and into
the shadows. Eddie watched it glisten for a moment, then
disappear in the darkness. He shielded his eyes from the
lowering sun to see if he could find the bottle.

He saw, under the white concrete, in the dim blackness
of the space between the water and the dock, perhaps five
feet back from the edge, an object he hadn't been looking
for, something he hadn't expected ever to find, something
he recognized immediately. It was a hand, moving lightly
on the water, up and down, up and down. His eyes were
just barely able to discern the outline of the body further
in the shadows, at the end of the outstretched arm. The
hand seemed to be pointing directly at Eddie's eyes.

Eddie shuddered, tried to stop himself, then shuddered
again. He moved his hand away, let the light blind him to
the shadows. With his hand away from his eyes he could
see nothing in there. But he knew what he had seen.

It had to be the drunk. The body must have moved into
the area under the dock while he stood there looking for it

in the water. It had been there the whole time, just under his feet.

He turned and looked at the bridgemaster's hut. There was no movement. No one else was in sight. He turned and walked back toward the cobblestone street, his shoes ringing on the metal bridge, then tapping on the old smooth stones. When he crossed Niagara and was on regular pavement, he no longer heard the sounds of his feet. His heart was beating too loudly for him to pay any attention at all to sounds so far away.

He got home out of breath, and it wasn't until he sat down at the table that he realized he had just run the last mile for nothing: there was nothing to do now but wait. The hours of evening had to be undergone before he could do anything at all.

The clock moved slowly, unbearably slowly. He watched television for a while with Betty, but he couldn't get involved in the stories. He kept waiting for the commercials because each one meant it was later and later. For the first time he could remember, the commercials came too seldom.

"I'm going downstairs for a while," he said when he could stand it no longer.

"Why?" she asked. "You're done with that chair."

"The place is a mess. I want to clean it up."

"You don't have to do it now."

"It's as good as any other time."

He took with him a broom, a dustpan, and a small brush. He closed the door to the cellar stairs behind him and put the broom and pan on the workbench. He leaned the broom against the wall, then turned on the scanner. During the whole time he worked, he listened to the scanner, terrified that they wouldn't find it. Now that he had exactly what he needed, he wasn't sure he was brave enough to do what he had planned.

At eleven-thirty he unplugged the scanner and carried it out to the car. He came back inside and looked over the cellar one last time. It was spotless. All the dust was gone, the tools were hung up properly, the oily rags were in a covered metal container. He carried the broom, pan, and brush upstairs and put them in their proper place in the kitchen.

She was watching the "Tonight" show, with Johnny Carson. That meant the movie on Channel 7 was really awful, because she always preferred stories to conversation. "I'm going out for a little while," he said from the kitchen.

"I'll be here," she said without turning around.

He backed the car out, feeling his fingers trembling. There was an uncomfortable sensation in his thighs: fear, excitement, he couldn't tell which. Perhaps they came to the same thing. He parked the Volvo in the usual place. When he got out, he carried a small bundle under his arm.

Across the water the lights of Canada winked faintly on the river beyond the canal. To his left the Peace Bridge soared across the open space, making a brilliant shimmering reflection in the moving waters below. During the day the bridge was rather dreary.

He reached the concrete dock and crouched in shadows for a long time. When he was sure no one was nearby, no one was watching, and that he was perfectly alone, he undressed, paused for a moment on the edge of the concrete, and slid over the edge into the water.

It was much colder than he had expected. Even this late in the summer the water was cold enough to give his body a sudden shock. He understood why so many people drowned so easily. The current sucked at his legs, and he held tightly to the support columns. He took a deep breath, then swung his body underneath, into the blackness.

His head and shoulders were above the water; his left arm held him steady against a slimy column. He waited for his eyes to adjust to the darkness. They didn't adjust. No lights seemed to come underneath at all. He moved around in the cold water, feeling for the arm wth his outstretched fingers.

A scurrying noise to his left snapped his body taut. His body knew the noise before his mind understood what his body knew. Something squeaked, then there was silence again. He shivered, not from the cold but from knowing that rats were nearby. He hated rats.

What if the rats had been eating the body? What if he reached again for the arm and found instead—

He told himself he had to stop thinking. It only made him sick now. Now he had to act. The body must have moved further back. He made a lot of noise with his hands on the water to scare away any rats still back there, then he moved deeper into the darkness.

It took him ten minutes to find the arm. He was surprised, then, how calmly he managed to pull it forward, almost as if it were alive and someone he knew. The terror of the rats had been enough to neutralize his revulsion at swimming with a corpse.

Getting the body up on the dock was more difficult than he had expected, and it took longer. He had to be careful not to scratch it on the concrete edge. He didn't know if the police would notice scratches, if they would show after so long in the water, or if they were expected because bodies smash against stones and other things when they drown in swift current. But it seemed a reasonable precaution. He skinned his own left leg badly and cut his elbow. He hoped the wounds wouldn't infect.

When it was done, he sat on the cold concrete, trying to catch his breath. He pictured coming on the scene and he found it almost comic: Eddie Argo, naked and dripping-wet, shivering with cold and fear, sitting on a concrete dock next to a drowned alcoholic bum.

But he knew that if anyone came along, anyone at all, it wouldn't be taken as the least bit comic.

He looked around again to be sure no one was watching, then he checked the dead man's pockets. There was no identification at all, and there were no keys. The man probably didn't even have a home. Perfect.

Eddie undressed him, which was extremely difficult. He had never undressed anyone before, except Betty, and that had been years ago, when they were courting and she was at least partially helpful. When the body was naked on the stones, Eddie rolled the dirty clothing into a tight ball and bound it with the dead man's belt. Now there were two of them, pale and naked in the faint light from the distant bridge.

He took his own clothing, which he had left in a neat pile nearby, and dressed the body. Socks, underwear, shirt, trousers, shoes. The shoes didn't fit very well, so Eddie took them off and, after making sure the laces were tied, threw them into the water. The shoes often came off in the water, he had learned, so that would cause no suspicion. He made sure the pocket with the wallet in it was securely buttoned. He didn't want the wallet to get lost. He put his ring on the man's finger. It was difficult getting it on because the finger wouldn't bend at all, but it finally slipped over the thick knuckle.

Eddie stood up again, naked, looking down at the dead man dressed in his clothes. At once he felt sick with revulsion at what he had just done and free as he hadn't felt in longer than he could remember. He looked at the lights on the water far away and gradually his stomach stopped churning wildly.

One more step. He climbed down to the thin ledge at the water level, reached up, and pulled the body over. It went directly into the water, making a loud splash. He held onto the arm. The body sank out of sight. Only the arm and the fingers interlocked with his were visible. Then the body rose again.

Eddie slid into the water, which seemed even colder than before. He swam underneath the dock and pushed the body before him until it butted against a wall slick with moss.

He was terrified of the rats, but he did the next thing anyway: he ran his fingers along the back wall until he felt a protruding spike just under the water level. He hooked the jacket onto the spike in a way it might have caught itself naturally.

When he climbed back onto the dock, he shook off as much water as he could. His teeth chattered, as much from cold as from fear. Perhaps more from fear. It was worse because he was naked. He wished he had thought to have carried a towel. He unrolled the bundle he had brought from the car—dry clothes—and quickly dressed. Nothing moved except some cars high on the bridge and a truck on the Thruway.

It was now Tuesday morning, six hours before first light. The weather was cool. Hardly anyone would be out in private boats until the weekend. Eventually the fibers in the part of the jacket wrapped around the spike would pull out and the body would float into the canal and resurface. Someone might see it moving around under the dock during the weekend. It was a few feet further in than when Eddie had spotted the hand, but people at the water level could see further in than someone up on the iron bridge.

The weekend was time enough for the water to do its work. Especially with the rats. Now that he was dressed and done with the dark water, the rats were his friends.

There was another possibility: the body might drift out into the lake and sink and never be seen again. It seemed a distant possibility. There was nothing Eddie could do about that. He was prepared to be a missing person, but it would be much easier if he were a drowned man. He preferred that. The odds were that he would soon be a drowned man.

As he unlocked the door on the driver's side, Eddie realized he had made his second mistake.

Out of habit he had transferred the car keys to the trousers he was now wearing. He should have left them with the body. Now he would have to leave them in the car so it would look like he simply forgot or didn't bother to take them out of the ignition. If the keys weren't on the body and not in the car either, they might get suspicious, so throwing the keys into the water was no help.

In the morning Betty would probably call the police and they would come looking for him. If they noticed the car right away, they would probably look in the canal. It would be awful if they found the body right away, before the water and the fish and the rats had a few days to work. But he couldn't move the car. If it were found too far from the water, that would make the later discovery improbable. Why would anyone—even a man who was just going to sit on the ledge for a while to mull over his problems—park more than a block or two away?

He could go back there again and climb down and put the keys in one of the pockets. No, he decided, he couldn't do that. He couldn't face the black water again; he couldn't handle that body again. He threw the keys far under the driver's seat.

Then he slid down and began unhooking the scanner. He heard, faintly at first and then louder, heavy footsteps running toward the car. He slouched lower and held his breath, and cursed himself for a fool for not having found an isolated spot for the car. His heart was pumping wildly; he heard it deep in his ears and felt the beat in his throat.

The footsteps raced alongside the car, then passed by without slowing. They began to fade. Eddie raised his head just enough to see over the dashboard. A tall man was turning the corner. He wore a gray sweat shirt, dark shorts, and white sneakers. A jogger. Nearly one in the morning and a jogger ran through the empty city streets. A lunatic. The city was full of lunatics.

He wondered what the jogger would think of him.

Eddie took the radio and quickly walked to the garage; then he drove away in the van. He had several things to do before he got to sleep.

He parked the van near City Hall in the gas station directly opposite the Statler. It looked like any other vehicle parked there for service. The square was empty.

There was no problem getting into the building. He had a key to the side entrance. He had never used the key before and for a moment wished he had checked it previously. But the lock turned easily.

Except for emergencies, no one worked there at night except the janitors. The janitors were time-studied, so he knew exactly where they would be at any particular hour. They had finished with the upper floors at 1:30 A.M. and they were not allowed to start on the lower floors until 3:30 A.M. The union and the city had worked out what seemed to them a fair rate for the work. Once in the cafeteria Eddie heard some of them talking contemptuously about a new man, a summer worker, who had asked why they couldn't just work through all the floors directly and then go home two hours early. The summer worker was someone's son.

Eddie took the stairs. He didn't want anyone to hear the elevator or see where the indicator lights stopped registering. Two flights per story, eighteen flights in all. He had to stop twice to catch his breath. As he walked down the corridor to his office, his breathing sounded louder than his footsteps.

He turned on the small fluorescent lamp at his desk. He

had the programs he would need ready in a small folder under the blotter. He switched on his console. The blue-gray light from the screen cast an eerie glow on the far wall.

First he ordered the computer center to access the current county tax roll tapes. There was a humming noise from his machine, then the word READY appeared on the screen.

This particular operation was dependent on something he had done almost a year earlier. The city had gotten an optical scanner that could transfer certain kinds of type directly onto the tapes without having to go through manual encoding first. Eddie had the entire telephone book— Yellow Pages and all—encoded.

"Why?" his boss said.

"Why not?" Eddie said. At the time, he didn't have a reason for doing it, but it seemed like fun.

"Yeah," his boss said. "Why not? May be useful sometime."

"Never know," Eddie said. "As long as we got the gadget here, might as well be ready."

"Good idea. Don't take too much time with it."

"I'll have one of the girls do it. She'll just have to turn the pages. The scanner does the rest."

"Oh," his boss said. "That's really good. Not Gladys."

"No, sir," Eddie said, "not Gladys."

The boss considered Gladys his personal secretary, and none of the other people in the office was allowed to use her, even when she was just sitting there knitting sweaters. There were stories, but Eddie didn't know anyone well enough to have been told any of them. He knew they were there.

After the tax rolls were accessioned, Eddie ordered another machine to access the Yellow Pages. That took a little longer. The ready indicator flashed again. He ordered the second machine to isolate the names of all entries under "Churches."

There was silence for a moment, and the screen was blank.

WHICH CATEGORY CHURCHES? the screen asked.

Eddie told it to give him the categories it knew.

ADVENTIST, AFRICAN-METHODIST-EPISCOPAL (SEE METH-

ODIST), APOSTOLIC, ASSEMBLIES OF GOD, BAPTIST, BYZANTINE RITE, CHRISTIAN DISCIPLES OF CHRIST, CHRISTIAN AND MISSIONARY ALLIANCE, CHRISTIAN SCIENCE, CHURCH OF CHRIST, CHURCH OF GOD, CHURCH OF GOD IN CHRIST, CHURCH OF JESUS CHRIST OF LATTER-DAY SAINTS, COMMUNITY, COVENANT, EASTERN ORTHODOX, EPISCOPAL . . .

The machine was reading out at a furious rate, and he tried to get it to stop, but the machine was programmed to fully answer any question put to it. It flashed away.

FRIENDS, INTERDENOMINATIONAL, JEHOVAH'S WITNESSES, JEWISH (SEE SYNAGOGUES), LATTER-DAY SAINTS, LUTHERAN, MENNONITE, METHODIST, MORMON, NAZARINE, PENTECOSTAL, POLISH NATIONAL CATHOLIC, PRESBYTERIAN, QUAKER, ROMAN CATHOLIC, SALVATION ARMY, SPIRITUALIST, UNITARIAN UNIVERSALIST, UNITED CHURCH OF CHRIST, UNITED METHODIST, VARIOUS DENOMINATIONS, ETC., WESLEYAN. END OF CATEGORIES.

By the time Eddie found the code for interrupting an answer, the machine had flashed out all the Yellow Page categories. He switched on the printer, then told the computer to type and total a listing of all property owned by all the church groups in the city, broken down according to denomination, and broken down again for all denominations according to property use. The machine interrupted to ask what categories of use he meant. He told it he meant church services, clerical residences, schools, and non-church business but rented for income.

The typing console chattered away for a long time. Its printing rate was nearly one thousand words per minute, figured at five-letter units. Eddie watched the first several feet roll through to make sure the paper feed was working properly, then went down the hall to the men's room. On the way he saw that the coffee machine was broken again. He went into the men's room, let his eyes adjust to the dark, found the urinal, pissed, washed his face at the sink, then walked down a flight of stairs to another bank of coffee machines, where he put in some coins. He drank the first cup there, leaning against the wall. He put in more coins and went back upstairs. When he reached his office, the console was still typing furiously.

The typewriter paused a moment, skipped a few spaces,

then began typing out the tallies. Eddie was astounded. He had expected a lot, but nothing like this.

The church property was valued at about eighteen million dollars; the residential property was valued at about sixteen million dollars; the school property was valued at twelve million (but, the computer told him parenthetically, the properties exempt from tax rolls had not been reevaluated in any of the past six property surveys done by the county, which meant the current evaluation was based on 1940 values and dollars), and the rented property excluded from tax rolls was worth about twenty-two million dollars. At current tax rates, the computer said, it all came to an annual removal from the tax rolls of property that would otherwise contribute slightly over four million dollars to the county treasury.

The current school deficit, the *Courier* had reported only two days ago, for Buffalo and Cheektowaga, the only two towns in the county of substantial size with substantial budget problems, was less than two million dollars, total.

When the machine fell silent, Eddie clipped off the sheet. He circled in red the significant numbers, folded the thick packet neatly, and put the pages in a large brown envelope, which he addressed to the business editor at the *Courier*, a man named Klipp. Klipp had been trying to get that information for years. He had come in and looked through the tax rolls and made his tabulations. The problem was, he had to look at every single entry to know whether or not it was tax-exempt. What the computer had done in the past twenty minutes would have taken Klipp—or anyone else—ten years. No one had told Klipp that the city and county computers were programmed to extract such information. Both bishops—Catholic and Episcopal—were heavy contributors to the party, which everyone knew. The Catholic bishop was frequently photographed on the county chairman's boat, especially when the governor made his rare visits to town.

Eddie ordered that the tax roll and Yellow Pages tapes be returned to storage. A few seconds later the video screen told him they had been returned to their appropriate storage locations.

Eddie smiled at the screen. He loved the computers. They would do exactly what you told them to do and they would never lie to you. Two inhuman characteristics. People who complained about the inhumanity of computers were right. They didn't know how to care or betray.

The next operation was more complicated. He had prepared for it some time before, and the preparation had required many separate inquiries.

He pulled the names of all people over sixty-five who were getting county assistance. He ordered the check-writing computer to give every one of them a $750 bonus over the next three months. He inserted a random delivery factor: the check increases wouldn't go out all at once, none of the recipients would get the money at one time, and there would be alphabetical distribution. By the time the overpayments were noted—next spring at the earliest—the money would have been spent. The county would perhaps try to withhold the overpayment from subsequent checks, but the elderly families on county assistance lived so marginally the press wouldn't let the politicians get away with it.

When he had finished with that, Eddie called again for the tax roll tape. He had it correlate with the old age assistance tape and entered a 25-percent across-the-board property tax reduction for everyone in the assistance group listed as owning a home. He couldn't do anything here for those who rented and he certainly wasn't going to give the reduction to the property owners who rented to poor old people, most of whom were slum landlords who kept their buildings in miserable repair and let them go until they were worth nothing, at which point they stopped paying the taxes on the buildings, which meant that the city or county a few years later repossessed a worthless shell. If they were adventurous and in a hurry for cash, some owners hired someone to torch the buildings for them. A fire inspector had told Eddie that they could easily prove most of the tenement burnings were arson; the problem was proving that it was the owners who did it or ordered it done.

"But no one else has a reason to do it," Eddie said. "No one else stands to profit."

"Sure," the inspector said. "You know that and I know that and the insurance company knows that. You know what the owners say? They say, 'Someone must have had a

grudge. How come you guys don't catch the sonofabitch?"
And the insurance company pays."

The owners who let the city repossess their buildings
had to wait longer for their money, but they made more.
The law was such that a man who lets one building go and
has paid no taxes on it for years could lose that building,
but he wouldn't have to lose any of his other properties.
They were all separate accounts; the building was the of-
fender, not the owner. Eddie thought it was crazy.

Eddie's gift to the elderly homeowners was an adjust-
ment that might not be noticed for years. Next March the
computer would automatically type out the tax bills. Only
by comparing actual printouts with the handwritten rolls
would anyone know what had happened, and the homes
affected were scattered throughout the city, so it would be
impossible to find them all without thousands of hours of
cross-checking. The only way to find all of them without
using a full-time platoon of clerks would be if someone
knew exactly what Eddie had done. The only place that
information resided, except for Eddie's brain, was on the
operational tape of the computer now clicking away.
When that computer had finished with the operation,
Eddie would erase the order and it would be as if it had
never existed. Computer tapes are full of erasures; information and commands come and go constantly; the
Nixon pitfall isn't there. As far as a computer is concerned, what is electronically erased from its memory
never existed at all, and blank spaces on a tape have no
more meaning than nothing on a scale.

Eddie did four more operations, three of them involving
county and city payroll checks, all of which were handled
by the same computer. He gave an across-the-board raise
of fifty dollars per check to all teachers in the ghetto
schools. He deducted an equivalent amount from the
checks of the city's highly paid political appointees. Then
he erased the tapes for outstanding private residential
water bills. People, he decided, shouldn't have to pay for a
drink of water or to be able to flush turds down a toilet.

The final operation was one he hadn't thought of earlier; it had come to him during the night's work. It was
easy enough with the information he now had.

He ordered the computer to print out the addresses of

all buildings that were delinquent in their tax bills and that had suffered apparently arsonous fires in the past ten years. He also told the machine to print out the addresses of all buildings that had been repossessed by the city because of tax delinquency in the same period. He told the machine to list the buildings by owner name.

A lot of properties were listed, but only a few names were involved. One man, owner of a fancy nursing home, was the owner of record for seventeen of the torched buildings and twelve of the tax repossessions. Eddie took those sheets of printout paper and, as before, circled what he thought the most interesting tabulations, then he put them in the envelope with the church property information. Klipp would be a busy man for a while. Perhaps he'd get a Pulitzer for investigative reporting.

It had taken four hours. By the time he switched off the machines and cleaned up his work area, it was nearly dawn. He looked around carefully to be sure he had left no trace. He took his work notes and the empty paper coffee cups with him rather than run them through the shredder. Someone might notice in the morning that the supposedly empty bag had some garbage in it.

He walked down the stairs very quietly. He wasn't sure where the janitors would be at this time and he couldn't afford to have any of them see him. He couldn't afford to have anyone see him.

As he neared the ground floor, he heard voices. Three members of the crew were sitting on the bottom step of the main stairway. The other two were slowly polishing the large mosaic that had been carefully cemented into the floor when the building was finished by WPA workers, the last time a city could afford that kind of luxurious detail in its official life.

Eddie backed up carefully and silently. He opened the door at the first landing and walked to the interior fire stairs. Their ground floor exit led directly outside.

He saw no one on the way back to the van. A cold wind blew in off the lake. He hummed to himself, wishing there were some way he could get access to the tapes of the gas and electric companies. But, so far as he could tell, they were much better protected than the tapes belonging to the government.

There was no traffic on the Kensington Expressway. He exited at the sign for the Thruway east and immediately got behind a large truck that had painted on its rear doors the letters P.I.E. At the toll booth he got close enough to see that the letters were an acronym for Pacific Intermountain Express. For years he had seen the enormous trailers with the big P.I.E. letters on their sides and backs, and he had never before known what the letters meant. He hadn't even known there were any Pacific mountains. The truck was a long way from home.

And Eddie, for the first time in his life, was without one.

# SEVEN

Betty did not call the police the next morning. She had no reason to call them. It was a Tuesday and she didn't wake until a little after ten. She assumed Eddie had come home after she had gone to sleep and had gone to work before she had gotten up; that had happened often enough before. A charming man on "Phil Donahue" told her about life on other planets.

When he didn't come home for dinner that evening, she thought it was more of his craziness. He had been acting very strangely in recent months. Lately he had been going out at all hours, and he had started snoring. She didn't remember him ever snoring before. It woke her up a few times, his snoring.

It wasn't until after the late show that she began to get really worried.

And it wasn't until the middle of the next morning that she called his office and was told he hadn't been seen there since Monday afternoon.

That night, just before the evening news, Betty called the FBI. She got the number from Information. She could have looked it up and saved the charge they had recently created for Information calls, but it seemed appropriate to dial 555-1212 and say, "Operator, I want the FBI." Betty was certain that Eddie had been kidnapped; there was even a possibility he had been done away with. She suspected the reason he was so crazy: he knew something about what was going on down there at City Hall, something he couldn't even tell her about because it was so terrible or because knowing the facts was so dangerous. Something crooked was always going on there, and he had probably uncovered some of it working on those computer machines of his. So they had kidnapped him. Or done away with him.

Special Agent Francis X. Kelly was alone in his office when the telephone rang. He was arranging pictures and framed citations on his wall. He had just gotten the office.

The telephone rang for a long time. The chances were excellent that it would be about something he couldn't do anything about, so he decided he wouldn't answer. He would only have to make a note for someone, and he didn't think a bureau SAC should be taking telephone messages for his inferiors. The person would probably call back the next day anyhow, during regular business hours.

Kelly was six feet tall and in excellent physical condition. He had bright red hair, red eyebrows, and the gray hairs he knew were there didn't show at all from a distance. He was a graduate of Canisius High School and Canisius College, both in Buffalo. He had considered becoming a Jesuit, but something told him he'd be better off in law school. He went to Notre Dame and, during his second year, met Mary Ellen Walsh, a junior at St. Mary's College across the way. They were married the day after he got his law degree, and she was, if his calculations were correct, pregnant within hours of the time they left the reception. They honeymooned a week in Cape Cod. Then they moved to Washington, where he spent three days helping Mary Ellen arrange their small apartment out in the double alphabets before he began his training at the FBI academy.

The Bureau had been the only employer he ever had, and he never once, in all his fourteen years of service, regretted his two decisions: the first not to take the cloth and the second to apply for the badge. For someone of his temperament the Bureau was better than the Jebs: he got an annual report from the Director's office that told him exactly how well he had been doing. In the Jebs, as far as he could tell, you never knew where you stood, and a lot of them were crazy.

Kelly had just been transferred back to Buffalo, his home town. It was the first time he had ever been stationed in Buffalo, and he was pleased to be able to come home as Special Agent in Charge of the Buffalo Field Office. It was a great honor for his mother, who arranged a party at Sodality, attended by everyone who mattered, even the bishop, who hardly went anywhere anymore.

Francis X. Kelly now got mail addressed, "Mr. Francis X. Kelly, SAC, FBI, Buffalo NY." It was like he was an air base: Kelly—SAC: SAC—Omaha. The acronym bore a fine tone of lurking power. Roaring engines ready to deliver the payload anywhere. The first time he picked up the phone to call Washington and said, "Kelly, SAC Buffalo, for the Assistant Director," he nearly had tears in his eyes.

The telephone began ringing again.

He could leave. There was no reason he had to finish hanging the pictures and framed citations tonight. He could hang them whenever he damned well felt like it. He was the SAC.

Kelly leaned back in his leather chair and saw the door to the outer office open. His right hand darted to the holster on his belt, but then he saw that it was only the Assistant SAC, a young black fellow named Purvey. Purvey was the only black A-SAC in the Bureau, and Kelly didn't know whether he should feel good or bad about that. Politics in the Bureau were very hard to understand sometimes. Purvey wasn't a bad sort, even though he did occasionally remind the others that he had graduated at the top of his class at Yale Law, but he wasn't the kind of agent Kelly had grown used to over the years. The night he first met Purvey, he had gone to his mother's house for dinner. She asked how he liked the people he worked with. He told her about Purvey and said he wasn't sure about him, that all of the agents he had worked with in the past were whites.

"But some of them were Protestants, weren't they, Francis?"

"That's true, Mama. Some of them were."

"So it started a long time ago."

"I guess it did."

Purvey waved and threw his tan London Fog raincoat on someone's desk. It wasn't his own desk.

"Want me to get that, chief?"

"Yes," Kelly said. "Just started ringing."

"Yes, sir," Purvey said.

Kelly wondered what Purvey was doing here. He had already gone home for the day and now he was back. Checking up on him? The Bureau did things like that. It had people spying on people who were spying on people.

You couldn't trust anyone, which was what Mr. Hoover had always said.

"Ma'am," Purvey said into the telephone. He didn't get to say anything else. He held the instrument a few inches from his ear, and even across the room Kelly could hear a shrill female voice barking away. He was very glad he hadn't taken the calls. There was a pause and Purvey leaped into it. "Have you called the city police, ma'am? It's their jurisdiction."

There was rapid and shrill chatter from the other end of the line.

"I know that, ma'am," Purvey said, "but you don't know for sure that it's a kidnapping. Not yet, anyway." The chatter burst forth again. "I'm sure of that," Purvey said, "but at this point—with no note or anything—we can't assume kidnapping. What's that? . . . My supervisor? You want to talk with my supervisor?"

Purvey looked across the room at Kelly, Kelly shook his head and waved his hands furiously.

"I'm sorry, ma'am, my supervisor has gone home for the evening. But I'm the Assistant Special Agent in Charge of the Buffalo office. I'm responsible. Now here's what I want you to do. You call this number"—he read her the number of the Buffalo Police Department detective bureau "—and you tell them everything that you've told me. If they decide that it was a bona fide kidnapping, they'll call us. They'll know just what to do. . . . That's right, ma'am. . . . You're welcome." Purvey replaced the handset in the cradle and shook his head.

"Hubby didn't come home?"

"You got it, chief. She says he was kidnapped."

"Why?"

"Because he didn't come home. He never *didn't* come home before."

"With a voice like she's got, maybe he's deaf. Maybe he got hit by a train because he couldn't hear its whistle."

"Maybe he jumped in front of the train to get some rest. We should hire somebody just to screen the calls. We waste a lot of time on the phone these days with crackpot calls. It's not very efficient."

Kelly wondered why Purvey had said that. Kelly had learned over the years that it was not good in the Bureau

to come up with too many ideas too fast. People wondered
about you. Purvey had been around long enough to know
that, but he hadn't been around long enough to start coming up with operational ideas. Kelly wondered about Purvey. He didn't tell Purvey that.

"Who's the guy?" Kelly asked.

"She says he's a computer programmer for the city.
Works in the city's general accounting office."

"What's somebody like that make a year?" Kelly asked.

"Maybe fourteen or fifteen thousand. I don't know.
Hardly anyone without a political appointment makes
much more than that in local government around here."

"So who'd kidnap somebody who makes fourteen or fifteen?"

"Nobody I know. A moron, maybe."

"Morons hold up liquor stores. So the guy wasn't kidnapped."

"I didn't say he was," Purvey said.

"Who did?"

"The wife."

"He skipped, that's what I think. A voice like that, I'd
skip too."

"Right, chief," Purvey said. Purvey lighted his pipe with
a small gold butane lighter. He blew columns of smoke
into the room. The pipe, like all his others, had a small
white dot on the top part of the stem.

One of the other agents in the office, an older man, had
told Kelly that the white dot was the trademark for a very
expensive British pipe manufacturer, Dunhill's. "What's a
nigger doing smoking a hundred-dollar pipe is what I'd
like to know," the agent said.

"What I'd like to know is what's he doing smoking a
pipe at all? I thought they all smoked Camels and Luck-
ies."

"I'm going home now," Purvey said. "I don't think she'll
call back. Anything you want me to take care of, chief?"

"No," Kelly said. "That's all right. I'll close up."

Purvey left leaving a broad trail of slightly sweet smoke
behind him.

Why, Kelly wanted to know, had Purvey come into the
office? What was he doing here? All he did was answer the
phone, which he couldn't have known beforehand was go-

ing to ring, talk about the call, and then leave again. Kelly turned out the lights, not feeling as comfortable as he would have liked.

Betty Argo was perfectly furious. If there had been someone around the house to yell her anger at, she would have yelled like one of those women in the John Wayne movies. Well, maybe not them . . . Maureen O'Hara always seemed to wind up getting spanked by Wayne, and Betty didn't think that looked like much fun. Maureen O'Hara always looked pretty happy afterwards though. Like Archie Bunker. She'd like to yell in anger like Archie Bunker. When he was mad, Archie knew how to yell.

On television Efrem Zimbalist, Jr., had always taken all calls from citizens seriously. That was when he was in "The FBI." The calls always led to an important break for the agents. These people seemed hardly interested.

She called the city police and told them what she had told the FBI agent who took her call. The detective said that people went off all the time. He asked if she and her husband had had any serious arguments recently.

"We've *never* had an argument."

"Christ," the policeman said, "I don't know anybody who can say that."

"I can," she said. "So now you do know someone. Eddie and I never had an argument."

"Why don't you come down and I'll fill out a missing persons description. They'll put it on the wire. Do you have a car?"

"He took it. Or it disappeared the same time he did. I don't know which."

The detective grunted. "I'll tell you something: they don't ever get excited about these reports until at least forty-eight hours after the last appearance."

"Kidnappings? They wait forty-eight hours in kidnappings?"

"When there's no note, lady. When there's a likelihood that it wasn't a kidnapping after all."

She said she would come down the next morning. He said that was a good idea, why not give the guy another night out before you call in the dogs.

She was furious at that. "Something *has* happened to

him," she snapped. "He's not having nights out, as you say."

"Whatever you say, lady," the detective said, sighing. "Room 203. Anytime after nine."

The police found the car late Sunday night. One of the patrolmen on the four-to-twelve shift remembered he had seen it parked in one spot since just before he went off duty Tuesday night. He checked it through the computer in case it had been reported stolen somewhere. The headquarters operator told him the Volvo with those plates was listed on the alert sheet all patrolmen had been given at muster every day since Thursday. She switched him over to one of the detectives.

"How come you guys are just calling this in now?" the detective asked.

"Because I just noticed that it's still here near the corner where it's been all week, but it's been stripped clean. Yesterday it hadn't been stripped clean. The tires are gone, the radio's gone, the trunk's popped wide open, and there aren't any tools or spares. I found the keys under the front seat. Nothing else in the car at all."

"Why didn't they steal the whole damned car?" the detective said.

"Maybe they didn't find the keys. Maybe they already had a car."

"Okay. You guys leave the car alone. A detective car will check it out."

"You want us to keep an eye on it?" the patrolman said.

"What for?"

"Preserve evidence or something."

"It sounds like everything worth taking has already been taken. Just get back to your beat."

The policeman rehooked the microphone and drove to an all-night diner not far away. He left his partner in the car in case they got any calls. He went inside and ordered two containers of coffee, both with three sugars and cream. There was a waitress in the diner he had been trying to make out with for two months now, but she only smiled at him the way she smiled at everyone else. Maybe one night he'd catch her speeding and they could have a conversation and work something out. Other cops told him stories of trading off traffic citations for a quick piece of ass or a blowjob from some sexy broad, but he always just ran up on dogs or couples. The waitress wasn't a dog, but she didn't pay him any attention at all. Maybe those other guys were lying to him. Some cops did that.

The detectives came at three thirty-two Monday afternoon. They were very busy these days. There had been major cuts in police personnel, and this wasn't an emergency kind of thing. Cars were stripped clean all the time. If someone had been reported with a gun or something like that, they would have come quickly. Or would have tried to come quickly.

They searched the area and found nothing. While the car was being towed away, some kids came over and said there was a man floating under the concrete dock. He was face down in the water and didn't have any shoes on. The detectives ran to the bridge and saw that the kids were right. There was a body in there.

The senior detective, whose name was Marcus Felice, told his partner to watch the scene and not let anyone near the dock. Then he ran to a nearby pay phone and called a reporter from the *Courier*. He walked slowly back to the car, smoked a cigarette, and then picked up his microphone and called the report in to headquarters. The reporters who monitored the police frequency would pick up the squeal, but the *Courier* reporter would get there first—which would mean he would use Marcus Felice's name two or three times in the story.

The underwater team came and seemed disappointed they didn't have to do any diving. They were all wearing their black wet suits. "Hell, Marcus," one of them said, screwing up his face, "all you need for this one is a rope."

"I don't have a rope," Marcus said.

"You should have called for one. Instead of hauling all of us down here."

"You guys got a rope?"

"Of course we have. We have everything necessary for operations of this type."

"So there you are."

Marcus called Betty from the morgue. The body had Eddie's wallet and ring and wristwatch. The wristwatch was a self-winding Timex and it was still working. Marcus thought about writing the Timex company and telling them that; maybe they'd use it for one of their commercials the way the BIC lighter people did. But, he decided, they'd maybe think it was a little morbid. He told Betty they could send a car to bring her down for the identification.

"I'll call you right back," she said, and hung up before he could say anything. She waited for a dial tone and pushed the buttons for the telephone number she had written on a piece of paper she had taped to the refrigerator door. She had known for days she would have to make this call. She had known it all along.

Kelly's desk buzzer buzzed. Purvey was sitting in the chair across his desk, giving him the daily activity report. "Yes," Kelly said into the intercom.

"A Mrs. Argo. She insists on talking with you."

"I'm busy. Give her one of the agents. Somebody must be out there."

"I tried that, sir. She insists on the SAC. Says last time she called she was given misinformation."

"What's the name again?"

"Argo. Mrs. Argo."

Kelly switched off the intercom. "Who the fuck is Mrs. Argo?"

"The woman who called last week about her missing husband. The guy from the city accounting office."

"The skipper?"

"You said that." Purvey puffed his pipe.

Kelly scowled at Purvey and reactivated the intercom. "Put her on." He heard a clicking noise. A woman's voice shrieked at him. When the voice stopped, he said, "Kelly, FBI district office, Special Agent in Charge."

The woman gabbled at him so quickly he couldn't understand a word she was saying. When she paused for breath, he told her that.

"I-said," she repeated, with a long space between her words, "they-just-found-my-husband's-body."

"That's very good, ma'am. I mean, I'm glad that the police were able to—What I mean is, uh, where?"

"In the canal. Foot of West Ferry. They're telling me he drowned."

"So the person you talked to here, the man who told you to call the Buffalo police, told you the right thing. You didn't have to call to thank us. I'm sure that—"

"No," Betty said, talking quickly again. "That's not why I'm calling. They said I have to go down to the city morgue to identify the body."

"Yes, ma'am. That's an awful but necessary part of this kind of thing. I'm sure the city police will send a car so you don't have to try and concentrate on driving in your ordeal. We don't—"

"That's not why I'm calling you. I'm calling you because I am sure this is a plot. There's more to this than meets the eye."

"Do you have a reason for thinking that, Mrs. Argo?"

"It happened like that on 'Columbo' once. This is just what happened on 'Columbo.' A man was found floating in his swimming pool and it was supposed to look like an accident or suicide, and really it was his partner who did it all the time. His partner turned out to be a gangster. That's why he killed him."

"Mrs. Argo, do you have any reason for thinking this is a gangland slaying? Other than what happened on 'Columbo'?" Purvey was rolling his eyes and laughing without making any noise. Kelly gritted his teeth at him. Purvey kept on rolling his eyes. Then he relighted his pipe.

"Why else would anyone kill my Eddie? Everyone liked him. Everyone who knew him, I mean. He didn't talk to very many people. He was kind of moody lately, if you want to know the truth."

"Mrs. Argo, please. Let the city police take care of this. If there's any organized crime involvement, they'll call us. I promise you. And we'll investigate every lead thoroughly."

"You promise?"

"Yes, Mrs. Argo. I promise."

"All right, then." She hung up.

"You know what, Purvey?" Kelly said, staring down at a spot on his carpet he didn't remember seeing there before.

"What, sir?"

"I really preferred dealing with plain old-fashioned bank robbers and people like that. They didn't talk to you, you know?"

A policeman came in an unmarked blue Plymouth sedan. Betty talked all the way downtown, and he said, "Yes, ma'am," several times. He walked her to the room where a man in a white coat waited.

"Are you the detective who called me?" she asked.

"No, Mrs. Argo. He had to go out on another case." She grunted with displeasure. "It's standard procedure, ma'am. The detectives aren't needed for this part of the job. This is my part of the job."

She followed the man in the white coat to a gurney covered by a white sheet. It was obvious that a dead body was underneath it. The face was covered, but the toes stuck out from underneath the sheet. She wondered why they covered the face but not the toes. Then she noticed the tan cardboard tag tied to the big toe on the left foot. It was so they could see the tag without having to lift the sheet. The toe was a terrible color.

"Now prepare yourself, ma'am. This is always kind of difficult for some people."

"Go ahead," she said. He pulled the sheet from the face. "Aw," she said. "He looks just awful. Just awful. What's happened to his face?"

"That ain't nothing," the attendant said. "Some of them go down in the fall and don't come up until after the ice breaks up in the spring. Their faces get *completely* eaten up by the fishes. This is just a little nibbling here and there. Probably rats."

"That's my Eddie," Betty said, and fainted in a heap.

Not many people at all came while the body lay in state. The coffin was closed, of course: the undertaker said it was impossible to do anything with drowning victims because they were always so bloated. "You understand, madam. It's easy to build up something that's not there, for someone who's been in an automobile accident, say. But it's impossible, without being vulgar, to remove things that are there. It just doesn't look natural. If you can't look natural, then close the lid on the entire affair. That's my policy. Don't you agree?"

"Whatever you say," she said.

"We'll close the lid, then. It's a lovely piece of work. People will comment on that, you can be sure."

For a moment she didn't know what he was talking about, then she looked at his hand with the gold pen fluttering and understood he meant the coffin. He didn't ever use that word, though, he called it a casket or he just pointed. When she used the word coffin once, he winced.

About forty people came to the funeral service in the church. Betty knew about ten of them. She asked Eddie's boss, whom she met for the first time there, if he knew who the others were.

"Never seen them in my life. Just that one—she works in automobile registrations. Don't remember her name. These others, well, there's a lot of people who just go to funerals. Don't care who's being put away." He said he would like to go to the cemetery, but he really had to get back to City Hall for urgent business. He was sure she would understand.

"Oh, my dear, yes," Betty said. "And Eddie would, too."

"I'm sure," the boss said. "He'll be very difficult to replace. His absence will be felt for a long time."

"I'm very happy to hear that," Betty said, wiping away a tear with a small lace handkerchief she bought especially for today and promised herself she would never use again. "I really am. It's important to be missed."

After the funeral Eddie junior drove back to the house with his mother, sat around for a while, then said he had exams he had to get ready for. He had to get back to Ithaca right away.

"But it's only the second week of school."

"They have exams early now."

Betty told him to take some of his father's suits and sweaters. He said he didn't wear that kind of suit and he had plenty of sweaters. She was always giving him sweaters. "Sweaters are always useful presents," Betty said.

Days later Betty sat alone in the kitchen and wondered how things would be different. She couldn't think of anything significant except there wouldn't be as much money coming in. Of course, she wouldn't need very much because the house mortgage and the Volvo loan and several of the charge accounts were all automatically paid off. She wouldn't have to spend as much for food. The insurance company had already had the tires and radio replaced on the Volvo; it was sitting in the driveway, nice and clean. The agent, a nice man from State Farm she had never met before, told her he had made sure the car had a full tank of gas. With Eddie's pension benefits and the Social Security she would do all right. They might even get a tuition remission for Eddie junior at Cornell.

She would miss Eddie, she was sure of that. Not that they talked all that much. But it had been nice knowing someone was around in case you did want to talk to him or in case something needed fixing. She tried to remember conversations they had had recently, but the only one she could remember was about some bills and it wasn't a very nice conversation. She remembered when he fixed the upstairs toilet and they didn't have to call the plumber instead.

It was almost seven o'clock. The "Andy Griffith Show," reruns of "Mayberry, RFD," was about to start on Channel 29. She opened a beer and went into the living room. It didn't look any different. The set came on immediately. It was brand-new, a large Sony she had bought with some of the insurance money to console herself. She loved the transistorized television sets that didn't need any warm-up period at all. The set had a remote control so she could change stations without having to get up from the couch.

Later, maybe later she'd think about some of the nice conversations.

Andy walked down the road with a small boy. One of the newspapers said recently that the small boy was the same one who played the lead in "Happy Days." It was wonderful to be able to watch someone grow up before your eyes, she thought.

The following Saturday afternoon there was a knock on the kitchen door. Betty was surprised. No one ever just came knocking. She peeked through the curtain and saw a portly man in a green suit. He was holding a large cardboard carton and was sweating along his upper lip.

"I'm Mr. Farthold," he said when she opened the door. "Eddie's supervisor."

"Oh, yes. I remember you from the funeral."

"I brought his things by. I thought you might want to have them."

"That's very kind of you. Please come in." She held the door and he squeezed past her.

"Thanks," he said, puffing lightly. "Where should I put this?"

Betty pointed at the kitchen table, which was cluttered with dishes. He looked at her without moving. "Oh, dear," she said, "I haven't cleaned up from breakfast. I didn't know I'd be having company." She moved some newspapers off the counter next to the sink. "Here will be just fine," she said.

"I don't know if any of it's important," Farthold said. "It's everything from his desk that wasn't city business."

Betty opened the box. It was almost empty. There were some notebooks with nothing in them, a few maps, his notes from the computer refresher course he had taken recently, a pair of driving gloves, a comb, and a flashlight. "Why would he have a flashlight at work?" she asked.

"Who knows? In case the lights went out. He was a very *careful* person."

"It's very kind of you. I said that, didn't I? It doesn't matter: it *is* very kind of you. Would you like a beer?"

"You must be busy. I don't want to impose."

"It's no imposition at all. I'm not doing anything. I was just going to watch 'Emergency.' It's on a full hour now. You ever watch 'Emergency'?"

"I haven't for a while."

"You want to watch it with me?"

"Well, I don't want to impose . . ."

"It's no imposition, Mr. Farthold. I promise you."

Betty realized she had never heard Eddie say Farthold's name. Eddie had always referred to him as "my boss" and "that asshole." Farthold didn't seem like such a bad person.

After "Emergency" it was time for "Bewitched," then "Hogan's Heroes," and then the "Saturday Night Movie." She and Mr. Farthold had several more beers while they watched and they had cold chicken sandwiches on the couch during the movie. During one of the commercials she asked if he liked "Barney Miller" and he asked if she liked "Cannon," and she said "Cannon" wasn't on anymore but she had liked it while it was on and he said he missed it because all of the current series heroes were skinny and that didn't seem fair. She said he wasn't fat, there was no reason for him to think of himself that way. He said he was too fat. She said he was just portly, quite reasonable for a man of his position. He thanked her and got them two more beers from the refrigerator. During the eleven o'clock news Mr. Farthold commented intelligently on the city's economic problems. She said it was a pleasure hearing the stories explained by someone who really knew what was going on. He looked down at the floor for a moment and said it wasn't often he got a chance to tell half of what he knew.

By then it was quite late. Mr. Farthold said that he wasn't married and he lived in Tonawanda. Betty said in that case he should stay the night because it was a long drive home. He said it was only twenty minutes, but if she was sure it was all right he would stay. She said it was now raining out and there was no sense risking an accident, and anyway, tomorrow was Sunday. Mr. Farthold agreed and went to get them two more cans of beer. While he was in the kitchen, he gathered up all their empties, put them in the green plastic garbage bag next to the sink, and put the plastic garbage bag in one of the green plastic garbage cans just outside the door. When he returned to the living room, she was leaning back on the couch and smiling. Her left hand held the remote-control device. She had the channel selector button pushed down and the screen was rapidly going through all the available options.

"That's some fine set."

"It certainly is . . . and thank you for getting the beer."

"My pleasure," Mr. Farthold said. He took off his shoes.

"I bet that feels better."

"It certainly does."

"I thought so." Betty lifted the cold can to her mouth and let the channels go.

# Part Two

■ ■ ■ ■ ■ ■ ■ ■ ■ ■ ■ ■ ■ ■ ■ ■ ■ ■ ■ ■ ■ ■

## EIGHT

The cabin remained in perpetual cool, shaded by the close circle of high trees. Only at noon, with the sun almost directly overhead, did the rooms flush with bright direct light. The circle of trees was partially broken in two places. The wide break was for the dirt road, just a little wider than a car, which curved around some oaks and disappeared on its way to a slightly wider gravel road a quarter mile away. The gravel road went the rest of the way down the mountain. At the bottom it joined a paved road that ran parallel to the river for several miles, usually separated from it by a thick growth of underbrush and shorter trees. To the north along the paved road was a small town which consisted primarily of stores and gas stations for the people who lived in the area; Eddie had never seen very many people in the town at one time. To the south the paved road wound back through the forest and eventually joined the highway that went to New York City and Albany.

The other break in the circle of trees was for a narrow footpath. The shade of the oaks and maples kept it clear of obscuring underbrush—though last year's leaf fall was still undisturbed on the ground, dry now, so Eddie's footsteps made a gentle crunching sound as he walked. The path led through a dense growth of pines and then to a clear stream. The stream was about ten feet wide and no more than two or three feet deep. A little further along, still on the property, the water burst brilliantly into sunlight where it came out of the tree line. Then it curved further down the hill and disappeared into another grove of trees just short of the beginning of the property belonging to the neighboring cabins.

When Eddie first came to the cabin, he tried to swim in the stream even though it was shallow. But the water was too cold. His arms and legs ached immediately; it wasn't any fun. He found a wheelbarrow in the shed behind the cabin and for the last two weeks he had been carrying rocks from the field to the stream. He was constructing three dams.

The first dam was at the high edge of the open field; the other two were about twenty and fifty feet further along. The first dam created a pool about thirty feet wide and almost six feet deep in the middle. The second dam did the same thing; the only notable difference was the water was several degrees warmer. His plan was to finish the third dam, creating a third pool to let the water warm even more. That one would be comfortable enough for swimming. The three pools would give the mountain water time to bask in the sun.

Before he finished the third dam, he found he no longer minded the temperature in the middle pool. He found the coolness invigorating. He abandoned the third dam halfway across the stream. The rocks created small rapids, a flash of white frothy water that calmed almost immediately. It was prettiest in the late afternoon.

He had taken to swimming naked in the second pool. At home, when he was still with Betty, he had worn pajamas to bed. Now he went swimming in the middle of the day with no clothes at all, and he would lie on the tickly grass and let the warm sun high in the sky dry him off.

The cabin had been easy to find. He thought of it while driving east on the Thruway. He had seen country places advertised in the newspapers for years. He stopped at a motel in Kingston and the next morning went to a real estate agent's office. The agent's name was Fleischer. He was a narrow man with thin fingers he regularly clenched and unclenched; he wore wire-rimmed bifocals and smiled when he talked, though the smile never went further than the edges of his mouth. Eddie disliked him immediately.

Eddie told Fleischer he had just retired after an accident that no longer let him do the sort of work he had done previously. Fleischer didn't ask about the nature of the accident or the nature of the work, which was fortunate: Eddie wasn't very satisfied with the stories he had made up for them. Fleischer did look a little concerned, and Eddie decided he was afraid Eddie might not be economically reliable without his job.

"I'm really quite all right now," Eddie said. "Just not quite what I was. I'm sure you understand that."

"Yes, sir," Fleischer said, still a little doubtful.

"And the settlement," Eddie went on, "was generous enough that I no longer have any money problems. I thought I would give you, say, six months' rent in advance."

Fleischer brightened immediately. He took out a handkerchief and wiped his hands several times, then smiled again. Anyone who was paying six months' rent in advance had to be a decent person.

"I want a place with a rural atmosphere, a place with total privacy, a place with electricity and a telephone. Not a party line. I want to get away from everything for a while, but I don't want to have to do without the basics."

"Of course," Fleischer said. "I know just what you mean."

Now Eddie smiled. For Americans of his generation the "basics" meant instant access to a long-distance operator, at least three television channels, and a garbage disposal unit in the sink.

The agent showed Eddie several photographs. One place was beautiful and, according to the map, perfectly located. Then Eddie noticed in the photograph what seemed to be the corner of another building. He asked what it was.

"Ah," Fleischer said, "that's the doctor's house. He lives next door. He owns the property. He won't bother you. He's retired and never talks to anybody."

"Too close," Eddie said. "I really want to live privately for a while. And that means everybody. Away from everybody, I mean."

Fleischer pursed his lips and interlocked his fingers. The fingers never quite stopped moving. After a while he looked up and said, "I think I have the place you want. It is totally separated from any other houses by trees; the nearest house is at least two hundred yards away. You could shoot rabbits off your porch at midnight and they probably wouldn't hear a sound. And most of the other cabins there are empty now anyway. The few summer residents left will be leaving their places for the winter very soon. The weather will be good for a while, but for some reason people don't stay around here long after Labor Day." He showed Eddie the photograph. "It looks like a country log cabin," Fleischer said, "but it's well insulated, it's really a year-round place. It's empty now. The owner lives in Florida and is making up his mind whether or not to keep renting it summers or just sell it outright. If you really like it, there's a possibility he might sell it to you. And there's a village nearby where you can get supplies. It's only about twenty minutes from the interstate. And the road that goes by this cabin dead-ends just a short way up the mountain, so there's no through traffic. How's that sound?"

"Perfect," Eddie said. "I'll take it."

"Don't you want to drive down and look at it first?"

"Not if it's exactly what you said it was."

"It is," Fleischer said, rubbing his hands again. Exactly."

"Then I'll take it."

Fleischer drew up the papers in the name Eddie gave him, then Eddie examined and signed them. "There's one slight problem." Fleischer's face clouded. "I'm in the process of changing banks, because of my retirement, you know?"

"Yes?" Fleischer's voice was suddenly weak, as if he were afraid it was all slipping away.

"So I wonder if you would mind taking this payment in cash. I've got the money with me." Eddie took from his jacket pocket a small sheaf of hundred-dollar bills. "I know it's irregular."

"Oh, sir!" Fleischer said, beaming. "That's quite all right. That's just fine. I thought you were going to say—Well, never mind. Money is just fine. It's been years since anyone has paid for anything in cash here. It's all checks and credit cards nowadays. No one uses real money."

"I like the feel of real money once in a while," Eddie said.

"So do I," Fleischer said, "so do I." He put his hand forward and watched Eddie count out the bills. He didn't look up once until Eddie had finished.

When he left the office, Eddie decided Fleischer had been a good choice after all. He was a loathsome person, Eddie thought, but there was a very good chance that the Florida owner would never learn that his house had been rented. Eddie wouldn't have been surprised to know that the forms he had just sighed were already on their way into the agency's trash can. Fleischer could pocket the money and it would be tax-free. No one could know, except Eddie, who certainly wasn't going to say a word. As far as he was concerned, the fewer records about his identities, the better.

The cabin had two bedrooms, a large living room with a high beamed ceiling, a small kitchen, a deep basement, and a low attic. A long porch ran across the entire front of the building.

After he had been there a week, he stopped closing the curtain in the bathroom when he used the toilet or took a shower. It seemed pointless.

He slept a lot, took long walks in the woods, and worked on his calculations. The van, with the equipment nearly installed, sat in the driveway alongside the house, waiting for him to finish getting ready. All it needed to become an active operational center was for Eddie to plug the telephone connector from the computer terminal into the telephone jack from the house, then run a power line to the van from any of the house's wall outlets.

On a beautiful Thursday afternoon, exactly three weeks after he had moved into the cabin, Eddie made the discovery that made his operations nearly infinite. He was swimming naked in the pool, wondering if it would fill with fish, wondering if he could clean fish without becoming nauseous while pulling out the slimy guts. He had never done that.

Something clicked in another part of his mind and he knew he was about to become a portable computerized superpower.

The question had been puzzling him for some time. It had to do with program access. If one had a program—if one knew the paradigmatic structure of a set of encoded information—then one could do nearly anything one wanted with that information. If it was simply material stored, then one could learn everything that was stored; if it was operational material, then one needed the program to do the work, and the utility of the programs he had taken with him when he left Buffalo was limited.

The cold water swirled around his legs and the ripples moved out from where his hands paddled the surface. Suddenly it was as if the answers had typed themselves out on the console screen.

> QUESTION: HOW DO I FIND OUT WHAT PROGRAMS EXIST WHEN I DON'T KNOW WHAT QUESTIONS TO ASK?
>
> ANSWER: ASK THE COMPUTERS WHAT QUESTIONS THEY CAN ANSWER FOR YOU. IF YOU HAVE THE ANSWERS, YOU KNOW THE QUESTIONS.

He ran home through the woods without even bothering to dry off. Mosquitoes pecked at his face. He dressed quickly, hooked up the van, and sat down at his keyboard. He addressed IFFI, the central law enforcement computer in Baltimore. The acronym stood for Information Filed for Future Investigations. He asked IFFI a question that translated as, "What discrete sets of information have you on hand and what are the access codes for them?" He set the machine for a printout rather than a readout on the monitor.

In seconds the Selectric began typing away. It typed for a long time. Office Selectrics can handle about thirty characters a second, faster than any human can go, but the ones built for information processing went almost three times as fast. Nearly one thousand five-character units of information a minute, and the machine seemed to be typing faster than he had ever seen it go before, faster than when he had requested information on church real estate holdings.

Eddie walked around the van for a few minutes, then checked to make sure the computer was still giving him the information he had requested. It was. He made an iced tea and sat on the porch, listening to the rapid chatter from inside the van. A rabbit scampered across the dirt road and disappeared into the shadows. Two robins chased one another through the branches of the largest oak in view. A squirrel on one of the limbs paid them no mind.

He still wasn't sure what he was going to do. He was calm about that. There was time to learn what was possible, and then he would decide among the options. The important thing, for him, was that he was finally using the computers against themselves, finally getting himself to a position where he could turn that incredible weapon for impersonal victimization that had so poisoned his life against the impersonal poisoners, the executives who used the giant machines to release them from the obligation of caring about other people as human beings.

When the computer stopped reporting, Eddie closed down the van. He folded the printout sheets and locked them in one of the cabinets. There would be time to think about uses for the information he had gotten, and about questions he would ask other computer centers.

Right now he had other work to do. Before he got much more involved he had to get a much larger reserve of cash. It was possible that he might be traced sometime, and if that happened he wanted to be immediately mobile. Money was the key to immediate mobility in America.

Someone might start tracing computer conversations and might somehow trace them to him. He was sure he had some time before that could happen. He would work out a program for the law enforcement central computer that would alert him if agencies began using computers to find him. In fact, if things worked properly, IFFI would tell him where they were going to look as soon as they decided to look. Things were too complex to look by eye; the eye was an obsolete organ in this game. They had to ask the machine . . . and the machine was Eddie's friend. His only friend. How many people, he wondered, had friends they knew would under no circumstances ever tell them a lie? People lied to one another all the time; it was part of the way people dealt with one another. But the computers didn't have that particularly human facility—a nicer aspect of their inhumanity.

There were two ways they might catch him. One had to do with telephone calls. The telephone company kept records of long-distance calls, so it was possible they could scan back over all sources for all computer input calls, check them out for legitimacy, cross-check all the affected data banks and operational centers, then kick out the cabin's telephone number. That would take a long time, because they would have to determine *when* the inquiries or instructions were made, and Eddie had already made some of his instructions operative only in the future—like the real estate tax breaks he had set up for elderly poor people in Buffalo. So it would be difficult getting an accurate time fix on his operations. And the calls all went through a black box to an 800 exchange, many of which were on a flat rate basis paid by the receiver of the call, and not automatically encoded according to source. They would first have to realize something odd was going on, then understand that it was being done through the computers, then scan all the conversations the intruded computers were having, and finally validate all the calls before the conversations terminated. It would not be an easy correlation or chase.

If they were smart, there was one thing they might do: they could program computer systems with multiple operations to constantly examine themselves for apparently irregular inquiries: a nighttime conversation, for example, when such conversations did not usually occur, or an inquiry for program information not usually requested. They could have it set up so the conversation, while in process, would immediately key another computer that would tell whoever wanted to know that the inquiry had come in or a command had just been given.

Eddie worried about that one for a while, then came up with a very simple answer; he would ask the computers if they had any such self-inspection instructions in their programs. It would become part of his regular greeting: HELLO. HOW ARE YOU AND ARE YOU PROGRAMMED TO TRAP ME?

The black box was his key to safety. He could make the calls nearly impossible to trace. He could call a computer in Albany an hour or so away by car, but have the call routed through a telephone exchange in Los Angeles, and have it routed through St. Louis and Miami before it came back to him. By the time anyone traced that kind of conversation, he would be off the wire. He would have to carefully limit his conversations with the machines; no long and casual interrogations were permissible. When a line was open, he could be found, however complex his telephone network; when the line was shut, it would be a totally empty world for the tracers.

Eddie thought about the problems he would have to solve and felt a great wave of pleasure. It was the first time he could remember that his work was a complete joy to him—joy in the results as well as joy in the getting of those results. And he could do exactly what he wanted to do, whenever he wanted to do it. The perfect job.

But first he would get more money. Early the next morning, he would get up, make a nice breakfast, then go out and get himself a big pocketful of money.

# NINE

Some leaves had already started changing color on the maple nearest the house. The van started right up, and Eddie headed down the gravel road toward the dock at the bottom on a small inlet off the river.

Just before he reached the intersection with the paved road, he saw a young woman walking alone. As he passed she waved, and he waved back automatically. Country people, he decided, were very friendly. In the city you never waved at people you didn't know. He hoped she had seen him return the wave, although he knew it didn't matter. She was wearing a pale blue T-shirt, a faded pair of jeans, and leather sandals. He wondered if she got stones in the sandals when she walked on the gravel road. Probably. They weren't very practical on roads like that. But she didn't look as if she were having any difficulty.

He stayed within the speed limit all the way down to the city. The CB chattered away, warning of speed traps, asking for road information, getting the time, checking the radios. He didn't talk at all.

A few times he thought of the girl in the pale blue T-shirt. Rather he first thought of her T-shirt, the body moving inside it, and then he thought about the girl. He hadn't gotten a very good look at her face because he had gone by quickly and his eyes were first locked on her body. It was a surprise to see such a lovely body so far from where he thought he would see anyone. Perhaps she lived in one of the cabins on the lower part of the mountain; there were a number of small dirt roads around there that went back into the woods. It had been a long time since Eddie had been with a woman and he felt an aching need. During the past several weeks, working hard and alone in the forest, he hadn't felt the need at all. But the brief vision reminded him of things he had managed to forget.

Then he neared Kennedy Airport and had no time for visions in his mind. The signs around the airport were confusing at first, and he managed to completely circle the place before he found the correct entrance to the short-term parking lot. He hadn't had much experience with airports previously. He sat in the van with the motor off until he was sure no one was nearby, then he got out and walked across the busy road to the main concourse of the nearest terminal.

In the middle, exactly as it had appeared in the television advertisement, was the American Express check dispenser. There was a small device, similar to a touch-tone board, on which one was to type the special code assigned his card and the amount of money—up to five hundred dollars per day—one wanted. The machine was programmed to issue no more than five hundred dollars in any twenty-four-hour period to any single account, but Eddie had fed the AmEx memory unit ten separate codes for the card he was using at the time.

The airport, as he had hoped, was very busy. He had learned from television that it was easier to be inconspicuous when there were a lot of other people being busy around you.

He inserted the plastic card into the proper slot. It was one of several new ones he had gotten recently. He punched the first code number, waited for the indicator to say the account was clear, then typed a five and two zeroes. The machine made noises, and in the small tray in front of him a thin stack of checks appeared. He immediately pushed another code number and another five-zero-zero. He didn't touch the checks, now worth one thousand dollars. He looked at a small piece of paper in his wallet, so anyone watching would think he had been having trouble getting the machine to work. He punched two more sets of numbers in rapid succession. Then he picked up the checks and went into the airport bar. He ordered a beer and drank it slowly.

The people in the lobby all looked like they were doing the things travelers were supposed to do. No one hung around too long. No one was watching the machine or him. After a while he got up and went to the machine again. He got another thousand dollars' worth of checks quickly.

There was a bank across the lobby. Three people were in line at the open window. There were two other windows, but both were closed. The woman handling the customers seemed very casual about her movements, though the men in line were very fidgety. It was something about airports, perhaps. Maybe they had planes to catch. The whole idea of bank branches in airports was to service people on the go, people in a hurry. But the woman didn't seem interested in that. She chewed gum.

The man in front of Eddie handed the woman a bank charge card. "I want three hundred dollars," he said.

She looked at the card a moment, punched some numbers into a small console, the console clicked back at her, and she pushed a slip of paper to him under the bars. "Fill out the slip. And I need some other ID. A driver's license."

The man slowly filled out the form. She stood there, her jaws pumping away. There were four people in line behind him now.

The man finished writing: she compared his signature to the signature on the card and on the license. "Okay," she said, her lips making a big O for the word so Eddie could see the fat pink wad of gum sitting on her tongue. She counted out the money.

"Would you cash these, please?" Eddie said. He slid ten fifty-dollar checks under the grille.

She looked at the checks for a moment, all of them. Then she took the gum out of her mouth and said, "These checks aren't any good."

"What?" he said horrified. "Of course they're good. I just got them." His stomach was turning over.

"Not like this they ain't." She pushed the checks back under the grille, then reached alongside the keyboard and handed him a ballpoint pen. "Not until you sign them they ain't."

*Idiot.*

Eddie signed the checks in both places; she gave him a slim packet of fifty-dollar bills; he thanked her, folded the money, and put it into his jacket pocket. He felt a little shaky in the knees, but he nevertheless walked back to the main concourse and stopped at the machine again, where he punched out another two thousand dollars' worth of checks.

He could have gotten more money that day, using other

cards and other code numbers, but he didn't want to hang around too long. There was no reason to be greedy. He could always get more. He didn't need the money now anyway: except for the van and what he had spent for food and rent on the cabin, he had most of the tax refund money left, almost nineteen thousand dollars. He was just building up a bundle in case a day came when his techniques couldn't be used any longer or he wanted to be dormant for a while.

Through Queens and the Bronx he made eight stops and got rid of the rest of the checks. He was careful to sign them properly, and there were no problems at all. He bought wine and more records. In Westchester he stopped at a bookstore and bought a stack of paperback books. At the last minute he decided to pay cash for them. It wouldn't do to start a trail heading north out of the city.

He got home a little after dark. He didn't like coming home to a dark cabin. In the future, he decided, when he went out he would be sure to leave a light on. Maybe he'd even leave the radio on. He hated Betty's constant television programs, but he had become used to the chattering noise reaching him from another room. He didn't miss Betty at all, but he did miss coming home to the noise.

While the steak began cooking on the broiler, he hooked up the telephone and power cables to the van. He punched the access codes for the AmEx record bank, then called up the records of his check purchases that day and abolished them. There would be no record of the transactions.

When the canceled checks came through—he figured he had at least a full week on that since this was Thursday—there would be some consternation at American Express's accounting office, but there was nothing he could do about that. He couldn't abolish real pieces of paper. But the pieces of paper would be connected to no account number. All they would have would be his false signature and the serial numbers on the checks, which would tell them where and approximately when the checks had been purchased from a machine. By the time they questioned the bank clerks—if they did—his face would be gone from memory.

He had read a lot of newspaper articles about the lack

of utility of eyewitness accounts. When the crazy killer, Son of Sam, was slaughtering young girls in New York, the police had gotten from eyewitnesses two composite drawings that all the other witnesses agreed looked just like the killer. When they caught the guy, he didn't look anything like the face in either drawing. Eyewitness identifications, a police inspector said, were usually good only if the witness and the accused knew one another. The rest of the time they were a pain in the ass. It was only if a person was memorable for some special reason that people remembered him.

One thing Eddie knew, he wasn't memorable. No one had ever noticed him for anything.

American Express would have a difficult time figuring out what had happened with the checks. They knew the machine issued checks only to currently valid cards and only in names that had accounts with banks that would cover the checks withdrawals. The money wasn't put on the AmEx monthly bill; instead it was billed directly to a bank and subtracted directly from a person's account, just as if it were a check for cash. But there was no contracting bank in the records for any of these checks. There was nothing. They would search for the name and find nothing. They would examine the numbers and find nothing. Finally they would assume it was some kind of screw-up in their own accounting or a crook in their own ranks.

It wouldn't involve enough money for AmEx to revise their operation; that was the beauty of it. They had advertised the program heavily on television and in magazines, so if Eddie didn't do it too frequently, they would simply write it off as a malfunction. They would set some programmer to finding the holes; he wouldn't find them. Eventually they would call the FBI. It would do them no good.

When he was done, he locked up the machines, unhooked the cables, and went into the cabin. The steak was just starting to burn. He turned it, let it cook on the other side just long enough to brown lightly, then sat down at the table. Even though he rarely drank alcohol, he opened a bottle of wine he had bought in Queens. He deserved a celebration.

He went to bed early. He was tired and tomorrow was

another long day. He was going to Hartford and Boston, both of which had airport check-dispensing machines. On the way home he would write another ten thousand dollars' worth of checks on this card, all of which he would cash in Boston on Monday morning, after which he would abolish the records, as this time, and destroy the card. He didn't need it: he could get all he wanted. By the time the AmEx accounting computers first started alerting their human masters that something was out of order, the account in question would never have existed.

The New England trip went according to plan. After he got all the money, he did something else, something that occurred to him while driving through the lovely hills of Massachusetts.

He took one of the registrations for the van he had gotten in New York, a set of plates he hadn't used, and signed the ownership over to one of the names he hadn't used yet, a name on another New York driver's license. Then he went to a Massachusetts motor vehicle agency, said he had just moved to Boston and wanted to get a new license and local registration. They gave him a pamphlet to read and said a road test wouldn't be necessary since he had a current license with an exchange-agreement state. He would only have to take the written test.

By noon he had a Massachusetts driver's license, registration, and license plate for the van. He walked two blocks to where the van was parked and put the license, registration, and plate in the tire well along with the spare New York registration. There might come a time when he wanted to dump all his New York connections, and this was the sort of transaction that was impossible to trace. Vehicles were sold out of state all the time. The address he gave for the Massachusetts license and registration was a large apartment complex in Boston. It was not likely that anyone would ever know the transaction and registration were bogus.

# TEN

For two days he watched on television the Senate hearings having to do with Wilmer Thibault, a man Jimmy Carter wanted to appoint ambassador to England. Eddie liked Thibault. He seemed the kind of man Eddie always would like to have been. Thibault was very calm, he listened very carefully, he forgot nothing anyone said. The senators never frightened or ruffled or intimidated him at all. He knew exactly what he was talking about and he knew he was right.

Two of the senators kept coming back to some loans Thibault had taken out, years before, with a bank he subsequently came to control. The loans were all to bail out members of his family who had been having difficulties keeping their small farms afloat. Two of Thibault's cousins declared bankruptcy, and since they were cosigners of the notes, there was something of a scandal. Eventually all the money was paid back.

The senators kept coming back to the defaulted loans again and again, even after the questions were answered very reasonably. Eddie couldn't believe the senators were so stupid they didn't understand. Apparently they hoped to give people the impression that Thibault was hiding something sinister and they were trying to ferret it out. Eddie didn't think it was fair. One of the senators had eyes like a snake and kept saying he was just trying to help Thibault, followed by remarks like, "The only thing I don't understand is . . ." And then he'd say something nasty.

The other senator had once been a primary candidate for president, but he hadn't gotten very far. Eddie was sure the man was trying to get an early start on the next presidential campaign and was using the hearing to get national exposure. He was grandstanding for the television cameras the way that other fellow, Baker from Tennessee, had grandstanded during the Senate Watergate hearings several years earlier. Baker, he had learned from a newspaper article, had acted like a hot and moral investigator

135

while the cameras were on, but in all the secret votes in the committee room, he was the Administration's boy. Baker didn't have the snake eyes, but Eddie hadn't liked him anyway. He was a tiny self-righteous man, very shallow and petty next to Sam Ervin, who was like everyone's nice grandfather.

Thibault couldn't do anything about those people who were using him. Eddie thought perhaps he could do something.

After dinner he climbed into the van and hooked up. He used the book of codes he had stolen from IBM. He scanned the bank records of the communities where the two hostile senators had their home offices. He also scanned the records in Washington. The operation was simple enough, though it took a while to run.

When the printouts were done, Eddie laughed aloud. The self-righteous senator, the one with the deep mellifluous voice who sounded as if he were running for president, had been born a multimillionaire, so there was no reason for him to ever have any financial problems. And in his home town account he hadn't. But his Washington accounts were a financial nightmare: they were full of enormous deposits and withdrawals, and not infrequently the withdrawals weren't within ten thousand dollars of the current balance. On top of that he had the bank pay his wife's bills at stores automatically, and there were records of a number of reminders from the bank to the senator that they would stop paying the bills if the senator didn't start putting money in his account. The senator was on the Banking Committee, and the bank never did take any drastic action, but it seemed several of the stores had finally canceled out his and his wife's accounts. There were also records of a number of very large checks to Las Vegas casinos.

The senator with the snake eyes didn't have such problems. He wasn't a rich man. At least he hadn't been a rich man five years ago. Something happened to his balances the past few years: they grew progressively larger. Every few months there was a large withdrawal, sometimes a large check made out to Merrill, Lynch. He was buying stocks. But it seemed that no matter how much he invested in the market, his bank accounts kept getting larger and larger.

Eddie folded the printouts and put them in a large manila envelope. That night, he drove down to White Plains and mailed the envelope to the *Times*. He didn't want a postmark from a local post office.

Since he was in the city anyway, he drove over to Kennedy and picked up another four thousand dollars' worth of checks. Even though it was nearly midnight when he started back, he had no trouble cashing all of them before he reached the top of the city.

# ELEVEN

The first Thursday in October he met the girl. She was young and rather pretty, and for some reason she looked vaguely familiar. He knew he had never met her. He would have remembered meeting someone like her. She had dark brown hair and hazel eyes.

She didn't seem surprised to see him. If he were a lone girl in such deep woods and met a stranger, he would have been surprised. And a little nervous.

"Hello," she said. He nodded. "You're the man who lives in the cabin on the bluff."

"How do you know that?"

"I saw you driving down the hill one morning. You waved at me, remember?"

"I remember. It was early in the morning. I didn't get a good look at your face." Of course it was the same girl; he felt stupid.

"I was going down to the river to watch the boats. There aren't so many of them anymore."

"I hadn't noticed." He felt very strange, not quite comfortable. He looked around carefully to see if anyone was lurking in the trees.

She laughed at him. "Nobody's there. Just me. I saw you swimming yesterday. In that pool you made with the rocks in the stream."

"I didn't see you."

"I'm good at that," she said. She smiled at him, even white teeth and slight pretty crinkles at the corners of her eyes. She was perhaps a little older than he had thought. Closer to thirty than twenty. "In fact, I've worked hard at it."

Eddie felt his face burning; she had been watching him swim naked.

"The water's cold in there," she said, "but it's nice. Putting those dams in was a good idea. I've swum in there several times when you weren't around or early in the morning. I like it better than the river. But I can't stay in there too long. My legs get numb. I hate that, when they get numb. They're all achy when I get out while the feeling's coming back to them. If it were just a matter of getting out and feeling good right away, it wouldn't be so bad, but that time in between, that's what I don't like." She stopped talking suddenly, looked at the ground, then looked up at him with the same fine smile. "I'm babbling on, aren't I? Sorry."

Eddie thought it a wonderful stroke of luck to have met such a girl in the woods. Woman in the woods. But the rational part of his mind told him that he couldn't afford such luck. He should move on. It would be better if no one knew him. Even if the police found his cabin, they wouldn't know who he was, or even what he looked like. There would be nothing in the cabin to connect him with the computer operations since all the equipment was kept in the van and there wasn't a slip of paper connected to that activity in the cabin. Nothing. And the black box system would keep anything but the most sophisticated and expensive equipment from tracing his calls. The most recent transactions with AmEx, to anyone looking at them from the AmEx terminal, would have seemed to originate from the Mission District of San Francisco.

"My name is Carla."

"Carla," he repeated.

"It's an ugly name. They wanted a boy they could name after an uncle with a lot of money. He didn't leave them anything anyway; it all went to the aviary at the San Diego Zoo. I thought of making up another name for myself, but it's hard getting used to another name. It's like part of your face. You know what I mean?"

Eddie said he did.

"When I was in high school, I made up nicknames for myself. Every time we moved and we started at a new school, I'd tell them a new nickname, hoping it would take. None of them ever took. Everybody called me Carla anyway."

She looked at him without saying anything. They were walking slowly toward the pine grove. He knew what she was waiting for. For a moment he looked back toward the taller trees, as if they offered a line of escape. But he sensed she knew these woods better than he, and if he turned and tried to disappear among the oaks and elders, she would appear on the path somewhere ahead of him.

He told her the name he had used to rent the cabin. "I'm Craig Hemsworth."

She burst out laughing. "That's a funnier name than mine. It sounds like the kind of name they give a movie actor when they decide his own name won't do. Did you know that Roy Rogers' name was Leonard Slye? I *always* loved that. He's such a good-goody squint-eyed twerp. He had his horse stuffed and mounted on his front lawn, until the neighbors complained and all his friends told him it looked a little kinky. And Cary Grant's real name is—"

"I had nothing to do with it," Eddie said. "It was just there one day."

"I understand the problem," she said. "I understand it perfectly."

"Not many people do," Eddie said.

She motioned with her head. "You want to see where I live?"

"Well, I don't know . . ."

"Come on. You were just walking through the woods. You weren't going anywhere. I could tell. People walk differently when they're going somewhere. You were just walking. Come on over. You can meet my friends. We never see anybody. I've told them about you."

"You've told them . . ."

"That there's a guy living up here. All alone. He minds his own business. That's what we do."

"That's not what you're doing now?"

"Not really. We met in the woods. I didn't plan it. Really. You know, you're not usually out walking at this time. It's not like I came up to your cabin and knocked on the door. I never did that. Though I could have. Lots of times."

"I guess so."

"So it's just an invitation, nothing more. You can go back to your place if that's what you want to do. We won't bother you. And if I accidentally come upon you while you're swimming anymore, I'll turn my face and close my eyes until I'm beyond the trees and over the hill. How's that?"

"You move from serious to something else very

quickly," he said. She shrugged and smiled at him again, her lips lightly together. It was just enough of a smile to crinkle the corners of her eyes.

She was framed by the line of pine trees. The sandals looked as if they had been worn a long time. The jeans were a very pale blue. When his got that pale, they always began ripping at the knees; he would have to ask her how she got hers that color without them ripping at the knees. She wore a white sweat shirt with sleeves cut off about five inches below her shoulders. When she shrugged, he could see her breasts moving neatly underneath the sweat shirt, the nipples clear against the soft fabric.

Betty had always worn a brassiere. He had once asked her why she always wore it, even around the house. Her tits were little and she didn't need the damned thing. She looked at him as if he had suggested she stop brushing her teeth.

Carla saw Eddie's look. He knew it and was embarrassed. He turned his eyes away quickly, looking at the tops of the pine trees.

"What's the matter?"

"Nothing. I didn't mean to—"

"Why shouldn't you? If you like them, you should look. That's what they're for. It's natural. It's one of the ways you tell the difference. Haven't you read any biology books?"

"I'm not sure I—"

"Of course you are. You haven't seen anybody for a long time, have you." It wasn't a question.

She smiled at him again. He was very tense for a few moments, and then he began to relax. He smiled back at her.

"About time," she continued. "You like the way my tits look under the sweat shirt. I saw your look." He was blushing again, but he didn't say anything. He had never known any women who called them tits; he thought only men called them that. "You want to see something really nice?" she asked, cocking her head slightly to one side.

"Yes," he said, knowing what she was going to do before she did it.

He was astounded at how quickly she took the sweat

shirt off. He had a momentary urge to look away, which he immediately knew was crazy.

"They're beautiful," he said.

She smiled. The jeans hung around her hips, just above the widest part. The brass button flashed in the sun, just below her navel.

"What's the matter?" she asked.

"Matter? Nothing's the matter."

"Then how come you still have all your clothes on?"

He began unbuttoning his shirt; his fingers were unbearably thick and clumsy. "This is crazy," he said. "You don't know me."

"You don't know me either, so why is it crazy?"

"I've never done anything like this."

"You sound like a girl. Don't worry. You won't get hurt."

"That's not what I'm afraid of."

"So what are you afraid of?"

"I don't *know*." He almost shrieked the last word.

"Then you're very silly for being afraid, aren't you?"

"I guess so."

They were both standing there without any clothes at all. For a moment he had a feeling of being watched, as if some platoon of boy scouts would appear, in formation, at the top of the ridge in moments, dutifully plodding behind some fat scoutmaster.

"No one's here but us," she said. "You know that."

He remembered that in all the time he had been at the cabin he had seen no one this far up the mountain, not until her today.

She took his hand. "Over there," she said, pointing to the open field.

"Why? It's pretty here."

"Sure it is. But it's all pine needles on the ground here. That's clover over there. The pine needles are pretty and they smell nice, but one of us is going to get up with an assful of them if we stay here." She walked into the sun, turned and faced him, her body glistening in the brilliant light. He came out of the shade and felt the sun immediately warm on his shoulders and back. She sat down and smiled up at him, then reached up a hand and led him down.

Afterwards they lay on their backs, side by side. He felt her arm touching his. His eyes were closed and he felt the warm sun on his eyelids. Then he moved his head and looked at her next to him.

Her eyes were closed and her breasts moved up and down as she breathed. The dark shadow they made on her abdomen moved back and forth. Her body glistened brightly with perspiration. Her tongue moved quickly across her upper lip, then disappeared again into her mouth. She opened her eyes. They were a different color in the sun, greener than he had thought. The pupils were very small. They were so close he could see the tiny flecks of coloration in the irises.

"You fuck like a convict."

"What?"

"I said, you fuck like a convict. Like somebody who hasn't done it for a long time."

"I haven't done it for a long time. I've never done it like this. I've never done it outside. In the sunlight."

"Did you like it?"

"Yes. I loved it."

"Good. So did I."

"Have you done this before?" he asked. "Done it in the sunlight?"

"No."

"Is that true?"

"No."

For a moment the only sound was the wind in the pine branches off to the left and the squabbling of some birds in the branches. Then they both laughed.

"I'm sorry," he said. "That was a stupid question."

"Stop apologizing. I'm trespassing on your property."

"So you are. Would you like to come up to my house for a while?"

"Later. I've already invited you to ours. Come on."

"I don't want to get up yet. The sun feels good."

"Then don't put your clothes on." She told him her house was halfway down the gravel road, a little way up one of the many dirt drives he had seen there.

"We'll have to walk through the woods to get there. There are mosquitoes in the shadows."

"I didn't say I wasn't going to put my clothes on." She

laughed, and ran to where she had left them. She put on the jeans first, then her sandals. He followed her slowly.

Betty had always put on her brassiere first. He thought that odd, so he once asked her about it, saying that if the purpose was to cover something private, that wasn't the first thing to cover. She said it was easier that way. He said he didn't understand, and she said she knew that.

Carla stood there a moment, wearing the jeans around her hips, smiling at him. She leaned over to pick up the sweat shirt, her breasts swinging as she moved.

"I don't know if I can stand this," he said.

"More later. Come on. Get dressed. Come meet my friends. I told you: we never see anybody. It'll be a treat."

Eddie was momentarily filled with an irrational terror that she was living in the cabin with a gang of men. He wouldn't be able to handle that. He knew it was silly, but he hated the thought anyway.

"Who are your friends?"

"No one you'd know," she said, laughing. She had the sweat shirt on. For a reason he didn't understand, she looked smaller than she had when she had been naked. And now she was fully dressed and he had no clothes on at all. He felt a shiver of embarrassment. Quickly, he dressed.

She sat on the stump of a tree, watching him, her arms folded around her knees. When he got his shoes on, she stood up and walked into the trees without saying anything. He thought about it for a few seconds, then followed.

Once he lost sight of her on the path. There was a fork, and both sections curved away quickly. He stood there, not knowing which way to go. He called out to her, "Wait for me."

"Come on faster." She was still moving ahead.

He caught up with her. "What's the hurry?"

"Your mosquitoes. They're biting like crazy. I hate the damned things. They always go for my ears and toes. Mosquito bites on my toes drive me crazy."

"They're not so bad if you keep moving," he said.

"What the hell does it look like I'm doing?" She took his hand and led him on.

He wished there were someone he could tell: never in

his life had he merely met a beautiful girl somewhere, made love, and then been told to follow along. But there was no one to tell. Even the people he had known before: none would believe him. Perhaps he could tell one of the computers.

HI, IFFI. GUESS WHAT HAPPENED TO ME IN THE WOODS?

NOT PROGRAMMED TO GUESS.

I'LL TELL YOU THEN. A BEAUTIFUL GIRL, WITH HAZEL AND GREEN EYES APPEARED AND WE TOOK OUR CLOTHES OFF AND MADE LOVE ON THE CLOVER.

CATEGORIES NOT IN PROGRAM. VERIFY.

YOU CAN'T VERIFY SUCH ENCOUNTERS, IFFI.

UNVERIFIED ENCOUNTERS ARE NONEXISTENT.

FUCK YOU, COMPUTER.

CATEGORY NOT IN PROGRAM. REPHRASE.

UP YOURS, COMPUTER.

CATEGORY NOT . . .

Their cabin was much larger than his. She stood on the porch steps and motioned Eddie inside. In the back, near a dense grove of trees and brush, was a yellow Dodge van.

The room was very dim. At first Eddie wasn't sure how many people were in there.

"This is Franco," Carla said, moving her hand to the left.

"Hiya." A man spoke from the shadows near a door that went further into the house.

"And this is Sheila."

"Hello." A woman's voice.

"My eyes haven't adjusted from outside yet," Eddie said. "I can't see you very well."

"That's okay, buddy," Franco said. "We'll be here whenever you're ready." He laughed, and so did the two women.

"Can you turn a light on?" Eddie asked.

"Nope. The electricity is turned off. And we're almost out of candles. Have to get some more. Wait a minute and your eyes will adjust."

"Craig lives in that cabin near the top," Carla said. "We ran into each other in the woods. We had a nice talk."

"That how you got the pine needles in your hair?" Sheila said.

"There aren't any pine needles in my hair," Carla said,

quickly touching the back of her head to make sure. "Why did you say that?"

"Just testing," Sheila said.

"You're crazy," Carla said. "Both of you." She turned to Eddie. "Don't mind them. They're really friendly."

"You own that cabin up there?" Franco asked.

"No. I'm just renting it for a while. You?"

"We're not even renting. We're what you might call poachers."

"He means squatters, I think," Sheila said.

"Whatever it is," Franco said. "We saw the people who lived here when they moved out. They locked the doors and the electricity was turned off. That means they won't be back for the season. So we just moved in for a while. The people who own the place must be rich. It's got all kinds of nice things. We found a ton of canned food. And booze, a lot of booze. You want a drink?"

"No, thanks," Eddie said. "I don't drink much."

"Man after my own heart," Sheila said. "Franco here, he'll drink anything."

"Not milk. I hate milk. Always hated milk."

"Anything that comes in a bottle," Sheila said.

"Milk used to come in bottles," Franco said. "You remember when milk came in bottles, Craig?"

"Yes," Eddie said.

"So do I. These two don't. Sometimes they don't remember *any*thing."

Carla's face was suddenly brightened by the glow from a match. He knew immediately by the odor that she was smoking marijuana. She inhaled sharply and closed her eyes. Sheila took it from her, took a deep drag, then passed it to Eddie.

He held it, hesitated, then dragged exactly as they had. He knew about holding his breath: he'd seen it done on television. He decided not to tell them he hadn't ever smoked it before.

"God," Sheila said, "I love dope."

"None for me," Franco said. "I'm drinking these good people's whiskey. Don't like to mix things up too much."

"Damned fool," Sheila said. "That stuff poisons your system."

"I know, I know," Franco said. "But it makes me feel

so *good* about it." He dragged out the vowed in "good" for a long time. Eddie heard himself laughing.

"Christ," Sheila said. "Don't encourage him. That's the last thing he needs."

"You gonna sit down?" Carla asked. "You've been standing there since we came in."

She was in the middle of the couch, an old wicker summertime couch, covered with what he now saw were bright yellow cushions. He sat next to her. The couch creaked and air hissed from the cushions. Her thigh and hip were touching his. For a moment it seemed as if all the sensation in his body focused on those points of contact. She squirmed slightly, then leaned over so their shoulders were also touching.

Her profile was very pretty in the twilight of the room. Her hand rested on his thigh. The fingers and palm were gentle there, not moving. Eddie realized he had another erection. It had been years since he had done it twice in one day. The way things were with him and Betty the past several years, they didn't even do it once a week. He had assumed it was him, something about his age; now he decided it was his context.

"It's getting cool," Sheila said. "Why don't you make a nice fire, Franco?"

"Why don't *you* make a nice fire? What's all this sexist crap? We get company and we turn into a family all of a sudden?"

Eddie looked at Sheila to see if she'd be angry. The tone of the words had been gentle enough. She shrugged. "You man. Go make fire. I'll stay here and knit."

"You don't know *how* to knit. If you knew how to knit I'd ask you to make me a red turtleneck sweater. Always wanted a red turtleneck sweater."

"Franco," she said, "the fire."

"All right, all right. This time. You make the next fire. Hey, man, you wanna help me make the fire?"

"No, he doesn't," Carla said. "He's a guest. My guest. And we're very comfortable just now." Eddie was glad she said that; he didn't want to move. Everything felt so nice.

"Okay, this time," Franco said. "But from now on he takes turns making the fire. You're a guest only once out here in the jungle."

"Fair enough," Carla said.

From now on? What were they assuming? Eddie wasn't moving in. This was crazy. He looked around the dark room and for a moment suffered the same kind of panic he remembered from the night he had changed identities with the drowned man.

"Here you go, Craig," Sheila said. "You'll be wanting this."

"What is it?"

"Cheddar. There was an enormous chunk in the cooler. It's really good. You want some crackers with it?"

He was about to say he didn't even want the cheddar, but he tasted it and found it was very good. He heard himself chewing. It seemed to take a long time. "Sure," he said. "I'd love some crackers."

The fire warmed and brightened the room. Carla made dinner for them all. Franco said he was going out to check his traps.

"It's *dark* out," Sheila said. "You'll get lost."

"Know these woods like the back of my hand. Been here man and boy for nigh onto—"

"—three weeks. You'll get lost in the dark."

"No, I won't.' He picked up a kerosene lantern and lighted it. "I'll hang this from a nail on the porch. A beacon to beacon me home."

"He's crazy," Sheila said after Franco went out, "but he's really very nice. He read about setting rabbit traps in one of the books we found here and he started building them immediately."

"But he's never caught anything," Carla said.

"I don't know what he'd do if he did. I can't imagine him skinning a rabbit. Remember how white he turned the time I cut my hand on that piece of glass? He can't stand blood."

"He'd bring it back here for us to skin," Carla said. "That's the way he'd handle that problem." She did some things at the stove. "Let's smoke a little more dope before dinner. Okay with you, Craig?"

"Fine with me," Eddie said. The cooking odors—he wasn't sure what they were—were the best odors he remembered. He leaned back and closed his eyes, listening to the sounds of the room, trying to separate out each aspect of what he was smelling. He was voraciously hungry.

Eddie remembered. He had been halfway through the design of a complex program when he took a break for a walk through the woods. And met Carla. That seemed a long time ago.

"I've got to get back."

"Where?"

"To my cabin."

"Now? Dinner's almost ready."

"No. Not now. But soon. I've got work to do. I'm in the middle of something."

"Up here? You're doing work that can't wait up here?" Sheila said, then cawed. "I don't believe it. You got a girl up at that cabin? Is that it? You holding out, Craig?"

"No. There's nobody up there but me. I mean, there's nobody up there at all now. I'm down here. I live there alone."

"That's true," Carla said. "Unless he snuck her in there today. I've peeked at him a lot."

"Maybe he never lets her out," Sheila said. "Maybe that's why you've never seen her. Maybe he keeps her hidden. Ropes. Chains. Soft cotton gags that taste of cinnamon and ginger. Maybe he's one of those weirdos we read about all the time."

"No," Carla said. "He's no weirdo. I've inspected his cabin carefully and there are no bodies hidden in it, no unaccounted-for persons tied down anywhere."

Eddie was getting nervous. He wanted to argue that he really did have work to do. Important work. But then both women started laughing and he found himself laughing along with them.

"I guess it can wait," Eddie said.

"I think you ought to stay here tonight," Carla said. "It's very dark out and you might fall and hurt yourself on the trail. Trip over a root. Then you wouldn't be able to work tomorrow."

"Or be attacked by a savage animal," Sheila said.

"Stay here and be safe," Carla said.

"How come there's not another man here?" Eddie said.

"Why should there be?" Carla said.

"I think there should be. Three is an odd number."

"So it is," Sheila said.

"But there is another man here," Carla said. "And it's not an odd three now. It's a well-balanced four. If you go out into the dark woods, it'll be an unsteady three again."

"I'm not going out into the dark woods."

"Terrific," she said.

Franco's boots clumped on the porch steps. He came in waving the kerosene lantern.

"Catch anything?" Carla asked.

"No."

"Did you find your traps?" Sheila asked.

"No. But it's sure a pretty night out."

"It's very dark out there," Carla said.

"I mean," Franco said, "that it's sure a pretty night out if you happen to like very dark nights."

After dinner they all did the dishes together. It got crowded around the sink, and Sheila said after a while, "Maybe I'd better finish these alone, before we wreck these nice folks' property."

"Just trying to help," Franco said.

"I admire the intention," Sheila said.

"Then we'll have no arguments." Franco put his hand under her blouse and scratched the middle of her back.

"You sonofabitch. You know what happens to me. Go on outside on the porch."

Franco turned to Eddie. "See, a guy tries to help out and they just turn on him."

"What happened to that wine we were going to have with dinner?" Carla said. "I saw you opening a bottle after you came in before."

"Oh, goddamn," Franco said. "Forgot all about it. Shall we have it now?"

"Why not?"

They sat on the porch and drank the wine. Eddie leaned against a wood post. It felt good against his back. Insects made a terrific noise in the brush and the wind rustled lightly in the dense foliage overhead.

"This is a good place," Franco said. "The trees are so thick no one can see our lights more than a few yards away. And noise doesn't travel."

"I never knew you all were here," Eddie said.

"I know," Carla said. "That was fun. Knowing you were there and watching you, and you not knowing I was doing it.

"She wouldn't tell us what she was doing out there those days," Franco said. "Once she said she had been swimming, but she wouldn't tell us where. And then this afternoon she said she'd be bringing a guest home for dinner. I thought she was crazy, to tell you the truth."

Franco told them about things he thought he saw in the woods when he had gone out earlier. Then he leaned back and sighed happily.

"The first few nights we were up here I'd hear those noises and I'd be scared silly. And then I realized it wasn't anybody, just the animals who lived around here. So now when I hear the noises, I try to follow them. I never catch up with anything, of course, but it's fun."

"He got lost one night," Sheila said.

"I really did," Franco said. "I kept following this noise, and it was never very far ahead of me. It would move, and then when I moved to follow it would stop. I'd stop to listen where it was and then it would scoot off again. It kept scooting and I kept following, and then it was gone. I had no idea what directions I'd taken or how far I'd gone. I looked for lights from the windows of the cabin, for the lanterns or the candles, but I couldn't see a thing. I listened for the girls' voices, but I couldn't hear them."

"What did you do?" Eddie asked.

"Only thing there was to do. I smoked a couple of joints and went to sleep. The ground was kind of lumpy, but I got into it after a while. Daylight woke me and I found I was maybe three hundred feet from the house. Right over that way." He pointed to the darkness on the left.

"We were worried sick," Sheila said. "I thought a bear had gotten him."

"There aren't any bears around here anymore," Eddie said. "There aren't any large animals, except for the deer."

Franco looked surprised. "I didn't know that."

"I thought he got lost and went to sleep in the woods," Carla said.

"That's true," Sheila said. "She told me that. I didn't believe her."

"She kept me awake all night," Carla said. "Wanted to go out searching for him. I said we'll get lost too."

"I don't get lost out here anymore." Franco said. "It's funny how quickly you get a sense of where you are once you belong someplace. Even in the dark."

"I haven't gone out much at night," Eddie said.

"We'll do it sometime," Carla said. "Not tonight. Enough talking. Let's go to bed."

"I'll take care of the candles," Sheila said.

"See you guys tomorrow."

There was just enough light coming in from the window for him to see the bed and Carla standing next to it. She undressed slowly, humming a tune he had heard but couldn't name.

After they made love again, she mumbled something into his shoulder. He asked her what she had said. "I don't know," she said sleepily. "I forget."

"Was it like a convict again?"

"Nope. Like a free man. And ain't it fine?"

He was going to answer, but the feel of her body and a change in her breathing let him know she was already asleep.

For the first time in many years Eddie slept close to a woman with whom he had just made love. He tried to stay awake and savor it, but he slid into the sensation and sleep at the same time.

The next morning when he walked up to his cabin after brakfast, it occurred to him that they had asked him no personal questions, nor had they told him anything about themselves. They hadn't asked what he was doing, living there alone in the woods, they hadn't asked where he was from, how long he was staying, where he was going. They talked about the things around them, the events of their days, but it was as if the past and the future didn't exist.

# TWELVE

Buffalo SAC Francis X. Kelly stared thoughtfully at a large map on his office wall. The map, which consisted of the forty-eight states with little offset boxes for Alaska and Hawaii, was stapled to a new cork bulletin board. The reason he requested the bulletin board was so he could stick pins into the map without ruining the plaster wall. Then he had come in one day to find the building's maintenance people drilling enormous holes in the plaster. "What the hell are you guys doing?" he yelled.

"Mounting the bulletin board you ordered. You want us to use nails? The thing'll fall down with nails and make a mess. Gotta use big Mollies."

"You've made a mess already."

"Won't see the mess once the board is up."

"What if I take the board down?"

"Wouldn't want to do that. It'd look like shit in here." The men went on working.

Kelly hadn't thought about bulletin board holes. Now, when this case was over, he would be stuck with the bulletin board. It really lowered the class of the office, but it would be either the board or the scarred wall.

Each pin in the map represented the location of a UCI—Unexplained Computer Incident. Green pins were for incidents involving private and commercial computers, red pins represented federal computers. Municipal, county, and state computers got black pins. There were now fifty-seven pins in the map.

The case had been taken over by the FBI after the seventeenth American Express check incident. At first the FBI and American Express assumed someone had gotten keys to the machines and had been taking checks out at night, when no one else was around. That would explain why the AmEx central computer had no record of the withdrawals. They installed sophisticated silent alarm systems on each of the units. Whenever one of the units was opened after normal airport working hours, the

153

alarms immediately transmitted a message to a central computer, which was programmed to automatically alert the local FBI field office and the airport police. During the period in which the alarms were used, three men were arrested. All turned out to be maintenance personnel legitimately replacing blank check forms. During the same period seven more check robberies occurred. Research people at AmEx said it had to be done through the computers. They had no theories.

An FBI agent in the New York office was first put in charge of the case. The man—Wilbur F. Walker—was supposedly a comer in the Bureau. He decided to put the machines under twenty-four-hour surveillance. After two days the surveillance was abandoned. FBI agents couldn't surround respectable businessmen and demand identification from them just because they used their credit cards to purchase traveler's checks. That was what the Director told Walker and his supervisor after Congressman Harry O. Potter was forced to identify himself one morning in Hartford.

Walker decided they would have to look for something unusual, for someone who didn't fit. During the two weeks the machines were watched after the Potter fiasco, there were four more robberies and no arrests.

Walker then developed a foolproof plan. All three machines would be put under continual film surveillance, using a special camera that had a clock mechanism that showed the exact time in the lower left-hand corner of each frame. The machinery would work just like the devices they used for bank robberies and watching Commies, with the differences being that the the cameras would be on all the time and no human monitor would activate the mechanisms. Then they could match up the hot checks, when they came through two weeks later, with the point and time of origin. It would take three cameras to adequately cover each installation so they would have sure film images of the culprit. Or culprits. Walker thought it was a gang at work.

It was a very elaborate plan, one sure to produce results. There were certain problems, however. The plan would require introduction to the check machines of a time-registering mechanism so they could subsequently synchronize the checks with the film. American Express said the devices would cost about $79,000. The FBI surveillance lab said the camera installations would run about $17,000 and there would be an additional expense of $24,000 for six new cameras. All the others they had, except three, were being used to monitor the movements of Jesse Jackson, William Kunstler, and Barbara Walters. Personnel costs for changing the film reels, camera maintenance, and transporting the film to the labs would run about $1600 per week. All of those were, however, minor expenses. Cost for the 16-millimeter film for nine cameras, running at eighteen frames per second for twenty-four hours per day, would run approximately $432,000 per month—exclusive of film developing and production of work prints.

American Express decided not to pay for the operation. Apparently the losses weren't so considerable, and they could write them off as a tax loss anyway. They said they might agree to support the FBI plan *if* losses reached a half million or so a month. But it didn't pay them to invest so heavily in a law enforcement operation designed to stop one sequence of crimes restricted to one operator. And the FBI handwriting experts had declared all the signatures were by the same person, though eleven different names were involved. An executive of the company wrote a senator on the Judiciary Committee asking what had happened to the quality of American law enforcement when a private company, one that paid a lot of taxes, was asked to subsidize directly an operation of the Federal Bureau of Investigation. The senator, who disliked the FBI intensely, wrote an angry letter to the Director, demanding immediate action.

The Director wrote back that the Bureau's estimate of the procedure outlined by the special agent in charge of the case—UCISAC Walker was the way the Director referred to him—would run the Bureau well over one million dollars per month. Given the current state of the Bureau's budget, there was no way he could responsibly authorize such an expenditure. The Senator was, the Director pointed out, on the Judiciary Committee. If he could get through Congress an additional appropriation of, say, four million to start off the operation, the Bureau would certainly give the case its usual intense attention. He reminded the senator that during the 1960s special programs set up by the Bureau to disrupt dangerous radical organizations and infiltrate others had enormous budgets and they weren't even accountable. "We don't have the funds to pursue potential Communists and subversives," the Director concluded, "so how could we commit so much money and staff to pursue one solitary forger?"

UCISAC Walker was furious when he was told his plan had been rejected by FBIHQ. He considered going to the press. He thought it outrageous that minor budgetary matters should stand in the way of criminal justice investigations. He knew how much the Bureau had spent during the 1960s and early 1970s on COINTELPRO and other political disruption projects. Millions and millions. He mentioned his concern to this bureau chief, who said he understood Walker's frustration. He had himself, several times in the past, been similarly frustrated in pursuit of criminals. He told Walker that the Director had written the Senate and reminded them of the discrepancy in the COINTELPRO and crime-fighting budgets, but the Senate did nothing.

"It's hard these days, Walker. But you know they *always* get caught in the end. You know that."

"No, I don't. A lot of people get away with it."

"No one we decide is guilty gets away with it," the chief said.

"That's true."

"Someday he'll make a mistake. And then we'll know who he is. And *then* it will be only a matter of getting the evidence and the man in the same place at the same time."

"Yes, sir," Walker said.

"The Bureau has a fine record for doing that," the chief said.

"Yes, chief."

"The best."

"Yes, chief."

"And it doesn't matter anyway, Walker."

"Why is that, sir?"

"Because the case has been transferred to the Buffalo office. The SAC there has been put in direct charge of it.

Walker was immediately furious again. He said it was

outside politics and it wasn't right that the Bureau should be subject to outside politics.

"No," the chief said. "It was transferred to Buffalo because Buffalo is the only place city government has been similarly victimized. The other cases we know about, in addition to American Express, all involve national corporations or interstate agencies. Buffalo has been singled out for particular attention by the Computer Bandit, and so the Bureau's CPPPD"—that was the Criminals' Psychological Personality Profile Division—"thinks he may be operating out of there."

The chief told Walker that city records involving tax exempt holdings, arson, and delinquency cases had been tabulated and mailed to a newspaper, which had printed them immediately and caused a series of scandals in both Democrat and Republican party organizations. Later a number of high-ranking city and county hall officials discovered that their salary checks had been reduced for no apparent reason.

"My God!" Walker exclaimed. "I've never heard of anything like this. Is there more?"

"Nothing reported yet, but there may be problems still undiscovered there. They're looking. And perhaps other municipalities have been attacked by the Computer Bandit, but none has reported anything. So Buffalo seems as good a place as any to start looking. You ever been there?"

"No," Walker said. "Why?"

"It's not good for much else, that's why."

Kelly had been pleased and nervous about getting the case. If he solved it, he would get national publicity, even a mention in the *Times*, and perhaps even the Washington *Post*. That would mean he could expect transfer within a year or two to one of the plum cities: San Francisco, Los Angeles, New Orleans, Honolulu, Las Vegas. But if he drew a blank, he would stay in Buffalo forever. Kelly didn't want to stay in Buffalo forever. The very thought made him shiver.

Kelly pushed the intercom button and had his secretary get Purvey. Purvey arrived five minutes later. He didn't say where he had been during that time and he sat down immediately, doubly annoying Kelly. In his day an assistant SAC was always available and he stood until his superior waved at an empty chair.

"We've got the Computer Bandit case, Purvey."

"I know that, boss."

"How do you know that?" Kelly's eyes narrowed with suspicion.

"You had Miss Leipzig post the current case activity on the outside bulletin board this morning. It was number seven on the list."

"Oh, I forgot about that."

"I read it every day, sir." Purvey sucked on his pipe.

"Good, Purvey. I'm putting you on it. Give someone else your other cases. Spread them around. Drop everything. This is going to be Number One. Got it?"

"Right, boss."

"I want you to check out every computer programmer and computer operator in the city, Purvey."

Purvey's brows drew together. "What do you want me to check them out for, boss?"

"Because I told you to, that's why." Kelly felt good about having asserted himself. But Purvey was sitting there with a blank expression on his face. He didn't ask Kelly for more justification, but Kelly knew he was thinking about it. "I don't have to give you more reasons, do I?"

"No, boss." He relighted his pipe, which had gone out.

"And I've told you not to call me boss."

"Right."

"Because we've got the Computer Bandit case. And they—the Bureau—think it may be somebody in Buffalo."

"That wasn't what I meant. What I meant was, what items do you want me to check out on these computer people? There's a lot of things to check people out for. You can't just check people out for everything. That takes forever."

"How the hell should I know what you should check them out for? You're the field agent."

"Sir, I'm Assistant SAC-Buffalo."

"But I'm the SAC and I've made you the field agent in charge of this case. Directly under me. That's what I just told you. I want you to go out and find out which computer person—it might be a woman—in Buffalo is the Computer Bandit. Is that clear?"

"Yes, sir."

"Any other questions?"

"No, sir."

"Then that's all for now, Purvey."

"Yes, sir." Purvey left. Kelly wasn't at all happy about what was happening to the Bureau. In the old days a man knew exactly what his position was and behaved accordingly. Now he had to continually remind these younger men about the real facts of life.

Three days later he saw Purvey in the cafeteria. "What's happening with the computer cases?" Kelly asked.

"Working on them, boss."

"Not *boss,* dammit."

"Right, sir. I'm working on it. There are approximately four hundred and forty computer people in the city. To be exact, we've turned up four hundred and thirty-seven so far. Checking them out takes a while. Some of them work at the university."

"God, you know about *them.*"

"Not really, sir. That's not why I mentioned it. But the campus is a way out of town now and it takes a considerable amount of time running back and forth. What you meant just now, I think that reflects another period. These fellows don't seem at all political."

"You never know, Purvey. Perhaps you read about the campus demonstrations they had out there ten years ago. That place was a hotbed, let me tell you."

"Yes, sir. But none of these people was even out of graduate school ten years ago. It's a whole new crew."

"Keep on it, Purvey."

"Right, sir."

When Kelly got home that night, Mary Ellen was livid with rage. She was waiting for him at the door.

"I don't know how to tell you what happened. I can't even talk about it I'm so furious."

"Now, Mary Ellen, if you can't talk about it, why don't we just sit down and relax a little while until the words come back? I'm sure you'll be able to talk as well as always in a minute or two. In the meantime I'll take off my coat"—he took off his tan trenchcoat—"and put away my briefcase"—he put the briefcase in the closet—"and just make myself a little—"

"Your martini is more important than your own children!" she shrieked.

"Mary Ellen. You know that's not true. But I've had a hard day. A rough case is getting rougher. And I've been looking forward for the last two—"

"You know what they did to him?"

"Who?"

"Francis. Your *son*. You know what they did to him?"

"I assumed you meant *that* Francis. Has something happened to him? Is he hurt?"

"He's all right now."

"Good. Then I'll just make my martini and you can tell me all about it."

"You listen to me first, Francis X. Kelly. It's the least you could do. You said we had to send the boy to that school."

"It's the best Catholic school in this part of the state."

"I wanted him to go to Nichols."

"Nichols is for a bunch of Episcopal faggots. Half the boys take dancing instead of hockey."

"Nichols is a fine school. Very nice people go there."

"All right. I'm not going to have that argument again. What happened?"

"Of course you don't want to have it again. Francis isn't going to Nichols, is he? This wouldn't have happened at Nichols, I'll tell you."

"What?"

"The sisters. You know what the sisters did?"

"I couldn't guess." In his mind Kelly saw a faint image of an olive, dull green inside a glistening cone-shaped pool.

"They rapped his knuckles with a ruler. Almost made them bleed. A *ruler!*"

Kelly roared. "Goddamn, I thought they'd stopped doing that. Some parts of the good old days haven't been wiped out by this liberal namby-pamby crap. What did the little sonofabitch do?"

"Francis! I'm talking about your own son—Francis."

"I know his name."

"He was beaten by nuns."

"And he probably deserved it. Must have been talking or something. He'll learn. Best thing for him. I remember some of those old nuns when I was a kid. One of them, Sister Rose Alice, by God, she'd give you one rap, just one. You'd remember it for a week. She was a fire breather. Probably dead now. All the good ones are probably dead now."

"I'm not going to listen to any more of this. That child is upstairs in his room in tears. You either call that school right now and have that woman relieved of her duties or tomorrow your son goes to—"

"Not Nichols, if that's what you're thinking. No son of Francis X. Kelly is going to a school where they can dance instead of get out there and play hockey like men."

She glared at him, her lips pressed tightly together. "You weren't like this before you became a SAC." She said it through clenched teeth.

"He never got his knuckles rapped before. This is the first opportunity I've had to be like this."

"You're a beast."

"Mary Ellen, come on. I've had a hard day."

"Torturing suspects?" She turned and walked quickly from the room. A door slammed upstairs.

Go after her and talk it out. That's what he should probably do, he told himself. That wasn't what he did. What he did was go into the pantry, where he took down an old-fashioned glass, in which he mixed the largest martini he had ever mixed himself. A couple of minutes later he mixed another one. By the time he mixed the third, he no longer cared that she was so mad she wasn't making dinner. By the time he mixed the fourth, it wouldn't have mattered if she had.

Purvey came into his office the following Monday afternoon. He said the examinations and career checks had turned up nothing.

"I don't believe *nothing*," Kelly said.

"I mean nothing of any use in the UCI cases. Some of the computer scientists had some kinky inclinations, but none of them seemed bent on criminal behavior of any other kind. The standing files—the material from IFFI on the computer—were a great help here. In one day I was able to get security-type profiles on over half the people on the list, and none of those profiles was more than twelve months stale."

"I'm always amazed at how many people have security clearance," Kelly said. "Though I don't know why I should be, after all the time I've spent doing background checks on people, watching them, talking to their friends. You know. And I suppose a large portion of computer people are in security-indexed jobs."

"Only twenty-six of the persons under investigation have any kind of functional clearance, sir," Purvey said. "The other information came about as the result of ongoing coverage of various political groups or people who got flagged for a variety of reasons."

"What kinds of reasons?"

"You would know more about that than I would, sir. I'm new at this. The file reports open to me don't indicate why people got flagged, just that they were, sometime in the past twenty-five years, brought to the Bureau's attention, and we've continued to watch them carefully. But it's more interesting than I'd thought. Some of these guys are *really* kinky. I mean *really*."

"That's not the sort of information we're looking for, Purvey. No reason for you to poison your mind and waste our time with filth."

Purvey smiled. "It's not 'filth,' sir, begging your pardon. It's FBI background information on persons under surveillance from the IFFI file, and it's very revealing. Some of you white folks is *strange*." He began filling a pipe Kelly hadn't seen before, another one of the kind with the white dot.

"Purvey, just go back to work and come see me when you turn something up, huh? I'm really tired."

"Been having a bad time at home, boss?"

"Why did you ask that?" Where was he getting his information? Kelly wondered. "Why do you think I've been having a bad time at home?" Mary Ellen still wasn't talking to him, but how could Purvey know that?

"You just been looking kind of wasted when you been

coming in the past few days. I thought you maybe haven't been sleeping too well. That's all."

"I've been sleeping fine, Purvey. Just fine."

"Right, boss."

Purvey was gone before Kelly could yell at him about calling him boss again. Ten years ago there were no blacks in the Bureau. Five years ago, when they started coming in, they never alluded to the fact that they weren't like everyone else and everyone else pretended not to notice anything odd about them. And now here was one who insisted on poking fun at the situation. "You white folks is strange," he had said. What could Kelly reply to a line like that? He couldn't even put it in Purvey's personnel file. How would it look, a line like that? *Strange.*

Purvey came back an hour later. "Sir," he said. "I've turned up two things. I don't know if either means anything, but I thought I should bring them to your attention."

"What?"

"Well, we turned up nothing at IBM. The university and the banks had nothing for us. The IFFI files didn't help on this caper either. But there was a bank programmer who was fired when he was caught trying to transfer funds from a large corporate account into his own overdrawn checking account. By the time they found him, he had used up about fifteen thousand dollars of a steel company's money. No charges were filed because the bank didn't want any newspaper articles, and he was allowed to quit his job."

"They covered up a felony? Oh, ho. You turned up something good there, Purvey. Good work."

Purvey gave Kelly a withering look. "I don't think this will amount to much."

"Covering up felonies is a crime," Kelly said defensively. "Sometimes it's a crime more serious than the crime itself. It may include conspiracy. Other things."

"It don't include shit if they don't report it. Banks can cover this sort of thing by internal accounting and they're responsible only for delivering deposited funds on demand, maintaining a rational accounting system, and showing depositors a reasonable profit. If the bank absorbs it soon enough and says no embezzlement occurred, then no embezzlement occurred, and you know it. That kind of mis-appropriation goes on all the time. There's no way to find out about such things unless someone chooses to tell us. And by the time we do get told, the cases are usually no longer actionable."

"That's ridiculous," Kelly said. "We can't have business-men going around deciding which laws they'll obey and which laws they'll ignore. That's—"

He was interrupted by a bellowing laugh from Purvey. Purvey laughed until tears ran glistening on his black cheeks, making them shine. At that moment Kelly hated Purvey.

When Purvey got his breath back, he and Kelly stared at one another for a long time. Kelly was about to burst into angry chastisement; Purvey was about to burst into another paroxysm. Both exerted magnificent self-control. Purvey succeeded at it first.

"One case at a time, boss, one case at a time. That guy is *not* our guy. He doesn't have any reason to be. He's got himself a very good job with another bank as a loan of-ficer, making more money than he made before, and he's working better hours. After the bank decided not to prose-cute, he agreed to submit his resignation, but only if they agreed to write him a decent letter of recommendation."

"That's more perjury. This is incredible."

"It may be incredible, but it's not demonstrable. He made them date the recommendation several days before the discovery of the shifted funds. You'll never nail any-body on that one."

"If it's all so well covered up, then how come you know all this? How did you get on top of it so quickly?" Kelly eyed Purvey suspiciously. "Are you telling me the truth about this? Have you made all this up just to frustrate me?"

"Boss! Sir! That's a rotten thing to say. Rotten."

"I'm sorry, Purvey. Now tell me how you know all this."

"I learned it all at lunchtime from my girl friend. She works there. She typed the letter of recommendation."

"Would she . . . ?"

"Not on your life. She likes that job. And she also wrote

the letter herself, so there's no one else you can get to contradict the story about the dating."

"They've got a secretary making decisions on matters of this kind? That's outrageous." Kelly didn't know what to say next. He rocked back in his leather chair. It had thick leather-covered arms. Only SACs had leather chairs with leather-covered arms. His fingers gripped the ends of the arms in frustration.

"Secretary?" Purvey shouted. "Betty Lou ain't no secretary. She's an assistant vice-president. Why'd you assume she was a secretary?" Purvey sat down and looked at Kelly, his face once again perfectly neutral. Kelly knew he was smiling somewhere inside.

Kelly gave up. "All right, that's a dead end, then. You said you had two."

"The other one is more dead. I was talking to the guy who runs the city programming office, a fellow named Farthold. He's the supervisor, but he doesn't know anything. He's an old political hack who got the job twenty years ago, and he's so well ensconced with the Democratic machine no one has ever bothered to fire him, or even find out if he knows anything about the job, which he doesn't. When he got the job, the city was using computers primarily to print payroll checks, keep tabs on school supplies, and schedule police cars and garbage trucks for oil changes. As the uses for computers changed, he hired assistants to do the real work. Anyway, his assistant, the guy who does all the work there, is a fellow named Copley, Bob Copley. Nice guy. But he doesn't know a damned thing either."

"But you just said—"

"Let me finish, okay? The reason Copley doesn't know a damned thing is because he's only been on the job two or three months. And the reason he's only been on the job two or three months is his predecessor drowned. A guy named Argo. Edward Argo. Either a suicide or an accident. Drowned over in the Black Rock Canal, where all those niggers go fishing and get drunk and fall in all the time."

"All those—"

Purvey raised a warning finger. "*I* can say it. You can't."

"I've heard that name before," Kelly said.

"Niggers?"

"Argo."

"It was probably in the paper. 'City worker drowns in canal.' Something like that."

"No, I've *heard* it. Someone said it to me for some reason."

"Maybe you knew the guy?"

"No. I'd remember if I knew someone who drowned."

"When did you hear it?"

"I don't know. You'll have to find out. Check back. There must be some memorandum somewhere. I write everything down. That's the only way you can find things later, if you write them down. Otherwise you forget things and you don't know if what you remember is all there was because you don't remember the things you don't remember, if you know what I mean."

"Uh," Purvey said, "yes, sir. I get what you mean." He was looking down at his shoes for some reason. "But I don't think it's going to matter much. This guy Argo has been dead for about three months. I don't think he'd be going around to airports generating hot American Express checks. The most recent check incident was only two weeks ago."

"But he'd know how to attack the city, wouldn't he? Maybe he had a vendetta going against the city. Maybe he's been doing things like this for years and no one ever noticed before."

"We've talked to several departments in the city and no one had anything irregular to report," Purvey said. "After the salary-adjustment, tax-exemption, and arson-report cases came up, we asked around. No one had anything of the kind they knew about."

Kelly opened his middle drawer, using a small key he took from a flap pocket in the special wallet that held his government identification cards and badge. He held up a thick manila folder. "My notes. I bet that name Argo is in here. Somewhere in here."

"Hold it," Purvey said. "You don't need them. I remember now. The shrieker lady who thought her husband had been kidnapped. Remember, she called and talked to me, and then after they found the body she called and talked to you. She was convinced it was a mob operation."

"Right, Purvey. That's it. I knew I'd heard the name."

"Was there any other time you heard the name, sir? In connection with anything else "

"No. That's it."

"That doesn't take us anywhere, then, does it?"

"No, I guess not. Damn."

Purvey looked at his notebook. "There is one thing interesting here." Kelly looked up. "The reporters who got the information in the mail; they printed their stories just a week after Argo died. Maybe the Buffalo Computer Bandit *was* Argo after all. How about that? Makes sense."

"Maybe it's been him all along. That's our man, Purvey. Now we just have to find him."

"No, boss. Not Argo. His wife made a positive ID on the body. There were no other disappearances in the city at that time. It was a clean death as far as the police were concerned. And as far as I'm concerned now. We can't stick this caper on a dead man and then walk away saying we've done our job."

"I wasn't saying we should do that, Purvey. I wouldn't do that. Why do you think I'd do that?" Purvey shrugged. "It was the wife who identified him. Maybe she's in on it. They're just waiting until he's got enough money together and then they'll hook up again. It's perfect. That's happened before. A lot."

"Yeah, but not this time. She's still living in that grubby house and she's about to get remarried. To that asshole Farthold. If she were in on a plot, she wouldn't marry Farthold. Nobody's that devious. Certainly nobody with a voice like hers. You know what I think?"

"How would I know what you think, Purvey?" Kelly knew Purvey was about to tell him.

"I think you've got it exactly right, chief: this Argo probably *did* hit the city computers before he did himself in. Why not? It would have been easy enough to do. Get that information and mail it out, do a little mischief, and then go down to the river and drown his sorrows."

"But what about the American Express checks, those New York equipment purchases, the enormous gifts to that school for blind kids in Ohio, paid for by stock tranfers from the Ford Foundation accounts, the release to the New York *Times* of the governor's personal expense budget that was covered by state funds, and all the other things on the UCI lists? A drowned man couldn't have pulled that off."

"Right you are. That's the *real* Computer Bandit. We've had two of them. Argo was a red herring. Maybe that's the wrong term. You know what I mean. An unconnected and irrelevant coincidence. After all, the Buffalo deeds were all done three or four weeks before the first traveler's check ripoff. That's just luck on the Computer Bandit's part: we got sidetracked on these Buffalo deals while he's been running around the countryside somewhere else. Why is it so surprising that we should have two computer crooks working during a short space of time? It's the most natural kind of crime in the world now. You can't steal much money with a gun anymore. Hardly anybody has much money except the banks, and only dummies rob them anymore. People who know how do it with computers. I bet businessmen do it all the time. What makes this guy special is he's an independent, he's working out there on his own someplace."

When Purvey finished, he was nearly out of breath. Sometime after he started, he had stood up and had been walking back and forth in front of Kelly's desk. He seemed almost embarrassed to discover himself standing at the side of the room. He sat down quickly. "What do you think?"

"You really think businessmen steal with computers all the time?"

"They must. They steal with everything else, don't they?"

"I don't think you should say that about all American businessmen."

"I don't mean *all* American businessmen, sir. Let's just say a number of them. But even if it's only two percent, that's a lot of goddamned crooks."

"Using computers."

"Probably."

"It's an area no law enforcement agency has gotten a handle on yet."

"Not that I know of, boss."

"Do you know anything about computers, Purvey?"

"Only what I've learned since I started working on this case."

"I think we should learn something about the computer industry. I think you've stumbled on . . . we've stumbled on something magnificent. After we catch this sonofabitch we can start on it. It's the wave of the future. And we'll be on the ground floor. *After* we catch this sonofabitch."

"Yes, sir. After we catch him."

"By God, Purvey, this can be big. Very big. For both of us."

"Yes, sir."

"I want that sonofabitch."

"And so do I, sir."

"Then stop standing here. Get out there and get him."

"Yes, sir."

When he was alone, Kelly rethought his options. It wasn't just New Orleans and Honolulu and San Francisco and Las Vegas, horizontal moves to pretty places with more interesting kinds of crime. Now there was a possibility of vertical mobility too. He had a new city on his list. *Washington.* As soon as they caught that sonofabitch.

He imagined the Computer Bandit in a large office somewhere. It had a beautiful mahogany desk. There was a telephone with several buttons. There was a computer console that put him in touch with any source of information anywhere in the world. There was a lovely carpet on the floor. Behind the desk were two large flags held up by brass rings attached to the wall. One was an American flag and the other was—

Kelly sat bolt-upright and rubbed his eyes. He realized he hadn't been imagining the Computer Bandit at work. He had been imagining himself behind the desk in the Deputy Director's office. He had been there once, when he got the Buffalo assignment.

He was sure that in Washington there were schools where the sisters were firm but didn't use rulers on the knuckles, and Mary Ellen wouldn't be mad at him because he didn't want to send his kid to a dingbat Episcopal school where the lads learned to curtsey and pirouette, or whatever else it was they learned in dancing class when they were getting out of hockey and football.

But first he had to nail the Computer Bandit. Somewhere out there a master criminal was running around. When Kelly caught him, a beautiful future would open up. Kelly could run pretty damned fast too. If he just knew where the track was. If he knew where the sonofabitch was running, he was sure he could catch him cold.

# THIRTEEN

Eddie spent the morning cleaning up, in case Carla visited during the afternoon. She had said she would walk up if he weren't going to be busy. He said he had some things to do, but would be free later on. She had laughed and said he sounded a little eccentric.

"Why do you say that?"

"Because this isn't the kind of environment in which one works on *schedules,* that's why. I mean preset work schedules. You use morning to tell you when to get up and darkness to tell you it's time to be inside. Anything else should just be when you feel like it."

"Well," he said, "I'm going to feel like doing some work during the first part of the day. Hangover from my compulsive past."

"You can take the boy out of the city . . ."

"But he takes his work ethic along with him. Right. And I'm no boy. Haven't been one for years."

"You do all right," she said. "I'll see you in the late afternoon. If you can take a break, we'll go for a swim."

When the cabin was looking nice, he took his work sheets from the van to design a program he hoped would give him neat piles of information on a small group of senators and congressmen whom he had decided were especially venal, men who did bad things but who got so much money from special sources there was no way anyone could beat them. *Unless* someone had information, which not even money could negate. He hadn't yet decided what he would do with the information when he got it, but the response to the *Times* articles about the one senator's scandalous checkwriting and account-dangling habits, as well as the other senator's enormous deposits, suggested that a lot of people were truly interested in such information, if only they knew how to get it. Eddie knew how, so he had only to decide how best to use it.

He wasn't quite comfortable with the morality of this role because he was making all the decisions himself. He was setting himself up as prosecutor, jury, and judge, deciding who the bad guys were and then getting the damning information. But it wasn't like he was a gangster. He didn't make a decision and then kill someone as a result. All Eddie did was get information, facts, the truth, and make them available to other people. It wasn't as though he were spreading lies on someone's reputation. And he hadn't asked any questions that might hurt an honest man.

So much information was now collected about people that it was impossible to keep it all on paper. That wasn't quite correct: it could be kept on paper, but no one could use it in that form. Moving those pieces of paper around took more time than anyone with a human life-span could spare; the computers permitted people to do things with information they never could do before, which was one reason they had become dangerous so quickly. There hadn't been time for an adequate morality to develop; they were already controlling lives and working solely for the people with the power to get to them and the money to pay for their time. They were like lawyers and high-priced whores: talented and amoral.

The difficulty was finding out what tapes were where and how one could gain conversational access. Every day he worked in the van, Eddie established more and more conversational relationships. Each one opened the possibility of others, and the possibilities fanned out like sunrays. It was like entering networks of people: befriend a man in a profession and you gain access to others in that profession. Meet a cop and you can meet other cops, then the people they deal with—lawyers and pimps and judges and junkies and thieves. Meet a musician and you can meet people who make recordings and arrange concerts and buy tickets and design posters. Meet a brain surgeon and you can meet people who specialize in knees or hearts or lungs or feet. Every new friend you make puts you in potential contact with a sparkling web of other friends.

A strange way for *him* to think, he decided, a man who had no real friends and socialized with no one.

Except for Carla and Franco and Sheila. That was the best afternoon and night he could remember, except perhaps for the night he attacked the city's computers and escaped.

The more Eddie thought about it, the more convinced he was that the computer conversations were just like meeting new people. Each computer complex had a different personality, a different style and rhythm of conversation, a different set of resonances. Some of that perhaps represented differences in the programmers, but Eddie was sure that more of it resulted from differences in the nervous system of the machines themselves. They were so complex now that no two were ever alike in anything but the grossest aspects.

If it would have made sense to the computers, Eddie very well might have begun his instructions with HI, IFFI. HOW ARE YOU GETTING ON TODAY? instead of a formal access code.

Not all of the information on congressmen was coming to him from IFFI, the law enforcement computer, but most of it was. IFFI was part of a survey and information system established by the FBI during the Nixon years. The access code was kept secret; it wasn't in his set of Buffalo codes or in the book he had stolen from IBM. He had gotten IFFI's address without difficulty shortly before he left Buffalo.

He walked into the Cheektowaga police station one day and asked for information about something he had made up. The desk sergeant was very helpful. When Eddie asked the sergeant about the computer clicking away a few feet from his desk, the sergeant said it was part of a new unit they had just gotten with $20,000 of city money and a grant of $250,000 from the Law Enforcement Assistance Administration. The sergeant was very proud of the unit. He showed it to Eddie and was about to describe its operation when his telephone rang. He said he would be right back.

On the left side of the keyboard was the access manual. Eddie flipped through it casually. He found the information he wanted immediately; the telephone code and general program interrogation sequence for IFFI.

The sergeant, whose name tag said he was Everett Hall, came back. "It's a beauty, ain't it?"

"It's all Greek to me," Eddie said. "I don't understand these things."

"Who does?" Sergeant Hall responded. "Nobody I know. But this little book tells you just how to do it. What buttons to push, everything. Want to see how it works?"

"Sure."

"What's your car license number?"

"720EUJ."

Sergeant Hall typed a code, waited for a clear signal, got it, typed an access number, got a response, then typed out the license plate number. Almost immediately the typewriter began going by itself. "That's to the state's auto registration computer. It's what we do when our cars call in and ask us to check for outstanding tickets. We can also ask the Feds for information, but that's more complicated."

The typewriter printed out Eddie's name, address, and zip code. He was hit with a brief panic. What if it said next that he worked as a programmer for the city of Buffalo? The machine paused, then started typing again. NO OUTSTANDING VIOLATIONS OR WARRANTS, it said.

"Ain't that great?" Sergeant Hall said. Eddie said it was indeed impressive. Sergeant Hall said they picked up a lot of people with outstanding violations that way. "The day of the moving-violation scofflaw is over," he said proudly.

Eddie remembered Betty's fire hydrant ticket; the operation had obviously worked perfectly.

"Police work sure has changed," Sergeant Hall said. "When I started out, everything you needed to know, you carried here." He tapped his head with his forefinger. "Now the only thing you carry there is your hat."

The program Eddie had the computers working on this afternoon had to do with quashed arrests for the members of Congress he was investigating. One thing he had learned about law enforcement data collection: even when something was proved wrong, the computer still held the information. Sometimes it let you know at the end that the charges had been thrown out, but it always let you know what had been thought at the time. The pity was double: innocent people had ineradicable records because the computer always reported suspicions, however unfounded they later turned out to be; and guilty people who had power could make arrests for cause look like errors, they could make them disappear somewhere between the policeman's notebook and the court calendar. Eddie was asking IFFI to scan the Baltimore and Washington police files for such discrepancies. His Selectric whizzed back and forth across the paper.

Eddie went into the house and got a Coke. He drank it standing by the sink, put the empty can in a plastic bag, then went back to the van. The typewriter was still chattering away.

He sat on the cot and read one of the paperbacks he had bought during his most recent trip to New York. This one was a science fiction novel set in the 1980s. Its premise was that the energy crisis had gotten so bad the economy of America—as well as of all the other industrial countries—was near collapse. Gasoline cost more per gallon than liquor cost per quart, and gas stations therefore became the favorite targets of stickup men. The problem was, the money didn't do them much good because inflation was rising so fast and because there was so little to buy. A mission was set up to bring back from Pluto a mineral that could create thermonuclear power generators on earth. The mission was sabotaged by a nut who smuggled himself aboard, and instead of stopping at Pluto the rocket ship shot out into deep space, where its passengers eventually found a habitable planet and started a new life. It was a pleasant enough story, though Eddie didn't feel it was very honest. He suspected the author knew quite well that there was no magic mineral that was suddenly going to turn the earth into a place made cheaply warm and fertile again. There were too many people and too much poison in the air and water. The sea was almost dead. His computers told him that the oil companies were still so powerful the federal government was putting almost no money at all into solar heating research; successful solar energy made cheap would put the utility companies out of business, and everyone knew it. Instead the government was pouring billions into nuclear reactors—which created radioactive garbage that would last a million years—and searches for new gas and oil fields— which couldn't whatever their extent, power the world for more than a century. Eddie hadn't learned that part from

his computers; he'd gotten the information from the New
York *Times*.

Sometimes he thought he was going a little crazy, hiding
out here in a cabin and playing with information and
money as if those things didn't matter outside his game.
Then he read the *Times* and felt he was saner than all the
politicians and generals. That didn't mean he wasn't crazy;
he knew that most nuts think they're the ones who have
the answers, they're the ones who hear the right questions.
But he didn't *feel* crazy. He simply felt that in a hundred
years if there was anyone still around, the *Times* would
read like a monument to institutional pathology.

He finished the novel and put it in a cardboard box
filled with the other books he'd read and finished since
he'd made his first trip to New York. Perhaps, when he finally left the place, he'd drop them off at some library or
some school. It seemed a shame to just let them go to
waste.

He looked at the printout sheets and was astounded. He
must have gotten access to a tape of miscellaneous things
that hadn't yet been assigned their proper categories.
There was information about a senator from Illinois who
had fourteen secret meetings with Arab oil executives anxious to boycott Jewish-owned firms in America. There was
a report about a senator who had a fetish for flat-chested
girls with very dark skin but who were not Negroid. There
was a report about a senator who had been picked up
three times in a sleazy section of Baltimore howling in the
streets. None of the three had been on Eddie's interroga-
tory list.

The stuff was a little too dirty for Eddie. He thought
people should have private lives. He put everything except
the report about the meetings with the Arabs in his burn
basket.

He had gotten to the point where he could ask twenty
different computers, WHAT CAN YOU TELL ME NOW? and
the computers would neatly type back for him questions
he might wish to ask sometime.

One of the books he had read was about when the Al-
lies cracked the German master code during World War
II. After that they were in on everything they wanted to
be in on. They knew everything the German generals said

to one another over the air. He felt like those Allied generals, but with one important difference: they had never themselves transmitted using that code because they couldn't afford to have the Germans know they knew it. Eddie could transmit whatever he wanted because his opponents couldn't know which information was theirs and which wasn't. They were totally dependent on what the computers told them.

It was like being the master voyeur of all time. It worked only for things that had been encoded and given to computers, but nowadays very little wasn't encoded and given to computers. Some of them even stored photographic information. The process had been developed by NASA for transmission and reestablishment of images from the Apollo and Mariner missions. Eddie wasn't equipped to handle visual imagers; they were very big and very expensive and very hard to get. But he could do everything else. Computers now took care of nearly everything for nearly everybody. And the machinery had become so fast and complex that people no longer even set and removed tapes; it was all done automatically from programmed data bank libraries. Only the most primitive units required manual accessioning, and Eddie had no need to talk to them.

He wiped perspiration from his eyes. In the past hour it had gotten hot in the van, even with the roof ventilator working and both front door windows open. The sun was high overhead. He turned off the machines, chopped up the sheets of paper in his burn basket, and carried it to the incinerator behind the cabin.

Until she said "Craig," he didn't know she had come up behind him. The papers in his hand flew into the air. "Hey, man," she said, "I didn't mean to frighten you. I'm sorry."

"I didn't know you were there." He was out of breath and his heart beat wildly in his chest.

"I won't do that again. I'll call to you from further away. It's all right. I'm sorry. It's just me."

It wasn't only that she had gotten so close without his hearing her steps approach; at first he also hadn't known who Craig was, so he was briefly confused. She knelt down and helped him pick up the slips of paper. She threw the handful into the fire without looking at them.

"You got a lot of confetti."

"Junk," he said, watching the strips brown, then burst into flame.

"It looks like confetti. You have to be more careful with that stuff."

"What do you mean?"

"Burning lightweight paper up here. When the fire gets going, the hot ashes fly into the air and they can start a fire in the trees." She looked around and picked up a blackened thin metal screen. She set it on top of the chimney. "That must have fallen off. Now you're not dangerous anymore."

She was dressed almost exactly as the day before, but instead of the sweat shirt she wore a blue work shirt with epaulettes. The top several buttons were open, and when she leaned to pick up the scraps he could see her breasts inside it, all the way to the brown and pink of the aureoles and nipples.

"The reason I came up here now," she said, "was to see if you were ready to go for a swim in the pool yet. I feel like going for a swim in the pool. I could go by myself, but I'd rather not."

"Sure," he said. "I've finished working for the afternoon. It's too hot to do anything now. But first what I'd really like to do, is—" He paused and found himself scraping the ground with the tip of his foot, just like a kid. Even after yesterday, the two times they had made love, the dinner with her friends, and the night of cool sleep, the words didn't come easily. He had never, in his entire life, directly asked a woman to go to bed with him.

"I was thinking about that too," she said. "You want to do it before or after the swim?"

He looked at her standing at ease a step or two away, at the open shirt, at the parts of her within reach, at her calm smile. "Let's try both," he said.

Later, when they were swimming, he watched her body disappear under the water. The ripples she made quickly moved out to where they were dissolved by the moving water heading toward the lower dam. She surfaced at his side.

"This is terrific," she said. "I'm really glad you made those dams. It's the only pool I know without chlorine. Doesn't need chlorine because the water is continually fresh. You know how many places in this part of the country you can swim in water that's continually fresh?" He shook his head. "Neither do I," she said, "but I bet it's not many. I think I'll take my bath up here from now on, if you don't mind."

"I wouldn't mind. I'll love it. Can I watch?"

"I insist. And I've got some biodegradable soap. It's an ugly word. But it means it won't do any damage." She laughed, swam away, deliberately splashing him. Then she swam back. "What are you staring at?" she said, seeing him looking at her intently.

"I've always wondered—this may seem crazy, but I've always wondered if they float."

She looked down at her breasts. The water came to just above her nipples, which were erect because of the cold. "You'll have to look again in five or ten years, pal. Or whenever it is they go saggy." She put a hand under one. "They're still pretty much in place. Not loose enough to do a study."

He reached out and put his hand under hers. She moved her hand away. The breast had a deliciously smooth texture in the water, cool and smooth. The nipple grew even harder as his thumb moved back and forth across it. He leaned forward and licked it gently, then he let his teeth lightly scrape where his tongue had just been.

"I just love that," she said, hugging him tightly. Suddenly he pushed her back. "What's the matter?" she said.

"My face was in the water. You were going to drown me."

"I'll *never* do that. I've never drowned anybody. Tell me, have you ever done this before? Felt a girl up in the water?"

"No."

"Is that true?" she asked.

"Yes," he said. She laughed. "You're making fun of me," he said.

"No. Yes, I am. Do you mind?"

"No. As long as I don't have to stop what I'm doing."

She moved against him. He felt the cold water and her body, warmer, firm.

"Let's go back to the cabin," she said.

"You want to try it in the water?"

"Wow," she said, "you are getting adventurous. For somebody who was a convict yesterday, you're a quick study. Some other time, maybe. The thing is, I'd concentrate on not drowning, and that's not what I prefer concentrating on. If you're really in a hurry, we can use the grass again."

"I suppose I can wait."

They walked to the cabin, holding hands. "To tell you the truth," she said, "I'm really a very conventional person. I prefer getting laid in a bed. It's more relaxed."

"I appreciate your conventions."

She stopped and looked at him directly. Her eyes were hazel this time. "Can I ask you a question?"

"You can ask anything you like," he said. "I won't promise to answer."

"What do you do in that van of yours?"

"Why?"

"Because I've seen you go in there and not come out for a long time. I was here for almost an hour before I came up to you at the incinerator. I didn't want to bother you while you were in there. I can't imagine what anyone would be doing alone in a van for so long a time when he's got a comfortable house not twenty feet away."

"Would you be offended if I didn't answer that?"

"Are you going to answer it?"

"No. I don't think I am."

"Then I won't be offended. I don't mean to pry. Well, that's not quite true. I'm just curious. It doesn't matter."

"Maybe sometime I'll tell you. But not now, okay?"

"Sure."

They made love for a long time in the bed. The curtains and windows were open. For a while the sun came into the room. He felt it warm on his back. Then it was warm on his chest, while her hands and mouth were cool, moving across his body. Afterwards they lay there without speaking, listening to the birds outside, watching the wind poke the curtain at the side of the window.

"The great thing about a bed is you don't have to get up and go somewhere else if you don't feel like it," she said. "You can just go to sleep?"

"You want to go to sleep?"

"Um. I do."

She just closed her eyes and was immediately away. He watched her for a while, listened to her breathing, listened to the sounds from the trees.

When he woke, she was sitting by his side, looking down at him. He moved his hand slowly across her back.

"You talked in your sleep," she said.

"What did I say?"

" 'Not to me you can't,' you said."

"What does that mean?"

"How should I know? You're the one who dreamed it. What were you dreaming."

"I don't have the faintest idea," he said. "I don't remember dreaming."

"At first I thought you were saying it to me."

"How many times did I say it?"

"Two or three. I don't know. It woke me up."

"Well, it wasn't to you. You can do anything you like."

"Anything?"

"Sure. You do fine things. At least you've done fine things so far."

She was quiet awhile. "Would you mind if I stayed here tonight? Would that bother you?"

"Why should it bother me? I'd love it."

"Because I know you're doing something you don't want anybody to know about and I worry you might not want anyone around. I wouldn't want to be around if it were a hassle. I've had enough of hassles, to tell you the truth."

"Please stay here with me tonight," he said. "That would be very nice."

"Thank you," she said. "I will."

She lay back on the pillow, close against him. Outside, the sky had gone a deep blue. He didn't know if it was late at night or if the moon was up. He tried to remember what phase of the moon it was. Last night had been dark, but perhaps they had been out before moonrise. Before he got it all together, he fell asleep again. At some point in the night she pulled the blankets over them. It had cooled, but he didn't waken enough to move. He felt the texture of the blankets, the smooth warmth of her body. He thought how curious it was that he felt perfectly at ease with this woman he hadn't known until yesterday, and how perfectly natural she felt sleeping at his side. And then he didn't feel anything for a long time.

When he woke, she was gone.

A strong odor of coffee had awakened him. The pot was on the stove, staying warm over a low flame. He poured a cup and walked to the porch. Nothing moved in the trees beyond the small clearing. The only sounds were birds in the branches and the wind. If it hadn't been for the coffee waiting on the stove, he might have dreamed the whole thing. He sat on the steps and watched the branches move, looked for small animals, tried to see the birds. Then he refilled his cup, went into the van, and started the day's work.

# FOURTEEN

The sun was low in the trees and his back ached because he had been in one position too long. He heard a man's voice outside yelling for Craig. He looked though the window, but couldn't see anyone, nor could he tell what direction the voice came from. As he stepped outside, he almost tripped; his left leg had gone numb. The dashboard clock registered three-thirty.

He didn't hear anything for a moment except the wind in the branches. Not even the birds. Then Franco crashed out of the woods. It was obvious why he never managed to creep up on any of the forest animals. Franco wasn't a creeper.

"Hey, man, when you didn't answer, I thought you maybe weren't around."

"I was doing something," Eddie said.

"Carla said you'd be around."

"And so I am."

"Right. She sent me up. She said to get you right away."

"Is something the matter?"

"No, everything's just fine. But she's all the way down at the inlet by the river. Actually, I volunteered to come up and get you. I didn't realize it was this far to the top. I've never seen your place. It's not bad. Not very big though."

"I'm alone here. If it had more room, it would be more work keeping it clean."

"You should do what I do."

"Travel with two women? I don't think I could manage that."

"I'm not sure I can either," Franco said. "And I'm not sure who's traveling with who, if you really want to know. The van is Sheila's. And Carla can be a difficult person. She makes me do the dishes one night out of three. And they make me do all the heavy stuff even though they're both as strong as I am, probably."

"I doubt that."

**183**

"Well, the heavy stuff usually ain't that heavy. But listen, the reason I came up: we've got a boat for the afternoon and we're going out on the river for a ride. You want to come along?"

"Where did you get a boat? Is it stolen?"

"Aw, Craig, that's not nice." Franco grinned, wide and friendly. "If we could have stolen it without getting into trouble, I maybe would have thought about it. But what happened was, the girls were in the village shopping for supplies and—"

"I thought you were living off the larder at the house."

"You get sick of canned things after a while. We did. We decided to spend a little of our communal capital and have a big dinner. It's Carla's idea. You're invited, of course, which is probably the idea. But they got talking with the guy who owns the grocery store and he told them he had a boat and they were welcome to use it."

"That's Toby Hinkes," Eddie said. "He owns the Mobil station next door."

"I don't know who he is because I've never been down there. I think they're crazy to go shopping around here. Someone may wonder where they're staying and we may get kicked out. But the girls said that people around here mind their own business, pretty much."

"That's true," Eddie said. "Most people."

"Anyhow, I thought at first he was trying to hustle them; you know, score by letting them know he had a boat and all that hotshot stuff, but they said he's about seventy years old. So if he *is* trying to hustle them, well, good for him, I say. So come on. They're waiting down below."

"All right," Eddie said. "Just give me a minute to lock up things around here."

"Lock up for what? There's no one here but us, and we're all going to be down there at the river."

"I just like to lock up."

"Whatever you say," Franco said. "Let's drive down in your van."

The computer equipment was all uncovered. He couldn't let Franco see the inside of the van.

"We can walk. It's a nice afternoon."

"It's over a mile back up the hill, man, and we'll be tired anyway by then."

"Okay. You go in the house and get a bottle of wine. We can drink it in the boat. I'll be ready in a minute."

Eddie went to the side of the van and unhooked the power and telephone lines. Then he went inside and rolled up the papers he had just been using and put them in a briefcase. He had covered the console and was just about to close the door on the monitor screen when he realized France was at the front door, watching him.

"This is one neat van," Franco said. "I've never seen one before with a TV in it. Not one this small, anyway. Do you get anything up here!"

"Not in the van. In the house I do. They've got an antenna and it's the highest point around. But not down here on the ground. Nothing makes it through the hills and trees unless you've got something really high. In the city it works okay."

"You got one of them funny roof antennas? I used to think they were for some kind of sophisticated radio equipment. I used to see this car all the time in my neighborhood that had one. Then I found out it was just a pimp with a small TV built into the dashboard to impress his women."

As they drove down the gravel road, Franco played with the scanner. He thought it was wonderful. "How come you don't have a CB?" he asked. "You got everything else."

Eddie showed him how the CB was part of the FM radio assembly. He explained that he could have the radio on and use the CB at the same time. Franco thought that was terrific. He said where he came from people always stole CBs from cars and trucks. "You'd think by now that everybody who wanted a CB would have one, but what I think has happened is they get stolen so much the radios are in constant circulation. One guy gets his ripped off and then he buys a hot one from someone else to replace the one that got taken from him, and then the guy who lost his to the first guy gets one. What's amazing is how they keep selling new ones."

The scanner stopped on the fourth red indicator light. Eddie explained that the light staying on meant there was a continuing transmission on that frequency. A voice from the speaker said, "Outstanding warrant inquiry. 1970 Buick. White. License plate 333EUB. Registered in the name of T. E. Arthur." The light went out and the row flickered again, one light on after the other in rapid succession.

"What's that about?" Franco asked.

"That's probably a state cop over on the interstate. It's the state police frequency. He's stopped a car for a violation and he's asking Albany if there are any violations outstanding against it. The computer in Albany will take a few seconds." The radio sequenced to another light. "That's the state police headquarters frequency." A woman's voice reported that there were no outstanding violations against Buick NY 333EUB. The trooper acknowledged the information.

"Hey," Franco said, "that's dynamite. How come you got that kind of radio? You're not some kind of a—"

"No, Franco. Not on your life. Don't worry. I just like to know what those people are doing sometimes, and this seemed a good way. It's illegal, by the way."

"Having a scanner? I see them advertised all the time."

"It's illegal having one in a car. You can have one in your house. If you have one in your car, you're supposed to have authorization from all the agencies using the frequencies you have crystals for."

"Do you?"

"Have authorization? No. Not for any of them."

"So you're parking there illegally, just like us in the house." Franco clapped his hands. "Wonderful! Now we've got something on you too."

"Were you worried that I'd say something to someone about you living in that house?"

"A little. You never know. You run into some weird people these days."

"But you know about Carla and me—"

"Yeah. But you run into some weird people these days. I don't think you're *that* kind of weird, if you want to know the truth. Maybe some other kind, but not that kind. Here." He handed Eddie a joint he had just rolled and lighted. "Might as well get in a fine nautical mood."

The two women were waiting for them at the dock.

Five boats were tied up there, all but one fitted with outboard motors.

"I thought you got lost again," Sheila said.

"I never get lost in daylight," Franco said.

"You never got lost at night before the time you got lost. That doesn't mean anything."

"You sure this is the right boat?" Franco asked. "They all look alike."

"They're all Toby's," Sheila said. "He rents them in the summer by the hour. He said we could use any one we liked, and I like the blue of this one."

"It's good we talked to him now," Carla said. "He told us he's going to be putting them away for the season before long."

They climbed down into the boat. Carla untied the mooring line. The boat drifted a few feet away from the dock.

"Don't you need a key or something?" Franco asked.

"No," Sheila said.

Franco looked at Eddie. "You ever drive one of these things?"

"No. You?"

"Nope." He looked at Sheila and Carla. Both shook their heads.

"It probably works just like a lawn mover," Eddie said. "Let's see." He leaned over the engine and found a choke control, which he set, and a toggle connnected to a rope. The throttle was on the steering arm. He held onto the steering arm and pulled the toggle. Nothing happened. He pulled again. Nothing happened. He jiggled the choke.

The boat was rocking gently. It had drifted out from the cove into the river.

"This damned thing doesn't work," Sheila said.

"Lemme try it," Franco said.

"We should have taken an oar," Sheila said. "We're drifting downriver. Oh, shit!"

"One more time," Eddie said.

"Lemme try it," Franco said, moving toward the stern.

Eddie pulled the toggle and there was a sudden roar, a plume of smoke bubbled from below the waterline, and the boat hurtled forward. Eddie almost fell overboard, but he grabbed the gunwale and held on. He realized he had the throttle wide open. He released his grip; the boat stopped turning and almost stopped moving. The engine dropped back to a slow idle. The two women were sitting down, staring at him.

"Well," Carla said, "it works."

"Yeah," Sheila said. "Now can we go back and get Franco?"

Eddie hadn't noticed Franco was gone. He looked over the engine and saw him treading water twenty-five feet behind them. He was slapping the water furiously with his hands.

"Maybe you better hurry," Sheila said. "I don't think he knows how to swim."

"Goddammit, Captain Ahab," Franco muttered after they pulled him aboard, "you got to learn how to drive."

"You're getting the boat all wet, Franco," Carla said.

"Very funny," he said, "very funny." His face changed. "Oh, shit! Oh, goddamn and shit!" He put his hand to his chest. "Damn!"

"What's the matter? What's wrong? Carla moved alongside him quickly, almost turning them over. "Did you hurt yourself?"

"No."

"Then what's wrong?" Carla asked.

"Goddammed dope got wet."

# FIFTEEN

The days were like none he had ever known. He worked most mornings in his van. Nights he spent with Carla. Sometimes she came up in the afternoon and they went down to the pools, though the weather was changing so quickly they hadn't done that much lately. Other times, if he was busy, she sat on the porch of the cabin and read, waiting for him to come out. It was very pleasant to sit at the console and watch the words appear on the papers or the video screen knowing she was out there whenever he decided he was done. She never again asked what he was doing. His information files grew thicker and thicker; he could talk to almost any information center in the country now.

One day the IFFI computer in Baltimore told him someone had been asking questions about him. The computer said it had been alerted to tell an auxiliary computer if questions were posed that did not have a secret preface number. Eddie asked what the secret preface number was and the computer said it had been programmed not to utter that datum. There was no way to break that command, Eddie found out, at least not with the information currently at his disposal.

HAVE YOU ALERTED THE AUXILIARY? Eddie asked.

AFFIRMATIVE, the computer said.

WHAT IS AUXILIARY DOING NOW?

TRACING you.

Eddie broke off the connection immediately.

He sat very still. It was like when he was a child, afraid of the dark, and convincing himself that if he didn't move at all, didn't make a single sound, whatever was out there would go away without doing him any harm, wouldn't even know he was there.

He waited an hour. There was nothing to do but wait, and he couldn't concentrate on anything else. He looked at his watch and decided he had waited long enough. He called IFFI and asked, DID THEY TRACE ME?

NOT YET.

He disconnected. He was safe for now. The second inquiry wouldn't have been long enough for them to get a trace going. But he didn't know how much they already knew, how far they had gotten, and he couldn't know which of his sources was covered . . . waiting for him. There was only one way to find out: ask the computers to find out for him, and do the asking from a place he could afford to abandon immediately.

Not here. He wasn't ready to leave here yet.

He told Carla he would have to go somewhere that night.

"Oh. Shall I come along?"

"I wish you could. But it's not possible. It's business."

"All right. Whatever you wish."

They had dinner and then sat on the porch steps drinking wine. An owl had taken residence a short way down the drive. He was calling out into the night. They saw him swoop down across the roadway and then disappear again into the trees.

"Scratch one field mouse," she said.

"You have to be very careful when you're alone in the dark," Eddie said.

"You have to be careful anyway."

When they finished the wine, Eddie said it was time for him to go. She asked if he was coming back.

"Of course I'm coming back. What kind of question is that? All my clothes are in the cabin. I wouldn't just not come back."

"People do weird things sometimes. I was just asking."

"I'll see you in the morning."

"Maybe I'll sleep up here tonight anyway."

"Do that. I'll wake you when I get back."

She sat on the porch with the empty glass in her hand and waved as he backed the van out into the turning space.

Eddie reached the highway, tucking his van inside a long line of heavy trucks maintaining a steady sixty-five. He didn't bother turning on the CB. The big machines would set a safe pace for him. He was thinking about faceless people hovering over computer consoles in distant cities, waiting for him to call back so they could capture him. It was like a game, except those people were deadly serious.

Just before Albany he saw a long strip of motels off to the right. The first was a Holiday Inn, which was no good for him because the vehicles were all parked in a large lot and access to the rooms was through the main lobby. He needed more privacy than that. There were a few sleazy motels, which he ignored. He didn't ignore them because of their sleaziness, which didn't matter for his purposes tonight, but rather because he had learned that such motels routed all telephone calls through a manual switchboard. At the end of the row was a new Ramada Inn. Its two parking lots were long black rectangles facing the doors of the rooms. There weren't many vehicles parked there.

The clerk smiled mechanically and pushed a form across the desk. Did the gentleman have a reservation? Eddie said he had no reservation. The clerk said that didn't matter. Then Eddie asked if there was a ground floor room away from the noise of the highway.

"All our rooms are sound-insulated, sir, but I can give you one on the back side of the building if you prefer. It's very quiet over there."

"That will be fine." Eddie filled out the form, using a phony name. He paused at the space for the vehicle license number.

The clerk took the form. "Can't remember it, huh? Happens all the time. Don't bother." Before Eddie could respond, the clerk called to a bellboy sitting on a soft chair near the door. "Jerry, check that tag for me on the van, huh?"

Jerry leaned over and tried to read the tag without getting out of his chair. He could barely see the plate.

"You gotta get up, Jerry," the clerk said.

"If I gotta get up, then you can go read it." Jerry leaned a little more, bracing himself by putting his hand against the large plate glass. He read off the numbers and letters, then leaned back and said, "See?" He folded his arms across his chest and went back to sleep. On the glass was a large greasy imprint of his palm and fingers.

Jerry had misread the two Bs as eights. The clerk wrote

down the incorrect number, took Eddie's money, and gave him a key.

"Hey," the clerk said as Eddie started through the glass doors.

"What?" Eddie froze.

"Forgot your receipt."

"So I did," Eddie said, walking back to the desk. "Thanks."

"Need it for Uncle," the clerk said.

"Thanks."

He drove to the room and sat for a few minutes with the motor still running. He had three options. He could leave the key in the room and drive back to his cabin right now. He could sleep the night and drive back to his cabin in the morning. Or he could go ahead with his plan and risk their tracing his transmission to this location.

On the card they had a bogus name and an incorrect plate number. Not much to go on. He had to know what the government computers knew about him, how close they were. If they were really getting close, he could continue driving, not go back at all.

He pictured Carla waiting for him in the morning, waking up and finding him still not there, staying awhile in the bed and then getting up and sitting on the porch, waiting for a sound of tires on the gravel road through the trees and then on the dirt driveway, not hearing the sound, and then walking slowly down the hill to the other place.

He would take the chance. It couldn't be very great. They might trace the call to the motel before he was done, but he could be gone by the time they came looking. They couldn't very well connect the man in the motel with Craig Hemsworth in that mountain cabin so far south. They would have a wrong name and useless plate number in their way.

He carried the console inside, then turned on the room's television set loudly so people in adjoining rooms, if there were any, wouldn't hear the sounds of the typewriter keys. He had read somewhere that people in motels weren't disturbed by loud television—it was part of a hotel environment—but they were disturbed by other noises. He didn't want anyone complaining to the desk about Selectrics in the night.

Very carefully he checked the telephone to make sure there wasn't a disconnect alarm, the sort of thing they had on the television sets. The wiring seemed standard. But there might be something in the wall circuit, so to be safe he simply took the plastic case off the phone and coupled the leads to his black box input without opening the telephone line's circuitry. Then he connected the black box to the console's touch-tone board.

The first trick was to make the automatic telephone device out front think he was making a local call, for which the motel did not charge—therefore the desk would not be alerted. He didn't know how long he would be on the line. He used an Albany 800 exchange, which meant he didn't have to dial one before the 800 number; it was a local connection that put him in potential contact with the world.

He turnd on the console. It was working perfectly. He then punched out six sequences of 800 exchanges. The final number was IFFI in Baltimore. His first question was, IS THIS CALL BEING MONITORED?

AFFIRMATIVE.

IS IT BEING TRACED?

AFFIRMATIVE.

TIME FOR SUCCESSFUL TRACE?

THREE MINUTES PER CIRCUITED EXCHANGE.

That meant they knew he wasn't calling directly. He had eighteen minutes, plus the local connection. Twenty-one minutes. A world of time on a computer. He was ready with his questions.

WHAT IS CODE FOR PROGRAM?

COMPUTER BANDIT.

WHAT IS KNOWN ABOUT COMPUTER BANDIT?

The screen rapidly filled with the dates and amounts of his American Express thefts, some of his recent information scans, the reports to the newspapers in New York. There was nothing about any of his delayed command operations, nothing about any of his inquiries of federal computers in Boston and San Francisco. And nothing about Buffalo.

He was astounded that there was nothing about Buffalo. He thought that would have been the first series of penetrations they would have discovered after the AmEx operations. He couldn't ask about Buffalo: if they hadn't connected him with the operations there, his question would do that for them.

TERMINATED ASPECTS OF COMPUTER BANDIT CASE? he typed.

FOUR BUFFALO INCIDENTS, IFFI said. The screen described some of his activities there the night he left.

WHY TERMINATED?

DETERMINED SEPARATE CASE. PENETRATIONS BY EDWARD ARGO. SUICIDE. IFFI gave Eddie the date of Edward Argo's suicide in the Black Rock Canal.

WHERE IS COMPUTER BANDIT?

SOUTHERN NEW YORK STATE PROBABILITY .6. BOSTON PROBABILITY .3. OTHER PROBABILITIES NEGLIGIBLE.

WHO IS IN CHARGE?

FRANCIS X. KELLY. FBISACBUFFALO.

IS KELLY NOW ON LINE?

AFFIRMATIVE.

TELL KELLY COMPUTER BANDIT SAYS HELLO.

MESSAGE TRANSMITTED.

He caught himself. It was foolish to spend time playing. He had only fourteen minutes left before they got a make on this phone.

And he had a nagging suspicion. Something was wrong. This was too easy. They couldn't be this stupid. They *could* be, but he didn't think they were. He couldn't count on the likelihood that they were.

REAFFIRM TIME FOR TRACE, he typed.

The screen responded immediately. THREE MINUTES PER CIRCUITED EXCHANGE.

IS THAT IFFI'S INTERNAL CALCULATION OR PROGRAMMED RESPONSE?

PROGRAMMED RESPONSE.

Goddamn! He had taken the computer at face value. He had assumed that since computers never lie they always told the truth. He forgot that men told them what to say and men lied regularly.

STATUS OF TRACE. REPORT.

BALTIMORE. ST. LOUIS. SAN FRANCISCO. NEW ORLEANS. THE BRONX. MONTREAL. ALBANY.

HOW LONG SINCE ALBANY ASCERTAIN?

THREE MINUTES PER CIRCUITED EXCHANGE.

YOU'RE LYING TO ME.

VERB FORM NOT IN PROGRAM. REPHRASE.

Eddie unhooked his cables and shut down the console. Within five minutes he was back on the highway. As he left the motel, two Ford sedans were pulling into the driveway. They could have been regular motel customers, late-arriving businessmen, but there was a good possibility they weren't customers at all, that they were the police, homing in on the trace.

A lying computer was a dangerous machine, as he well knew.

He kept scanning the rearview mirrors to see if he was being followed. There was no way to tell. In the dark he could see only distant headlights back there. He left the highway, drove a few miles west, then turned south again on a blacktop road. He found a quiet grove of trees and backed the van in with its lights off. He sat there with his hands folded in his lap, listening to the scanner. He heard an inquiry from a trooper for a violations check on a red Plymouth that had been speeding on the Thruway. The radio was silent after Albany told the trooper the Plymouth was stolen.

With his flashlight Eddie looked carefully at the map. It was no good sitting here. He had to get home and off the road in a safe place. But he was better off avoiding the main highways. Those safe wide roads with their controlled-access ramps were traps.

Eddie wished he had gotten a van with a more powerful engine, one that could really race. He imagined himself outrunning a line of police cars as he had seen Robert Mitchum do a long time ago in a movie about a moonshiner. *Thunder Road*. Then he remembered how it ended: Mitchum's car left the pavement on a curve and crashed into a high-voltage transformer. Eddie was no race driver. In a high-speed chase he'd wind up killing himself.

He drove quickly, listening to both the CB and the scanner. Except for an occasional exchange of talk between truckers, he heard nothing until he was twenty miles from home. An alert report came over the state police channel. They were to look for a van with the license plate number 838010. Close, but no cigar. The alert didn't say what kind of van or what color. No trooper called back to ask for more information, which meant none was working in the area. He was still lucky.

He reached the gravel road a little after 2 A.M. He felt a great sense of relief when he turned in and listened to the tires loudly crunching as the van whined up the hill. As he passed into the area where the tree's branches closed in overhead, the terror came back. He was blind everywhere the headlights didn't point directly. A hundred of them could be there, waiting on the side of the road.

The worst thing about paranoia, he decided, is there's no way to know if you are right or wrong until it's too late. If the beasts are imaginary, you could call yourself a fool for thinking they were waiting to leap; if they were real, the satisfaction that you were right would form cold comfort.

Halfway up the road he backed the van into the driveway of a cottage he knew was vacant. He pulled it far back so it couldn't be seen from the road. He sat awhile and listened to the night. Nothing but the wind and the owls. He got out and closed the door quickly, momentarily blinded by the interior light that came on automatically when the door was opened. If anyone was watching, they would have seen it.

If anyone was watching, they would already have seen the van. He had to keep himself in control. The most important thing was keeping in control.

He walked to the gravel road and headed up the hill. The wind in the trees grew louder. A crackling noise from the brush to his right made him gasp. He stood absolutely still and heard a small animal scurry across the road ahead of him.

His cabin was dark. There were no cars or other vehicles anywhere around it. He began to relax. The porch boards creaked as he took the top step.

There was a sudden movement inside the cabin, and immediately he jumped off the porch and crouched in the darkness. He heard from the doorway the *chu-chunk* sound of a shotgun being pumped.

"Who there?" Carla yelled. "Somebody's out there. You better show yourself, you sonofabitch, or I'll blow your goddamned head off."

"It's me, Craig."

"Goddamn you," she said. "You scared the living hell out of me. You said you weren't coming back until morning. I heard someone on the step. I didn't hear the— Where's your van? Did you have an accidnet? Are you okay?"

"Slow down, slow down. I'm fine. I left it down the hill, in one of the driveways. I'm sorry I frightened you."

"Why did you leave it down the hill?"

"I don't know. Something crazy. I just wanted to walk up the hill. Okay?"

"Sure. It's your hill. But, man, I could have *shot* you with this thing."

Eddie took the gun away from her and walked inside the cabin. He put it back on the two pegs where it had rested since he first moved up. "No," he said. "It's not loaded. The magazine is empty."

"It's not loaded? Shit. And what if I'd put some shells into it?"

"Then you could have shot me."

"I don't know where the shells are. What good's an unloaded gun? Some pervert could have assaulted me."

"And do you think you would have shot someone with it? Really?"

"If I knew it was a pervert? Goddamned right I would."

"And how would you find out if he was a pervert or not?"

She giggled. "I guess I'd have to invite him in for a test."

The cabin was still dark. He saw her silhouetted against the window, a black form against the deep blue of the sky outside.

"Let's go to bed," he said. "I've had a bad night."

She turned and walked to the other room without saying a word. After he got undressed and was in bed beside her, she rolled over so she could nuzzle against his side. "I'm glad you got back early," she said, "even if you did have a bad night and even if you did scare the shit out of me. Protect me from the goddamned perverts."

"My pleasure."

# SIXTEEN

Buffalo SAC Kelly was enraged. He was so enraged Purvey told the other agents in the office and Miss Leipzig, Kelly's secretary, that he was not to be disturbed for anything less important than a call from the Director's office.

"What's bugging him?" Miss Leipzig asked.

"I wish you wouldn't use that word around here," Purvey said.

"You know what I mean."

"The Computer Bandit said *hello* to him last night."

"What's so bad about that? I thought he had been trying to start a conversation with the Computer Bandit for three months now. It's all he's been doing lately. Ask me: I know." She pointed to a stack of papers on her desk. Purvey knew they were files Kelly hadn't had time to work through because of his concentration on the UCI cases.

"The Computer Bandit talked to him on his computer line last night and Mr. Kelly didn't catch him. That's why he's in a horrible mood."

"You mean that computer he's got in his house?" Miss Leipzig asked. Purvey nodded. "I knew no good would come of that. Craziest thing I ever heard, a SAC putting a computer terminal in his bedroom."

It's not in his bedroom. It's in his living room. His wife made him take it out of the bedroom.

"You know what I mean, Mr. Purvey." She heaved a heavy, matronly sigh.

"I certainly do, Miss Leipzig."

"I thought you would." She smiled up at him.

Miss Leipzig had never married. She had been the personal secretary to the Buffalo SAC for twenty-two years now. She had been here through seven different SACs and was generally regarded as the most reliable source of information in the district office. She was extremely reliable, and gave information only to people she liked and trusted, as three previous SACs had discovered, much to their personal dismay and professional malaise. She thought SAC

Kelly a likely candidate for a coronary or a bleeding ulcer within a few years; anyone who took a computer home with him had problems dissociating his private and professional lives, and such dissociation was necessary for physical and psychic survival. Miss Leipzig thought A-SAC Purvey a man who understood very well the terms for survival; when he was off duty and it wasn't one of his on-call nights, he was impossible to find. She knew where he was most of those nights, but she never told him that or called him there. Lately she had begun giving Purvey little bits of information on various affairs of the office he might find useful. She thought it likely that within a few years Purvey, even with his sense of humor, would be an associate or deputy director of the Bureau. Purvey didn't know it yet, but Purvey didn't know as much about the Bureau as Miss Leipzig did.

The auxiliary computer monitoring IFFI in Baltimore had automatically dialed Kelly's home telephone number when the conversation with the Computer Bandit started. It had been programmed to do that almost a month ago, after a meeting Kelly had with several researchers from IBM and a telephone company senior technician. IBM had found out about some of the UCIs, and was apparently a victim of more incidents than they had yet told the FBI about. They feared that widespread knowledge of such assaults could cripple the company's operations. If computer behaviors were subject to random intrusions by madmen and burglars, then nothing was safe. No computation was reliable, no information pool could be thought uncontaminated, and no money would be coming in.

Kelly had been authorized by the Director to utilize the classified unlimited budget fund. It was a great responsibility and a fine opportunity.

The first thing he did was have computer terminals with video screen readouts installed in his bedroom and his office. Mary Ellen told him she would not have that ugly device in her bedroom, and Purvey told him that they had no records of the transmissions they were getting. "We need a machine that types it all out."

"We haven't gotten any transmissions yet," Kelly said.

"But maybe we will. We'd better, after what this cost the Bureau."

"We will," Kelly said. "You can be sure of that."

The consoles were replaced with a new model which, the IBM representative said, took up less space than its predecessor and weighed less than one hundred pounds. It was exactly the same as the unit Eddie had bolted into his Chevrolet van, though Kelly didn't know that.

When the new unit was installed in Kelly's living room, the IBM technician said he would program whatever computer they were connected with to ring Kelly's home telephone number whenever a transmission was coming in. That way he would know when the Computer Bandit was working, day or night.

"Jesus, Mary, and Joseph," Mary Ellen said. "On top of everything else we're going to be getting calls in the middle of the night from a *machine*."

"Only a few," Kelly said. "And then we'll catch him."

Kelly's son complained that the terminal looked like hell in the living room, and he wanted to know what his father intended to do if the computer started working while he was watching one of his programs. It wasn't fair to bring an FBI office home and keep a kid from his programs, he said.

"What I'll do is have the nuns rap your *other* knuckles until you learn some respect, that's what I'll do."

Only young Flora didn't complain. Young Flora never complained. She was sixteen, did perfect work in school, and said she was going to be either a nun or a doctor. She had blue eyes and red hair, just like her father.

It hadn't been that easy establishing the computer system in the first place. The basic problem, according to the IBM technician, was they couldn't listen to the Computer Bandit's conversations and trace him if they didn't know what computer he was addressing at any given time.

"Why not just tell all the computer centers in the country to notify us when a suspicious inquiry occurs?" Kelly asked.

"Because," said the IBM technician, looking at him patronizingly, "there are now over 350,000 separate computer installations operating in the continental United States. It's impossible."

"Even for IBM?"

"Even for IBM."

"I didn't know anything was impossible for IBM," Kelly said.

"Few things are. It's not *technically* impossible, by the way; it's *financially* impossible. We have the technology, of course."

Kelly decided that the IBM man looked just like a lot of FBI men he knew. They wore the same kinds of suits and shoes and carried the same kinds of briefcases. It was too bad the FBI had to spend the 1960s infiltrating ratty little radical organizations for which they had to wear foolish clothes. It would have been perfect if they had some reason to infiltrate IBM instead. They could have worn their own clothes. He didn't tell the IBM man that.

"Let's ask the CIA," Purvey said. "I bet they've got machinery that can do it."

"No," the IBM man said. "They haven't. I know exactly what they've got working now and they can't handle this any more than you can."

"What does the CIA have operating now?" Kelly asked. It was the chance of a lifetime. The CIA never told them anything anymore.

"Not on your life, Mr. Kelly," the IBM man said. "That's classified information and you know it."

"But I'm an FBI Bureau SAC. I've got Q-clearance."

"This is R-double-Q."

"I've never heard of R-double-Q," Kelly said.

"Exactly what I've been telling you, Mr. Kelly. Now can we get back to your problem?"

"It's your problem too," Kelly said, trying to control his anger.

"It belongs to all of us, Mr. Kelly."

Kelly was furious that a minor functionary from a computing instrument company had higher security clearance than he did. That didn't seem right. The FBI was supposed to have access to everything, to all the secrets. That's what the FBI was paid to do, look at everybody's secrets.

The IBM man pointed out that on four separate occasions in the past month apparently spurious inquiries had been processed by the criminal information data bank in Baltimore, the IFFI installation.

"I'm familiar with that," Kelly said.

"Of course, sir," the IBM man said dryly. "We have no

idea what information was extracted in those inquiries because the nature of the transactions was electronically erased at the termination of each conversation. But we do know that the New York *Times*, subsequent to each episode, published articles they claimed had been researched by an investigative reportorial team. One of the articles had to do with a quashed bribery case involving two southern senators and a natural gas exploration consortium. Another was about a congressman whose wife recently opened a numbered Swiss bank account for over two hundred thousand dollars, all of which apparently arrived in Switzerland on a plane from one of the small Arab emirates. IBM and FBI officials both agree that the only way those *Times* reporters could have gotten that information was if someone had access to the IFFI files you fellows put together. Which means that was probably the data in those spurious conversations."

Kelly was annoyed that the IBM man talked about IBM and FBI officials as if they were on a par, as if they were the same kind of executives. Everyone knew that the FBI was a law enforcement agency while IBM was just an information-processing company. There was all the difference in the world.

"We should bug the New York *Times*," Kelly said.

"You already do," the IBM man said.

The IBM man suggested that they put a constant monitor on the criminal justice computer system. IFFI would have a standby mechanism in constant readiness which would, immediately on receipt of a spurious address, begin working through the telephone company circuits to trace the source of the call.

"Beautiful," Kelly said, "just beautiful. Hoist with his own petard, as they say, right?"

"Maybe, maybe not."

"What do you mean? Why 'maybe not'?"

"Your friend will be able to see us."

"What the hell does that mean? I thought these screens put out only words and numbers."

"That's not what I had in mind. If we set up a system to monitor his inquiries, he can inquire and the machine has to tell him we're on the line. But we can confuse him a little." It was his idea to have the machine give the three-minute-per-circuit statement, which required the computer to draw from its stored information rather than examine its current status. "The machines have to tell the truth," the IBM man said, "unless we feed the lies to tell. Then they tell lies which they think are the truth. It's easy. We do it all the time. It's no problem at all."

They were joined by a representative from the telephone company and Purvey.

The telephone company representative, whose name was Barstow, said his team was sure that the calls were all circuited through 800 exchanges. "No one this sophisticated with computers would be silly enough to dial directly in." The IBM man said that was their thinking too. Barstow said the company could do specific number searches on direct lines in slightly under fifty-four seconds. The equipment was linked together in a way Kelly didn't quite understand, but they told Kelly it came to this: if the Computer Bandit thought to ask IFFI how much time he had, he would be off by a multiple of three. "Actually, slightly more than three," the IBM man said. Barstow nodded in agreement. "If he's really got ten minutes, he'll be told he's got thirty. It's lovely."

"Elegant," Barstow said.

"Why not tell him he's got an hour?" Kelly asked.

"Because he's not an idiot," Barstow said. "And anyone who knows anything about the telephone company knows we can trace calls in only a few minutes." Kelly reddened, but Barstow ignored his obvious anger. "We've got to feed him an estimate that is believable—"

"—but totally inaccurate," the IBM man said.

"Right," Barstow said.

"It's like *Battleship*," Purvey said, smiling at Barstow and the IBM man.

"You understand perfectly," the IBM man said. "That's exactly what it is."

Kelly scowled. Purvey spoke without waiting for the question. "It's a game kids play, boss. You make a grid and try to capture the other guy's ships, you try to sink them. You know where your opponent's ships are only when you make a direct hit. The rules say he has to tell you when you make a strike, but you've got to decide where to hit, which is the same here as—"

"—where and when to ask the questions," Barstow said. "We've got to have our computers ready to ask other computers if he's talking. They'll tell us, but he'll know—if he thinks to ask them, which I'm sure he will since he's no dummy—what we've just found out."

"If the game works perfectly," the IBM man said, "any question by either side offers the opponent an opportunity to extract information. Neither of us can get information about the other without risking loss of information, and neither can get information when information isn't being requested. It's very interesting."

"So it is," Barstow said. Purvey nodded in agreement.

"We're not talking about *games*," Kelly said, his face an even darker color than it had been when Barstow implied he was an idiot. "We're talking about *crime*, gentlemen. *Crime!* We're talking about the theft of funds from one of America's most respected corporations. We're talking about interfering with taxes. We're talking about taking other people's information!" By the time he finished, he was standing and pounding furiously with his fist on his hardwood desk. The other three men looked at him blankly, carefully keeping their expressions neutral. They didn't look at one another.

"Well," Purvey said after a while, "crime is our problem, not theirs. These gentlemen are perfectly entitled to look upon it all as a game if they put us on the winning side. Right, chief?" He smiled. The IBM man smiled. Barstow nodded in agreement again.

"I want that sonofabitch," Kelly said.

One week later, a Wednesday just before midnight, the bedside telephone rang. Kelly picked it up on the second ring. A mechanical voice said, "Spurious intrusion in process. IFFI here."

"See," Mary Ellen mumbled. "I *knew* it."

Kelly leaped from the bed and ran to the living room, terrifying Flora and one of her boyfriends, a seventeen-year-old fellow named Roger. Roger still had acne.

Flora leaped up, grabbing at the front of her sweater. "Oh, Daddy," she shrieked, "I thought you were asleep." She seemed to have trouble breathing. The boy was backing toward the door. His face revealed his doubt; he wasn't sure he could make it before the old man cut him off. He was grateful only that the old man hadn't come into the room five minutes later, by which time he expected to have Flora's panties off and himself in the promised land, which he had been assiduously trying to penetrate for almost three months now. Flora did not give it away easily; she knew she had to be careful of her reputation. So far it had only been bare tit and mutual handgigs.

"Get out of here!" Kelly screamed.

"Yes, sir," Roger said, believing in sudden salvation for the first time. "I was just going. *Yes, sir*." He turned and raced for the door.

Kelly turned toward his daughter, who by this time had the sweater pulled down and the brassiere looking almost as if it were hooked in the back. "Daddy," she crooned, "I—"

"You, too! You get out of here, too. This is official business!"

Roger heard the words from the porch. He slowed down and allowed her to catch up with him, and the two of them ran for his car, still parked in the driveway. The father had never given her permission to be out after eleven on a school night before and it wasn't an opportunity to be missed. Especially considering Roger's advanced state of anticipation.

When they were gone, Kelly activated the screen and watched the conversation going back and forth between the Bandit and the computer. His telephone rang. He didn't answer it for a while.

"Well, answer it, Francis," Mary Ellen yelled from the bedroom. "It's probably your computer calling again."

"It's not the computer," he yelled back.

"Then it's another one of your bizarre friends. Answer the phone so I can get some sleep."

She still hadn't forgiven him for not letting Francis transfer to Nichols. The last time they had talked about it, he reminded her that it wasn't a Catholic school and they had agreed years ago on the importance of having the children get a good traditional Catholic education. "That was before they started torturing my children," she said. She reminded Kelly that he didn't go to church since Easter, and if the whole Catholic business was so important to him, *how come* he didn't go to church and *how come* he didn't object when she had her tubes tied? He told her it wasn't the same thing. It wasn't the same thing at all. She guffawed. It was impossible to argue with her sometimes, she was so damned Irish.

He picked up the phone. "What is it?" he growled.

"Purvey here, boss. They're communicating."

"I know that. How do you know that?"

"I'm down here at the office and the system just went on. Thought you'd like to know in case the phone device didn't wake you up or something."

The sonofabitch is checking up to see if I'm here, Kelly thought.

"You get on the tracing operation, Purvey. Alert all our standby units in Rochester and Albany and Binghamton and Yonkers. Everyone be ready to move as soon as we get a make on the telephone."

"I've already done that, sir. They're all standing by. I'm waiting for the phone company to call back now. Should only take a few minutes more."

"Call me back when you have something to say."

Kelly hung up. He felt his blood pressure boiling upward, and he knew that if Mary Ellen came into the room now, she'd forget her argument and worry about the color of his face. It was because of the questions that had framed themselves in his mind: what the fuck was Purvey doing in the office at midnight on a Wednesday and who was the sonofabitch really reporting to?

It occurred to him that if he knew how to operate a computer terminal, he could sit down at the console right in front of him and ask some memory bank somewhere those two questions. Just the sort of thing the Computer Bandit liked to do. The Computer Bandit, of course, knew how to do it.

If only he had an image of the Computer Bandit, his opponent, it would be easier. Then he could picture the man out there, have some sense of his physical movements. What if he was short? Or black? Or an Indian? The last was unthinkable. Who ever heard of Indians using a computer to help them steal? It wasn't their MO. He went back to picturing a middle-sized, middle-aged white man. The white man wore a business suit; his necktie and top shirt button were loosened. Maybe he was wondering about his opponent, the anonymous but powerful agent of justice out there, pursuing him with all the force of the United States Government.

Then the words on the screen snapped his fantasy shut:
TELL KELLY COMPUTER BANDIT SAYS HELLO.

Tell *Kelly?* The arrogance of the sonofabitch. Who was watching who?

The telephone rang. It was Purvey. "He's got your name, boss."

"I know that, Purvey. I can read."

"Right. And we've got *him.*"

"You've got him? You got the little sonofabitch?"

"Not exactly. We know where he is. Two cars are on the way now. They'll be on the scene in less than ten minutes. The Ramada Inn eight miles south of Albany."

The conversation on the screen stopped. Kelly read over the first part of the conversation between the Computer Bandit and IFFI. He roiled again when he saw the greeting to himself. He sat back in his chair and waited for the telephone to ring. It didn't ring. He poured himself a long whiskey and drank it. Then he poured another.

"You shouldn't drink so fast," Mary Ellen said from the bedroom doorway. "It's not good for you."

"I'm working," he growled. "Leave me alone. I'm busy."

"If you're working, you shouldn't be drinking at all. The Director never approved of drinking on duty."

She meant Hoover. Hoover was dead now. There wasn't much that Hoover had approved of. By God, Kelly thought, he had loved that man. He was like a father, but a father who never let you down as long as you did the right thing at the right time. With the Director there was never any ambiguity about what the right thing was: catch the bastards, make sure it gets into the papers, and do nothing to dishonor the Bureau. Kelly thought about it a moment and realized he had the order reversed. For the Director, the Bureau came first, a good press second, and catching crooks third. There was only one Bureau, but there were lots of crooks.

The telephone rang again. He picked it up before the first ring was completed. "Do you have him?"

"Uh, no, sir," Purvey said. "The boys got there a little

too late. He'd already left by the time the agents got to the motel. But there were fingerprints all over the room; they've already determined that."

"His prints?"

"Impossible to tell. A lot of prints. There weren't any on the doorway except the agent's who went in first. The telephone was absolutely clean, though."

"Idiots. Fucking idiots."

"Albany office, sir."

"What else? Do you have *anything*?"

"He had a van. We're trying to determine the color. And we've got the license number. Checking it out through the Albany state computer now. And we've got his name. He wrote it out for the desk clerk."

"What makes you think he chose to offer a correct name, Purvey?"

"Oh. You think he maybe used a phony name, huh?" Kelly was silent. "I guess he probably did. But there *is* the license number. I've put out a call to the state police to stop the vehicle if they spot it. They don't have any ears in the area right now, but they will as soon as their new shift gets out."

"The state police have no one patrolling the highways outside the state capital? That's insane."

"It's the time when the shifts change. That's what they told me."

"Call me when you have something definite. I'm going to bed. This had better improve, Purvey."

"Yes, sir."

Kelly poured another drink, stumbled into the bedroom, muttered some obscentities which Mary Ellen at first thought were directed at her, and passed into immediate unconsciousness.

She took the glass from his hand and put it on the night table on his side. She thought about dumping it out, but then he might wake up again and get angry again, and there was no reason to have him waste expensive liquor. Mary Ellen hoped he would be successful in this case soon so they would be transferred to someplace quiet where the weather wasn't too mean—like Hartford or Rahway, New Jersey.

The telephone did not ring again that night. When Kelly

got up in the morning, he saw the glass on the nightstand, remembered why it was there, took it into the living room, and poured it back into the bottle. No one else was up. He checked all the rooms and everyone was sleeping peacefully, especially Flora. He vaguely remembered that he had to talk to her about something, but he couldn't quite remember what it was. He had other things on his mind.

By the time he got to the office, he remembered why he was furious: the Albany team had blundered. He also discovered he had an outrageous headache. It turned out things were worse than he expected. The license plate number was also bogus.

"I don't understand that," Purvey said.

"Why shouldn't he have given a bogus number? You want him to hand himself to us on a platter? We've got to go out and get him."

"But he didn't give the clerk the number. A bellboy did. We found out the bellboy doesn't see too well and he didn't have his glasses on."

"*Wonderful.* Run a check through motor vehicles on all vans of that type and color. What type and color is it?"

"Well, we're pretty sure it's gray."

"Pretty sure?"

"That's what the bellboy thought. There are green spotlights in the driveway, though, so it might have been tan or off-white or even pink. That's what the lab says."

"You called the lab?"

"Miss Leipzig did."

"I'm glad somebody's thinking down here. What kind of van was it?"

"Chevy or Dodge. It may have been a Ford, though. The bellboy wasn't sure."

"That covers about ninety-five percent of all the vans on the road."

"We're running a check for all vans with combinations of those license plate digits. Maybe we'll come up with something."

"Not good enough," Kelly said. "Run it for all vans with any four of those digits in the order given. He may have read some of the numbers wrong. He must have read some of them wrong."

"Yes, sir."

"And then I want you to check out the whereabouts of every single one of those vans at eleven p.m. last night."

"Yes, sir. Uh, sir."

"What now?"

"That may be several thousand vans."

"Get out of here, Purvey. Get out of here right now."

"Yes, sir."

Kelly called Miss Leipzig and told her he needed some aspirin immediately.

She brought the aspirin and a glass of water.

"Things aren't going too well, Mr. Kelly?" she asked sympathetically.

"I couldn't begin to tell you," he moaned.

"We always get our man, sir," she said, standing very straight. He hadn't ever noticed how short she was. "Just remember that and it will make you feel better."

"I'll try, Miss Leipzig. I shall try."

"Will there be anything else, sir?"

"Yes. I don't want to see or talk to anybody."

"Anybody at all? Not even—" She didn't finish the sentence.

"Of course them. But nobody else. Not unless it's someone telling me they've got this sonofabitch."

"Yes, sir," she said, backing out of the office and making herself even smaller than she was.

# SEVENTEEN

They had the wrong license plate number, a weak description of the van, and a phony name for him, but Eddie knew better than to think himself safe. If they ran the approximate van description through the computers with an instruction for the computer to assume the logical errors of reading the bellboy might have made on the plate, they could come up with a list of suspect vehicles and plates which would include his. They could find and talk to each owner. It would take them a lot of time, but it was simple enough to do.

It was also simple enough for him to find out what they were doing now.

After Carla went down to her cabin, he hooked up and called the motor vehicle agency computer. It said it was not being monitored. He asked about inquiries since midnight. There was the inquiry about the red Plymouth sedan, another for a Buick with Jersey plates that had originated in a Staten Island precinct, and then the one-forty-two inquiry he heard just before he got home. At nine twenty-two this morning there had been a request for a plate survey on Chevrolet, Dodge, and Ford vans, approximately two to four years old, gray, beige, light blue, or off-white.

The computer had kicked out the names, addresses, and correct assigned plates numbers of almost three thousand van owners. One of the listings matched the plates he now had on the van. They would discover it was bogus soon enough.

And then they would just start asking people and someone might remember him. They perhaps knew he was operating out of this part of New York State; it was a logical assumption after last night's motel incident.

That fellow Fleischer, the real estate agent in Kingston who rubbed his hands all the time they talked, he had seen Eddie's van, and if there were an article in the papers he might give the police a call. It depended on whether or not he had done the embezzling Eddie expected of him. Then he was the kind of fellow who might make an anonymous call.

Or they might have local police departments and sheriff's patrolmen make routine inquiries of gas station operators and grocery store owners.

He imagined a patrol car stopping to chat at Hinkes' Mobil station, the officer getting out and leaning on his fender, spitting in the gravel. He would ask about the van and Hinkes would point up the mountain and say, "He lives up there somewhere."

Which meant he couldn't stay here very much longer. He had a little while yet, but not too long. It depended on how much energy they would put into the case, how annoying he had been to them. He would try and find that out.

He had gotten used to the name Craig Hemsworth, absurd as he knew it was. He would miss it.

He hadn't decided which name he should use next. He would have to use the Massachusetts plates when he left; it was unlikely, with so vague a description, they would bother a van with Massachusetts plates. Unless they noticed that he had a New York inspection sticker in his window. Maybe he'd use one of the extra sets of New York plates until he got to Massachusetts. That was better.

Selection of a name was important now. Before, the names had belonged to someone he knew was really Eddie Argo. Now, he wasn't so sure who the names belonged to.

In the morning and at night, when he stood in the bathroom and brushed his teeth, the face he saw in the mirror bore little relation to Eddie Argo, the guy who had drowned in the Black Rock Canal last summer.

His body was in better condition than it had been since he was a teen-ager, perhaps even better than it had been then. Chopping his own wood and walking through the forest had introduced a solidity to the muscles. He was standing straighter; the old bow in his back was gone, making him at least two or three inches taller than slouchy Eddie had been. Craig wore glasses only for reading small type; Eddie had worn them nearly all the time. Craig had long hair, cut off neatly in a thick bunch just at the collar line. Carla had done that: given him a haircut one afternoon sitting in the clover field by the pool. Afterwards he jumped into the water and washed off the ends of hair that had always made him so uncomfortable when he went to a regular barbershop and had to walk around the rest of the day feeling the free hairs tickling and itching his back. After she cut his hair, they made love on a patch of grass in the sun between three tall trees, both of them wet and making funny noises with their bodies. And Craig had a beard, full and neatly trimmed; Eddie had always been clean-shaven, his sideburns cut off about middle-ear.

And, most important, there were no fingerprints on file anywhere for Eddie or for Craig. Or for who he would be now. That was because Eddie had never gone into the army. He had been too young for the Korean War; by the time Vietnam stoked up, he was already married and too old. He had never been arrested for anything. He had never held a passport or applied for a job with a security rating that required an FBI check.

He might, if required, have a problem establishing where and what he was before last summer. Perhaps he would spend some time during the winter generating out a series of encoded experiences that would combine to form a personal history. He could put himself into the records of the New York City school system; no one remembered anyone in New York, and only the computer entries engendered an academic past there. He would create a college career for himself: he had his choice of any large college that used computers for records. Perhaps a nice vague liberal arts major at a Big Ten school, a place where he wouldn't have been remembered by anyone in particular. It was always possible that if they did an intensive investigation, if they went into the records kept by individual professors, they would find out that his identity hadn't really existed. But he doubted it would ever get to that: they would send for a transcript, get it—typed out automatically by the school's computer—and he would have existed in that time and place. He could, given enough time, create for Craig's replacement whatever kind of past he wanted.

There was the possibility that they would establish a connection with Eddie Argo, the man who drowned himself in the canal. They might try that, if they were desperate enough. Perhaps they would try fingerprints. It wouldn't do them any good. After all this time they couldn't find a set of prints that belonged to the real Eddie. All they would have were the prints from the man taken from the water, and Eddie was willing to bet that the man fished from the water hadn't had any fingerprints left that were worth taking. Worms and bacteria had taken his prints away.

No: Eddie Argo was safe, though Craig was in some danger. He would have to disappear soon.

That afternoon, Carla sat on a stump and watched while he chopped wood for the fireplace.

"We're going to be leaving soon," she said.

"I thought you were going to tell me that."

"Why?"

"I don't know. Something in your face. I'll be very sorry to see you go." It had gotten so he could talk without losing breath. He actually enjoyed the work now.

"What about you?" she asked.

"I'll be going soon too. Some things are happening that I've got to take care of."

"You could come with us, Craig."

"I'd really like to, Carla. I really would. But I can't. There are things I have to do. Some things I've started but haven't finished yet. I may have to move quickly sometimes."

"Something you've worked on with that computer outfit you've got locked in your van?"

"You know what it is?"

"Sure. One day when you were swimming. Before I even talked to you. I don't know what you've been doing in there, but it's obviously something you don't want anybody to know anything about. I haven't peeked at anything of yours since the day we first talked, by the way, I want you to know that. It didn't seem fair to snoop after we became friends. You don't do that kind of thing to friends."

"Thank you for that."

"And I never told Franco or Sheila either. And I won't. You're entitled to your secrets. But I can see it's all portable. You've just hooked the van up to the cabin's power and phone when you've worked in there. Why don't you come along with us and do it from wherever we light next?"

"I can't. I really wish I could." He knew it was miraculous: finding a woman like her, who would leave his secrets alone, who would let him work alone in the dimness of the van and never push for information about what he was doing. He knew it wasn't that she had no curiosity; she was willing to accept his terms. Just as he had accepted theirs: he never had asked where they had been before, why they were living this way, who they were.

The difference was, he suspected, if he asked her those questions now, she would answer. She was perhaps waiting for him to ask. He didn't.

She watched him swing the ax. He finished a section and moved further along the log. Finally he stacked the pieces on the porch.

Then she said, "Are the police looking for you now?"

"Why do you ask that?"

"I don't know. I just got that feeling. That they're looking for you."

"They may be." He smiled and shrugged.

"If that's why you're not coming with us, it's not a good reason. We understand that kind of thing. We'll be glad to help you any way we can. People have to help one another. If they don't, then what else have you got?"

"Just a bunch of machines."

"That's right," she said. "Just goddamned machines."

"I still have some things I'm going to be doing and I've got to be alone. I don't want to involve anyone else. That's a way of helping people, too."

"I hear you, Craig, and I appreciate it. But if you change your mind, say so. You're welcome."

"I appreciate that. More than you know. Where are you going?"

"We haven't decided yet. Someplace else. We've been here too long. If you stay in one place too long and get too comfortable, people find you. And they're not usually the people you want to find you. We're not anxious to be found." She laughed, light and charming, like the first day they had met. "You're not the only one with secrets, Craig. Or whatever your name is."

He started to tell her what his name really was. He didn't know why. It just seemed like something he ought to do. Even though he felt no living connection with Eddie any longer, he was going to tell her that name. She put a finger to her lips.

"No, don't say anything. I don't want to know your real name. You've got enough to worry about. If you tell me, you'll have to worry that I might someday tell someone. This way, if someone finds you out, you'll know it wasn't me."

"I wouldn't think it was you."

"Now you don't have to."

"I hope you guys make out well," he said.

"I hope you'll decide to come along with us, that's what I hope. We get along really well. It's not often that four people get along so well. I'd miss you."

He thought about it. There was a considerable difference in their ages. She was twenty-eight and he was forty. It hadn't seemed to matter so far, but he was sure it would eventually. They made him feel young, which was nice; it was something he had missed with Betty from the beginning. But he feared that one day they would also make him feel old.

She read him perfectly. "Don't worry about it. Come with us and stay for as long as it's good and then split when it's not. There aren't any contracts."

"There are always contracts," he said. "It's just that some of them don't get written or spoken out. You know that." She nodded. "Believe me: I would like to come with you, and if there were a nice way I would. But there are things I have to do and I can't have people around. I don't want to involve any other people."

"Will you be doing it forever?"

"No, I don't think so. I'll have done enough mischief after a while, and I'll stop."

"Will they kill you?"

"You've seen too many movies. It's not that serious."

"You haven't seen enough movies. It's always that serious. They're crazy out there."

She went into the house and came out a moment later

with a piece of paper. She put it into his shirt pocket. "That's the address of a very good friend of mine. If you want to catch up with us, write my friend and tell her you're my mountain friend. She'll know who you are. She'll probably know where we are."

They had dinner and afterwards they made love on the rug by the fireplace. She said she got achy sleeping on the floor and was going to get in bed. He said he would join her in a little while, he had something to do in the van.

He got a computer terminal in St. Louis that belonged to the Greyhound Company. He had routed the conversation through Seattle, Boston, and New Brunswick, New Jersey. He found out immediately that it wasn't a monitored terminal. His inquiry couldn't be traced back in less than an hour. He told the terminal to gather all the information it could from certain other data centers—he gave it the codes for IFFI and bank survey centers and the Justice Department personnel file—about a person named Francis X. Kelly, who currently resided in Buffalo, New York. He instructed the computer to print out the information and transmit it to the FBI office in Buffalo, New York, immediately attention SAC. It would give his friend Kelly something else to think about.

It had taken him only twelve minutes. She was already asleep when he got into the bed, and he didn't wake her.

When he got up, she had made coffee and left it for him on the stove over a low frame, just like the first time she had stayed the night.

He drank a cup and looked out the window. The leaves were mostly gone from the maples and the oaks; the few that remained had turned a dull yellow and red. He was amazed how quickly autumn happened here.

He walked along the gravel road, listening to the sounds of his boots. The morning was very cool. At several points he could easily see all the way down to the inlet and the river. Only a few boats were out. Winter was coming soon.

Even before he reached their cabin, he knew they were gone. The place felt silent and empty. When he got close, he saw that the lock had been replaced on the front door. Everything was swept and clean and a stack of firewood had been cut to replace the one they had consumed. The owners probably wouldn't even notice the missing liquor and food. It was as if they had never been there.

Eddie sat on the steps and watched some leaves blowing across the driveway. They were dry and light. The wind came in short gusts, moving them, raising them in the air, dropping them on the ground awhile, then picking them up and carrying them away again. He watched one golden oak leaf move all the way across the clearing. When it disappeared into the shadows, he got up and slowly went back up the hill.

# EIGHTEEN

The day he closed down the operation at the cabin for good, he put through his last operation there. He had been thinking about them for a long time. It was personal, but he felt his experiences with the firms involved couldn't have been unique. The firms were TRL, the credit agency that had caused him so much grief with the Volvo, and Penney's. They both had been terribly cruel to him, unwilling to listen to him as a person; he was just an account number, and if they happened to have the wrong person connected to the account number, it made no difference to them.

First, he introduced to the TRL memory bank an operational instruction. The computers were to establish criteria for the worst credit ratings possible. The next four hundred people who met those criteria were to be given clean bills: the reports that would come out on them would show no defaults, no judgments, no repossessions. For each case the computer would give the clean response three times only. After that the old case reports would again be issued.

Eddie figured it would take them years to work it out. The worst people in the world would get three good loans or charge accounts. They would probably default on most of them. The banks or stores would come back to TRL and ask how they could have declared such bums trustworthy. TRL would print out a report on the name in question and it would show page after page of financial irresponsibility. The woman with the crooked mouth would smile and say, "See? Our records are accurate."

Then the representative of the banks would say, "But see this: it's the report you gave us. *None* of that information is here."

And TRL, like Eddie would have to explain how such gross misinformation had come from its fine computers; TRL would have to convince the executives that they should continue using its services. Eddie doubted very much that TRL would stay in business very long. He was sorry about putting the drones on the consoles out of a job, but the firm did a lot of harm. The operators were cruel, careless people. They hid in technicalities of the law, and didn't have to tell the truth.

Penney's was more difficult. He spent a long time trying to decide how to revenge himself on them for their cold refusal to respond to any of his letters, their cruel branding of him—of Eddie, who no longer existed—as a bad person.

Eddie had no difficulty getting the access code for the Penney's account memory tapes: he asked the TRL computer the electronic address. And, as long as he was on the line, he got all the rest of TRL's addresses in case he wanted to use any of them in the future. TRL wouldn't be needing them much longer.

His solution was simple and immensely satisfying. It was also, in terms of dollars, his grandest criminal act. He knew it was a crime, but he felt he was at war, and in war the rules get changed. They had declared war on him with their computers and he was responding with his.

CURRENT BALANCE IN ALL OUTSTANDING CREDIT ACCOUNTS, he typed, IS NOW ZERO DOLLARS ZERO CENTS.

ERROR, the Penney's computer typed back. CURRENT BALANCE IS $27,677,543.24.

PREVIOUS WAS NOT A STATEMENT FOR CORRELATION; IT WAS STATEMENT OF FACT: IF YOU DON'T SHOW SAME FACT ADJUST YOUR MEMORY AND REPORT.

There was silence for about ten minutes. It took a long time for all those tapes to spin across the erase heads.

CURRENT BALANCE ON ALL OUTSTANDING ACCOUNTS, the screen said, IS NOW ZERO DOLLARS ZERO CENTS.

RECONSTRUCT PREVIOUS BALANCES, Eddie ordered.

PREVIOUS BALANCES DO NOT EXIST, CURRENT BALANCE ON ALL OUTSTANDING ACCOUNTS IS. CORRECTION. THERE ARE NO CURRENT OUTSTANDING ACCOUNTS.

Eddie went through the entire cabin, wiping clean all the smooth objects he could find: dishes, doorknobs, windowpanes, chair arms, toilet and sinks, faucets, light bulbs, the telephone. The walls and doors were rough unfinished wood, which carried no prints.

He didn't know how useful it was, this work of erasing all the fingerprints. They couldn't connect Craig with anything, not unless they caught him with the equipment. They might get a make on the van, but even so, they could never be sure it was the same van and the same person who had made the calls from the Albany Ramada Inn that night. The bellboy had made a mistake in two digits; he might have made others.

But he didn't like having the identity of Craig contaminated, even though he knew he would abandon it very soon—it was the first identity he'd had that was fun. But more likely it was because he had heard Carla say the name so many times. He couldn't imagine Carla's smooth body next to his and her voice in the darkness talking to an Eddie or some other name. He would be Craig when he left. Later he could come to terms with another name. Maybe he would get rid of the van and pick up another one. Perhaps he'd use a regular sedan for a while because of the developing gas shortage. There were all kinds of possibilities, and he had a lot of cash.

It was possible he had missed some places. Perhaps an ax forgotten in the woods, a small print missed by his sponges in the sink. But he knew that such fragments would do the FBI no good. Only in movies did they find a pinkie or thumbprint and pull a name out of a file of a hundred million people. In reality, fingerprints were useful only when they had a suspect in mind, and the only thing they had now in mind were sets of fantasies and hypotheses. He had left no prints in the Albany motel, the man in Eddie Argo's grave had no prints to give them, and there would be virtually nothing in this place. All they had were their copies of perfectly anonymous electronic conversations.

It took the entire day. He had never realized how many smooth surfaces there were in a place, even in so small a cabin. But he was methodical about it, and confident, when he was all done, that if the FBI picked up any useful fingerprints from the cabin, they would be their own.

For the immediate future he had three projects. He was sure he would discover others. The possibilities were nearly infinite.

The first was to insure that he had the funds he needed for whatever he wanted to do. He couldn't keep up the American Express business: that was already too dangerous and, whatever his feelings about the company, he didn't think it fair to take it all from one place. One option was to find the access codes used for congressional classified spending accounts. The funds were kept in Washington, D.C., banks and could be released—he had learned from the *Times* during the Watergate investigations—by presentation of a proper code sequence. The presentation didn't have to be in person; the money could be transferred to any account anywhere in the world, immediately, electronically. He could charge his own expenses to the open accounts of certain well-funded senators; they couldn't complain too loudly because then the public would learn just how lavish were the support accounts those people got, how little accountability there really was for expenditures—which would mean that their *real* utilization of the monies would come under scrutiny. As long as he kept spreading his money taps around, he could get by safely for a long time. He could also transfer more funds to charitable organizations. He could imagine the expression on the face of the senior senator from Mississippi when he received the enthusiastic notes of thanks for his generous gifts to the NAACP and the ACLU.

His second project had to do with the oil and gas companies. They talked of shortages and raised prices while year after year recording record profits. Even if the dollar were held constant, their profits would be spectacular. Some government agencies said reserves were low and others argued that reserves were not low—but the companies weren't telling the truth. The FBI said they couldn't investigate National Fuel, Gulf, and the others as if they were common criminals; they couldn't bust into the offices and take whatever information they found. They had to deal with the information the companies gave willingly or under subpoena, and that information partially substantiated the shortage claims. Eddie didn't believe it one bit, and he could, effectively, bust into their offices whenever he wanted, from anyplace he wanted. He would have to learn a lot about the fuel business to understand the information—and then he would send it to the *New Republic* and

*The Nation.* It was the sort of thing their reporters would handle more bravely than either the *Times* or the Washington *Post.*

It would take time, but he had plenty of time. As long as the computers continued talking to one another, they would talk to Eddie. They had a lot to say to each other, Eddie and the computers.

The third project was more ambitious; it involved one of the most closely guarded set of memory tapes in the United States: the IRS records housed at Andover, Massachusetts. It would be easier penetrating the security defenses of a missile base than walking into the tape storage areas at Andover. Only the CIA files were more inaccessible.

At Andover the IRS kept the duplicate tapes of the information in all the regional IRS processing centers, and it was at Andover that the permanent records were encoded and stored. The regional centers held onto the information only so long as cases were active, usually no more than three years.

In the spring the regional centers and Andover were on twenty-four-hour schedules, four shifts working round the clock, and on Sundays and holidays. He had once toured one of the regional facilities as part of his intern program. It was very impressive. It was the cleanest building he had ever seen.

Any of the centers could talk to the computers at Andover and also to any other center. They talked to one another constantly, checking up on people who moved or who had multiple residences; they passed information around so they could catch someone. During the summer and fall the work crews were smaller. Programs would be set up and people went home for the night, while the computers talked to one another automatically until the morning shift came in to see what had turned up. Much of the time people were necessary only to tell the computers what they should be concerned with.

He could get access to the regional centers because they, unlike Andover, were set up to talk to banks everywhere. That way they could get information on people's bank accounts whenever they wanted to. All he needed was access to the banks' information processors, and from them he could switch into the regional centers.

He wouldn't erase tax records. It would cost a fortune to reconstitute them, and the documents from which most had been compiled still existed. As yet he couldn't do anything about real documents. The money which the reconstitution would cost would appear in new taxes, so that wasn't fair to people. But there were things he could do. They would be simple, and were not likely to be noticed or traced.

First, he would order the computers to access all returns for income under twenty thousand dollars that had been tagged for audit. Then he would remove the tags from everyone in Watts, Harlem, east Buffalo, Roxbury, and several other ghettos he had read about or seen. That was easy. He only had to order removal according to zip codes. Then he would pull the tags from random name-letter combinations, say everyone whose last name began with Be, Ci, Mc, and Sl. He couldn't help everyone, but he certainly could help some. He couldn't believe that people making less than twenty thousand dollars could be taking from the government as much as the government would spend hassling them for more money. He would fix it so a lot of people who were barely getting by would be left alone in this one regard. And he would be able to do it every year, passing around the benefits to different neighborhoods, different initials.

Next he would get printouts of everyone with a net income, before deductions or with income from tax-free bonds, of over $250,000 who had paid no income taxes in any of the past three years. Those lists would be sent to the New York Times, the Boston Globe, the San Francisco Chronicle, the Detroit Free Press, and the London Times. Maybe even the Christian Science Monitor. It would be gorgeous.

If it turned out that the bank hookups were unworkable—if, say, they could communicate only with the IRS regional centers when IRS initiated the calls—there would be other ways in. County and state computers were keyed in as part of their work with the state income tax bureau, and the state computers were in constant communication with their federal counterparts. Eddie could do it, once he got the access worked out, from anywhere he parked his van. He would need only access to a telephone hookup.

His next van would have a small AC generator. That way he wouldn't need a connection to someone's electricity. Perhaps eventually he'd figure out a way to use the telephone lines without a mechanical jack. That would be perfect: he would be absolutely portable and absolutely untraceable.

He was just about ready to leave when the telephone rang. It was the first time the telephone rang since he had been at the cabin.

"Mr. Hemsworth?"

He didn't recognize the voice. It sounded like an older man. It was a long time since he had used a telephone for talking to people.

"Yes."

"This is Toby Hinkes, down at the Mobil station at the crossroads."

"Oh, yes, Toby. What is it?"

"Well," the old man said, "I just thought you ought to know. There were two suspicious guys in here a few minutes ago asking questions about you."

"About me?"

"Not about you in particular. They were looking for your van. They had a good description of it, except they weren't sure about the color, and they had the plates. They were a little off on the plates, too, but it was close enough. They didn't know your name. I thought I ought to give you a call and let you know. They were very suspicious guys, if you know what I mean."

"I really appreciate this, Toby."

"I'm glad to help out a good customer. They said they were from the FBI, but you know what?"

"What?"

"They looked like a pair of gun-thugs to me. I thought you ought to know that some gun-thugs were in the neighborhood. I didn't tell them anything, but somebody will. Somebody always tells. I ever tell you about my union days?"

"No, you didn't."

"Well, I ain't gonna tell you now, that's for sure. Sometime when you've got time. Saw plenty of no-good gun-thugs then, though. They got a look in their eye, which is how you get to know them."

"Thanks, Toby. I won't forget you."

"You be careful, Mr. Hemsworth."

"I surely will."

Eddie wiped his prints off the telephone and went out to the porch. He would have to do something for Toby. But first he had to get away from here. If they were at the bottom of the hill, he would have to take off on foot across country. He changed clothes and got ready. He had thought about this possibility before and knew exactly what he would do. It took him thirty minutes.

On the bluff Eddie sat on a fallen log and looked through his field glasses at the four cars gathered near Hinkes' wooden dock in the cove far below. There were eight men, four of them in state police uniforms. Some of them were looking up the mountain toward his cabin.

The couldn't see him. He wore his tan and gray camouflage suit and he had blacking on his cheeks. Except for reading small print, he had stopped wearing glasses weeks ago. Glasses reflected light in the sun, out of the question for someone in his position.

Two of the cars belonged to the state police; the other two, both Ford sedans, belonged to the FBI agents. They talked to one another on their radios. Eddie wondered why they didn't simply stand together and talk. Perhaps they liked their radios. He listened to their conversation on his scanner.

They were getting ready to come up the hill. He had a can of kerosene next to the van. In a minute or two he would empty it on the seats and the cot and the console, and he would set a twenty-foot section of slow fuse burning. It would give him time to get into the woods before the van went up. He was sorry to see the equipment go—it had served him well and the van was a good one—but there was no way he could get out of here in a van with them parked at the bottom. Maybe they would spend a while looking for a body in the flames and waste more time before they realized he had taken off cross country. And they were dressed in their pretty uniforms and their business suits. They couldn't follow him.

In his pack he had enough food for five days, a change of clothes, his condensed notebook of access codes, his packet of credit cards and drivers' licenses, and $189,000 in cash.

Everything he needed to get started again.

# NINETEEN

The man standing by the green Ford was obviously direct-
ing the operation. He had bright red hair. Eddie decided
that must be Kelly, the FBISAC from Buffalo. Kelly
opened the trunk of his car, took off his suit jacket, and
bent over where Eddie couldn't see him for a moment.
When Kelly stood up, he was wearing a green army-type
field jacket. He didn't remove his necktie. Kelly looked at
the black man standing near the front of the car and said
something. Eddie wondered if someone who was really
good at it could read lips at this distance. He decided that
if the field glasses or telescope were good enough, there
was no reason a person couldn't. The black man shook his
head. Kelly must have asked him if he wanted a field
jacket too. The black man lighted a pipe. It took him a
long time; the matches kept blowing out.

Kelly closed the trunk and raised his hand. Eddie got up
and was about to go pour out the kerosene in the van. He
thought it was the signal for the attack, but then he realized that the signal meant Kelly was going to take a piss
in the bushes before things got under way. Kelly walked to
some bushes about twenty feet from his car. The other
men leaned on the fender and puffed smoke into the air.

A sleek white motorboat whizzed past the dock, heading
south. A spreading wake broke the calm water in its path.
The boat was so far away it moved in perfect silence—
smooth and beautiful.

As Eddie watched the boat through his binoculars, he
realized he could perhaps save his van and avoid the rigors
of a cross-country trek.

He took from the van his PRC-6 portable transceiver.
In seconds he pulled the crystals and replaced them with
the FBI crystals from the scanner. Now he could transmit
as well as receive on their frequency.

He covered the microphone with a handkerchief, just as
he had seen people do in the movies. Kelly was still in the
bushes and the black agent was still leaning on the front

fender of the green Ford. Kelly had found a fine and private place.

"Goddammit!" Eddie yelled into the microphone, deliberately overmodulating and causing a fuzzy transmission. "That's him! Out there in that motorboat!"

"Who's that?"

"Who's talking?"

"Probably one of the troopers!"

"Kelly, you idiot. What are you jerkoffs doing just standing there? Look: there he goes. Get in those goddamned motorboats and get the sonofabitch!"

Even without the field glasses Eddie could see a great deal of movement toward the end of the dock. Kelly was still in the bushes. Eddie wondered if he had some sort of problem. Then Kelly came out and looked at the others scrambling into the small boats tied up there.

Eddie put down the PRC-6 and focused in again with the glasses. Kelly was leaning into his car, talking into a handset.

"What the hell is going on?" Eddie heard him yell over the radio.

"He's out there in the white boat. We're going after him."

"Goddamn!" Kelly said. "How'd he do that? I thought he was on the cliff." If Kelly identified himself, Eddie knew, it was back to the kerosene and forest journey.

"We all did," the trooper said.

Kelly threw the handset back into his car and ran for the boats, the black FBI agent a few paces behind him. The four state troopers and the other two FBI men were in two motorboats. The FBI boat took off first. The trooper boat had trouble starting, and Eddie was sure it was going to swamp before it got very far. Whoever was driving got it to stop wobbling and followed the first boat out to the river. Kelly and his assistant got into the boat which Eddie and Carla and Franco and Sheila had used the afternoon Franco fell in. It didn't start for a long time. Then it pushed out a bright plume of smoke. The black man cast off, sat down, and the boat chugged away, trying to catch up with the others.

By now the white motorboat was far to the south and moving much faster than any of the boats pursuing it, but none of the policemen seemed to realize that. The troopers and the FBI men in the front boat yelled back and forth to one another over their radios about who would catch the Computer Bandit first and what they would do to him. None of the voices came from Kelly's boat, and Eddie decided that Kelly didn't have a portable radio with him.

When they were about two miles out and at least fifteen minutes from getting back, Eddie took the can of kerosene from the van and put it back in the tool shed behind the house. He locked the shed. Then he put his backpack into the van, climbed in, and started the engine.

It would take him four or five minutes to reach their cars. All sorts of nice things were down there for him.

# TWENTY

Kelly sat in the bow and looked through his field glasses. He couldn't see the white speedboat at all because its wake sent spray rising in a glistening wall as it cut the water.

"Can't you make this damned thing go any faster, Purvey?"

"No, boss."

"They're getting away from us."

"This thing won't go any faster, boss."

*Boss.* The sonofabitch called him boss. Kelly thought about the envelope that had been delivered to him this morning. It had been sent by the IFFI computer in Baltimore. He knew the Computer Bandit had ordered it sent to him. He had been right about Purvey all along. What he hadn't guessed at all was what Miss Leipzig had been doing. Who could have known that that little shriveled fart had such a high rank in the Bureau? How could you work in a place where the spies spied upon the spies? Kelly turned and looked at Purvey. He wondered if he really was making the boat go as fast as it could. Purvey didn't know about Miss Leipzig. Maybe he did. Maybe that was another secret. Why else would she have said such nice things about him in those reports? Miss Leipzig! His eyes clouded with anger.

The white boat made a slight turn to the left, moving out to the middle, then it leveled, straightened, and headed south again.

"Shit!" Kelly screamed. "Shit and goddamn!"

"Sir?"

"You heard me. We're going the wrong goddamned way. There are four people in that white speedboat. All of them are girls. We're not after four girls. We're after the goddamned Computer Bandit. One man! Call them, Purvey. Call the others. We've got to get back."

"Can't sir." He was shouting over the noise of the engine.

"Why not?" Kelly shouted back.

"You left the PRC-6 in the car. We don't have a radio."

"Can't this goddamned thing go any faster?"

"No, sir."

"Then *shout*. Both of us. They'll hear us."

Purvey let go of the throttle and their boat fell almost dead in the water. It drifted slowly with the current. They screamed in unison until Kelly's throat was sore. No one in the other boats gave any sign of hearing them.

"Give me your gun," Kelly said.

"Sir?"

"Your gun. Give me your gun."

Purvey's mouth opened. He licked his lips. Go ahead and lick your lips, you goddamned spy, Kelly thought. "Sir,"Purvey said, "regulations say an agent—"

"Purvey! Give me that fucking pistol! That's a direct order."

"Yes, sir."

Purvey handed Kelly the pistol. Kelly looked at Purvey. Purvey looked sick. "Sir, you've got to understand . . ."

Kelly turned around, stood in the bow with a pistol in either hand. He pointed both forward, angled at a 45-degree angle into the sky. He fired both at once. Both pistols bucked. Then he fired again. The guns made a lot of noise. The third time he didn't get them quite in unison. He got them together again for the last three pairs of rounds.

Someone in the state police chase boat heard that. The trooper turned and waved at them. Kelly waved back. The trooper leaned forward and picked up his PRC-6. Within seconds all four troopers and the two FBI men in the front boat let go a terrific fusillade of bullets in the direction of the white speedboat. Even at this distance the noise was horrendous. It reminded Kelly of the SLA shoot-out in Los Angeles, which he had watched on television.

The firing stopped as quickly as it had started. Kelly looked through his field glasses. All the troopers and the agents were leaning over. He knew what they were doing now. When they finished reloading, they all began firing again.

The white speedboat was far out of range. Kelly saw little splashes from the falling bullets hit the water far behind it. Some of the bullets were far to the left or right of the boat's wake—meaning some of the men in the pursuit boats were wretched shots. He hoped it wasn't his men. Things were bad enough.

Kelly turned the field glasses back to the shore, a couple of miles away now.

The hoods on all four cars were up and a man was moving around quickly. He was too far away for Kelly to make out any details on his face. He wore a black watch cap and what appeared to be a camouflage suit. He was doing something inside the engines. He stood up when he was done with the green Ford, something round and black in his hand. He walked to the river and threw the object far out into the water. It skipped once, the way a stone does, then it sank out of sight. The man walked to another car, leaned into its engine, and came out with another black object. He threw it into the river just as he had the first object, except this one got two skips before it disappeared.

"Oh, shit," Kelly said.

"Sir?"

The man on the bank waved, then turned and disappeared into the line of trees near the road. Kelly wouldn't be able to see what kind of vehicle he was driving. He wouldn't know if it was a Ford or a Chevrolet or a Dodge. He wouldn't know if it was gray or tan or off-white.

Kelly sat down on the bow seat.

"He's pulled the distributor caps from all the cars."

"Then we'll be stuck for a while, huh?"

"There's that gas station down the road a few miles. You can walk."

"Me?"

"I'm SAC, dammit. *You* can walk. Now turn this fucker around and go on back there." As far as Kelly was concerned, Purvey could walk straight to hell.

"Maybe we can radio for help once we get to the cars."

"I suspect we'll find none of the radios functioning anymore, once we get to the cars. Did you see the way that sonofabitch threw the distributor caps into the water? He spun them, like a kid with a flat rock. He wanted to see how many times he could make them skip. He was having fun. You know what, Purvey? That sonofabitch isn't in this for the money, that's what I think."

"Then what's he in it for? Why go to all this trouble? Why do it?"

"If it's not money? Damned if I know. That's the only reason I'd have for doing it. Who knows what reason that maniac has got? Maybe he'll tell us sometime. I suspect we'll be hearing from him again before very long."

"And we'll get him then. Don't you worry about it."

"Sure we will, Purvey. Sure we will." Kelly sighed and leaned back. *Buffalo. He'd be in Buffalo for goddamned ever.*

# TWENTY-ONE

Eddie walked through the line of trees to his van. Its silver surface was pleasantly dappled by rays of sun coming down through the high branches. The only sounds were the wind and birds in the trees. The motorboats were still too far away to intrude.

He checked the cabinets to be sure the console and monitor were securely bolted down and cushioned. Everything was neatly in order. He took off the camouflage suit and put on regular clothes.

He felt very strong, and the feeling was more than the physical change he had experienced the past few months. The memories awaiting his black box telephone calls were constantly present in his awareness now, like friends asleep in homes far across the country. Friends might not be thinking of him, but he could instantly reestablish relationships merely by pushing ten or eleven buttons on the telephone panel. As a man was the sum of his relationships in the world and the result of the experience with those relationships, Eddie was now, in part, the sum of the memories and command potentials linked to his fingers. He experienced himself as part of an enormous nervous system, ready to respond to any question, ready to carry out any command. It moved from his brain and through his fingers into the keyboard, from the cool transistorized circuits of the console out into the black wires glistening on high towers across the country, hurled at incredible speeds by radio relays across the fields and mountains and rivers, buried deep under the sea for journeys around the world. The information was activated in miraculous fractions of a second, and the results of the orders were carried out miraculous fractions of a second later. As his fingers touched the keys of the silent console, he felt as if they could emit sparks, as if they alone could bring the circuits alive and make them both extensions of and part of himself.

The only thing he couldn't find with the wires was

someone like Carla, who lived far outside that kind of world. But she had told him how to find her when he was ready. He had a warm feeling, knowing he could find Carla when he was ready, and sensing the sparks ready in his fingers to command a complex electronic mind a thousand miles or more away. Wherever the wires of the world went, Eddie could go; whatever secrets were wound on automatic reels of brown magnetic tape, Eddie could listen.

Unless they caught him. There was always the possibility they would catch him. They would surely try. Even now that FBI agent, Kelly, was heading in his little boat back toward land, back toward the radio in his car dashboard. Eddie smiled at that: they would have a hard time using their car radios. When he had pulled the distributor caps, he had also done some work with his wire cutters.

Nevertheless, it was not good to stay around here any longer. He had finished here. It was time to move on. He locked the cabinets hiding the console and the monitor.

The motor started immediately. The tank was nearly full. In a few minutes he would be on the highway. They didn't know what kind of vehicle he was driving, nor could they know he was now the driver of a legally registered Massachusetts vehicle.

The van bounced lightly on the road, skidded a little on the first turn. He slowed to a more reasonable speed until the road straightened, then pressed down on the accelerator again.

He wasn't sure just what he would do next. There were a lot of things out there, a lot of territory, a lot of information to get and instructions to give. The tapes were full of secrets people had a right to hear. The daily newspapers were full of missions for him. The challenge was nearly infinite.

And Kelly would be out there, if he didn't get replaced by someone else just like himself, in constant pursuit. It was like war. And war it would be.

"Charge," Eddie said softly, smiling at the silliness of hearing his own voice when he was all alone.